Praise for Jess Dee's
Steve's Story

"I had originally read Tyler's story and fell in love with Steve, wanting his story right then. After making me wait months, Jess Dee more than delivers with Steve's Story. I can't say too much without giving away the story, which simply must be read to appreciate. Heartbreaking while at the same time being heartwarming, Jess Dee shows that while not every happy ending is perfect, sometimes you take the hand life deals you and love with all your heart. I found myself in tears several times. Truly outstanding."

~ *Melissa, Joyfully Reviewed*

"STEVE'S STORY is an emotional ride from beginning to end. The sexual tension between Steve and Pen is captivating. The CIRCLE OF FRIENDS stories have truly touched my heart and give me a newfound respect for life and those who choose to embrace everything life has to offer."

~ *Chrissy Dionne, Romance Junkies*

"The dynamics of this couple proved that Dee knows how to grip the readers' imaginations. There was a myriad of emotional highs and lows in this book. I shed enough tears to be glad I was reading in private. I laughed. I read some incredible sexual activity. The overall content of the story was breathtaking. I loved the story and I loved the outcome. I've found a new author to add to my automatic list."

~ *Brenda Talley, The Romance Studio*

Look for these titles by
Jess Dee

Now Available:

Ask Adam
Photo Opportunity
A Question of Trust
A Question of Love

Circle of Friends Series
Only Tyler (Book 1)
Steve's Story (Book 2)

Print Anthology
Three's Company

Steve's Story

Circle of Friends

Jess Dee

A SAMHAIN PUBLISHING, LTD. publication.

Samhain Publishing, Ltd.
577 Mulberry Street, Suite 1520
Macon, GA 31201
www.samhainpublishing.com

Editing by Jennifer Miller
Cover by Scott Carpenter

First Samhain Publishing, Ltd. electronic publication: April 2009
First Samhain Publishing, Ltd. print publication: February 2010

With Thanks

To Jennifer, for her editing brilliance (once again).

To my fellow Ozcritters, for ironing out all those creases and rough spots.

And to my boys... I love you.

Chapter One

"There's something else I need to tell you." Steve Sommers' stomach twisted as he wondered how his brother would respond to his news.

"You mean there's more?" Sam's voice echoed over the line. "The accident wasn't enough?"

"Yeah. There's more." He exhaled loudly. "Kate and I broke up."

His words were met with silence. "Sam?"

"I'm here."

"Say something." The connection was bad enough without his brother's meditative quiet.

"I'm sorry?"

That was the best Sam could do? He'd just announced that his forthcoming marriage was off and all his brother could offer was a questionable condolence? "You know," Steve sighed, "that might be a little bit more comforting if I thought you actually meant it." He slumped against the hospital wall, the stress of the past two weeks draining him of his strength and energy.

Static interference whispered through the phone.

"I honestly am sorry." Sam hesitated. "I can't say I'm too surprised. That's all."

Steve groaned in disbelief. "Is there not one single person in my whole family who believed Kate and I would get married?"

"Truthfully?"

Steve stared listlessly down the passage leading to ICU. Nurses at their station bustled about their business. "No, don't bother. That's answer enough." He raked his hands through his hair. Damn, Kate's decision to call of the wedding still stung. It shouldn't, but it did, and his family's intuitive knowledge that the relationship wouldn't last only increased the burn.

"Look, you know we're all crazy about Kate, and you know we'd all have welcomed her into the family, but you don't love her." A couple of seconds passed before Sam added, "And she doesn't love you either."

Nope, she didn't. Not like a woman should love her fiancé, anyway. "How do you figure that?"

"You know I always said the woman was in love with Tyler, mate. It was obvious to all of us. You included."

His brother had a point. Not only was Kate in love with Tyler, she had been for a very long time. "Yeah, maybe I should have given that a bit more credence before I proposed." But there'd been no reason. Tyler was out of the picture and Katie had never admitted to loving him. Steve had been aware all along that his and Kate's engagement was based more on friendship and trust than on passion and romance. Hell, they'd discussed it several times before they'd decided to get married. Based on those numerous conversations, Steve had figured they'd had a fighting chance...

"We just wanted you to be happy, man." Sam broke into his musings.

"I was happy." He was. Not head-over-heels, crazy-in-love happy, but content. Definitely content. Which was good, because before the engagement he hadn't felt that sense of contentment for two and a half years.

"I meant really happy." The line crackled. "Like you were with Pen."

A blast of pain shot through his chest. Followed closely by a shard of apprehension. Words failed him and he grunted into his phone.

"What happened?" Sam asked, obviously taking Steve's grunt as a signal to steer clear of the Penelope discussion. "Did Kate break it off after Tyler came home?"

Not the second he stepped off the plane. She'd given herself about two weeks—enough time to fall in love with him again. "It's a little more complicated than that, but basically, yeah."

At least the raw hurt and humiliation had subsided. Or maybe it had been masked by the trauma of Tyler's accident. Either way, he and Kate had reached a truce. They were talking again, which was a big step up from their situation a few days ago.

"Hey, Steve?" Sam's voice broke into his thoughts.

"Yeah?"

"You going to be okay?"

"Ask me when Tyler wakes up." Steve shut his eyes wearily. "*If* Tyler wakes up."

Silence resonated over the phone, and he could almost see Sam's grim nod. "What about you and Kate? You okay with that?"

"Sort of, I guess." He'd know better when real life resumed. When time was no longer suspended within the four walls of Tyler's hospital room.

"You going to be able to continue working with her?"

Steve grimaced. His initial reaction had been no. When Kate ended the relationship, he'd told her he would find new rooms, told her it would be too difficult to carry on working at their medical practice together.

Then Tyler was almost killed in a motorcycle accident, and his perspective changed. Funny how one's perspective changed in a life-or-death situation. "I want to. We both do. We're going to give it a shot and see how things turn out." Trouble was, neither of them had gone back to work since the collision. Neither of them wanted to leave Tyler's side. Kate had organized a locum to take over the practice until they were ready to return.

Steve felt a sudden pang for his absent brother. He could do with a friendly face right now. "You coming home anytime soon?"

"Two weeks," his brother said. The phone crackled loudly. "Shit, I'm losing my signal."

"That's okay. I need to go anyway. I have to see Tyler."

"No worries. Send him my..." Sam's voice either trailed off or got lost in the static. "Christ, I hope he pulls through."

He nodded slowly. "Me too."

"Hang in there."

"Thanks, mate. G'bye." Steve doubted Sam heard his last words over the interference. He closed his phone and leaned heavily against the wall. He knew he should push himself away from it and go into the damn ICU cubicle, but he couldn't. There was too much on the other side of the door stopping him.

For one thing, there was Tyler. His best friend lay comatose, the victim of a car smash. He'd been on his motorcycle when a four-wheel drive shot a red light. One minute Tyler Bonnard was fine and healthy. The next he was fighting for his life.

Then there was Kate Rosewood. Steve's ex-fiancée and the love of Tyler's life, hanging on to Tyler's hand for all her worth, wishing him awake by sheer strength of will alone. So far, it hadn't worked.

Finally, there was Tyler's sister...

Steve swept a hand over his eyes. He couldn't go there. Not

yet. Not until he had absolutely no choice but to face her again.

Mentally he shrugged off three days' worth of exhaustion. It was pointless standing outside. He needed to go into the room. Needed to see his friend and stand by his friend's lover. Ironic, really, that he and Kate were supporting each other after all they had been through, but there it was. The gritty facts of life. No matter what they might once have been, they weren't that anymore. Circumstances had changed, and now they needed each other to get through this god-awful time.

Besides, it was time to face up to his past. *All* of his past.

Taking a deep breath, he stood a little straighter, twisted the handle and pushed the door open.

The air in the room hung thick with tension. Thick with unspoken words and desperation. Steve longed to turn around and walk away, close the door behind him and pretend that none of this had happened. Pretend his life and the lives of the people around him had never been shattered by tragedy.

Instead he trained his eyes on the bed, on the deathly still figure of Tyler. As impossible as it was to face his injured, comatose friend, it was still easier than looking at the women on either side of Tyler's bed.

Steve suppressed the howl of agony that beat for release against his chest. He had to hold it together. For everyone's sake.

Reluctantly, he turned to his ex-fiancée. "Hey, b—" Steve caught himself. *Babe* no longer seemed appropriate. Such intimacy and affection weren't a part of their relationship anymore. "Hey," he corrected. "How's he doing?" It wasn't easy talking to her. It hurt, big-time, but he had to put his emotions aside. They weren't important now. Tyler's recovery was.

She sniffed, touched a knuckle to her nose and blinked. She looked awful. Her eyes were bloodshot and her skin pale as alabaster. Even her hair, which usually bounced with vitality, hung limp around her face. She looked about as good as he felt.

Her gaze darted from Steve to Tyler to the other side of the room, then back to Steve again, before she answered in a strained voice. "Same, same. Dr. Lavine was here a little while ago." She gave him a weak smile. "They're going to decrease the Hypnovel tomorrow."

Steve nodded in response. They'd kept Tyler drugged for several days, reluctant to bring him out of sedation. He'd sustained a head injury, and unable to assess the extent of the damage, the medical team had elected to sedate him until the swelling subsided. The induced coma had been necessary to decrease any risk of further damage to his brain. Now it was time to wean him off the drug and see how he responded.

If he responded.

Steve's composure began to crumble.

Not here. Not now. He had to hold it together. He forced a lungful of air into his chest—a futile attempt to regain his poise—nodded carefully and finally looked around the room.

Damn stupid thing to do, inhaling like that. The sweet, subtle scent of a perfume he had not smelled in a very long time wafted around him, teasing his nose with the memories it evoked.

His gaze settled on the chair he'd come to think of as his, and as if in on cue, the muscles in his neck went into spasm.

She rose as she greeted him. "Hello, Steve."

One look, that was all, and anguish barreled over him, knocking sense from his mind. She was here. In Sydney. In Tyler's hospital room. *Sitting opposite his ex-fiancée.*

God help him, she was still as dazzling as ever. Beautiful, with her luxurious, coppery hair falling in waves over her shoulders. Her presence still had the power to render him speechless. Or perhaps it wasn't just her presence. Perhaps it had something to do with the fact that the only two women he'd ever fully given himself to, the same two women who had rejected him, sat meters apart, both facing him now.

His chest seemed to constrict, screaming in silence against the lack of oxygen in the room. He couldn't breathe, couldn't move. Every muscle in his body froze, suspended in time. An act of self-preservation? If he so much as twitched now, he'd likely turn around and flee. Get the hell away from the most excruciating circumstances he had ever been forced to face.

Or worse, he'd likely grab the woman he loved and hold on to her, tight, so she wouldn't be able to leave him again. The question was, if he did grab her, which woman would it be? And what would she think if the man she'd dumped took her in his arms again?

"Hello, Pen," he answered at last, trying in vain to throw off the claustrophobia that threatened to choke him.

She smiled. "It's good to see you again."

Good to see him? Was it really? Bullshit. He didn't believe her, not for a second. It had to be every bit as agonizing for her as it was for him. Fuck, how could she look so composed? Her brother lay in a coma beside her, and her ex-lover stood bewildered before her. What gave her the right to take it in her stride without so much as blinking an eye?

"It's...good to see you too." No, goddamn it. It wasn't. It was shocking. It was gut-wrenching. It was un-bloody-believable. Penelope Bonnard stood in the same room as him.

In the last two and a half years not a single word had passed between them. Not a letter, not an email, not even a stupid text message. Nothing. Even at the airport, when she and Tyler had boarded their plane to London two years ago, they hadn't spoken.

Sure they'd communicated that day. He'd silently begged her to stay, pleaded for another chance. She'd looked at him with those enormous chocolate-brown eyes, infinite sadness written on her face, and neither of them had said anything.

At least Kate had spoken to him when she'd given him the boot. At least she'd given him valid reasons for ending things. Not that it made the hurt any less, but at least he understood.

Now Pen was telling him it was good to see him again. Yeah, sure. As good as it was to see her brother half-dead, he imagined.

"Kate..." His throat felt rougher than usual and he cleared it and tried again. How did you talk to your ex-girlfriend about your ex-fiancée while both of them stood in the same room? "Kate told me she'd called you. She said you were coming to see Tyler." He didn't tell Pen he'd been sitting next to Kate when she made the call. Didn't tell her she'd taken the responsibility of contacting Pen off his shoulders.

"I had to come," Pen said, stating the obvious.

"Of course you did." He couldn't shrug off the guilt. He should have called; he should have been the one to tell her about Tyler. But how did you pick up the phone to tell the woman you'd once worshipped like a goddess that her brother had almost been killed in an accident?

For a long moment he looked at Pen, incapable of coherent speech. She gave him a quick smile, then dropped her gaze to the floor.

Somewhere in his peripheral vision, he saw Kate's face soften in sympathy. Damn it. The last thing he needed now was her compassion. He maintained his focus on Pen. She looked older. A few lines around her eyes and her mouth marked her thirty years. She also looked exhausted. Dead on her feet. Her lids drooped the way they always did when she was tired. God, he used to love it when she looked at him with her eyes all sleepy like that. When she'd snuggle up to him and nuzzle his chin with her mouth before curling onto her side, spooning against his chest and falling asleep.

There was none of that cozy comfort in her gaze now. Instead the fatigue he saw there seemed to be mixed with distress. Pen might appear composed, but she was cut up. No doubt about it. But then, who wouldn't be tired and troubled after a long-haul flight from London and a trip to the hospital with her ex-boyfriend's ex-fiancée to see her comatose brother?

Christ, what a fucked-up situation. For all of them.

"Tyler would be glad you're here," he told her. That was good. Talk about Tyler so he didn't have to focus on himself.

She smiled at the floor. "Bull. Tyler would be pissed that I came all the way for no good reason."

There it was. A glimmer of the fun, joking Pen he remembered. However, Steve wasn't much in the mood for smiling right now. Not with his unconscious best friend and Kate and Pen all within the same four walls of the room where he stood.

He understood why Kate called off the engagement, and after a few days he'd even started to agree with her reasoning. At thirty-two he was old and wise enough to recognize when a relationship was doomed. Didn't make it easier to bear, but he understood it.

Pen's unceremonious dumping of his ass was still incomprehensible. Compounded by the shocking information he'd recently learned about her, he almost couldn't stand the psychological torture of being in the same room as her.

Almost. The only thing worse would be if she left now. Damn it, all he wanted to do right then was pull her into his arms. Tuck her head under his chin and gather her against his chest.

Some things didn't change, even after two and half years of separation. The need to touch Penelope had always manifested as a physical ache in his gut and only worsened with each passing moment. Therein lay an essential difference between

Pen and Kate. If he hugged Kate now, it would be for mutual comfort and reassurance. If he hugged Pen it would be because he couldn't stop himself.

He kept his arms at his sides.

"Yeah," he agreed with Pen at last. "Ty probably would be pissed." He shrugged guardedly, reminding himself to keep his distance. "He'd still be happy to see you."

"I wish he could see me," Pen whispered, more to herself than to him. "I wish he knew I was here."

She deflated before his eyes. Her shoulders sagged, her chin dropped against her chest, and her shoulder-length, coppery hair fell over her cheeks, hiding her face.

He touched her arm and then wished he hadn't, because touching Pen only ever led to heartache, more heartache than one man should have to endure. "Sit down," he said softly. "You look like you could use the rest."

The gentleness in his voice annoyed him. He didn't want to be soft and gentle. He wanted to rage against the world, against the accident, against his heartache. He wanted to yell and swear and kick the crap out of the walls. He wanted to, but he didn't. It just wasn't in his nature.

She stared at him with the depth of sorrow in her eyes. "Thanks, but I've been sitting for almost twenty-four hours. I'd rather stand."

Steve nodded placidly and took a few steps backward until his shoulders touched the wall. Then he leaned against it and folded his arms across his chest. He didn't feel placid. Not by a long shot. He felt trapped and frustrated and angry.

No, he didn't. Outside of his family, these were the three people who mattered most in his life. But Tyler was unconscious, Kate had ended their engagement, and Pen had walked away from his love. What he felt was far more basic than anger or frustration.

What he felt was pain. Bone-deep, gut-wrenching pain—
and he hated it.

Chapter Two

It was midnight when Penelope spoke again. It had taken her about two hours to regain her composure. She'd almost steeled herself against the trauma of seeing Tyler unconscious. Unfortunately, two years of fierce determination had not been enough to prepare her for meeting Katie or Steve again.

How was she supposed to respond to the fiancée of the man she loved? Moreover, how was she supposed to respond when she saw the man she loved for the first time in two years?

Her legs had turned to jelly the second he'd opened the door. Before she even saw his face or heard his voice, she knew it was him. It wasn't only the familiarity of his aftershave, the masculine smell of spicy lemon that preceded his entrance. It was the five million prickles down the back of her neck and the way the hair on her arms stood on end.

When it came to Steve, she just knew.

Like she'd always known. She'd developed a crush on him the first time her brother brought home his new friend. At thirty, she was equally besotted. At twelve, there'd been the childish, naive possibility of having him. Now there was none. As much as she wanted Steve Sommers in her life forever, she couldn't have him for even a day. Especially now that he was engaged to Katie.

She yawned and then shivered, her arms suddenly icy. "I'm sorry. I know you two don't want to leave the hospital, but if I don't get some sleep I won't be functional tomorrow." The room spun; such was the level of her exhaustion. She hadn't slept in two full days, not since Katie had phoned her. The muddle of jetlag, shock and desperation had taken their toll. Sitting next to her unconscious brother, between Steve and his fiancée, was breaking her heart. If she didn't get a little space, a little perspective and a good night's sleep, she knew her composure would crack as well. She would have no reserves to call on when Tyler woke up, when he needed her to be the strong one.

Katie swung her gaze from Tyler's face to Pen's. "Oh, of course. Come on, I'll take you to your apartment."

"No," Pen objected. One car trip with Katie was enough. "You planned on staying here through the night. Don't worry about me. I'll catch a taxi."

"You're not staying at Katie's place?" Steve asked. He hadn't moved in all this time. He'd stayed where he was, motionless, as though glued to the wall.

Pen shook her head. Katie had offered, but how could she possibly stay at his fiancée's house? At the house of the woman who'd rejected her brother? She and Katie may once have been friends, but matters were far too complicated between them now. It would be easier to stay somewhere else.

She forced herself to look at Steve. Even that straightforward task was difficult, since looking at him made her long for him more than ever. "I booked a unit at the Medina in Coogee." The furnished apartment would be more practical than a hotel room—especially if she needed to be in Sydney for an extended period of time.

Katie stood. "Don't be ridiculous, Pen. You can't take a taxi. I'll give you a lift and then come straight back here afterwards. It's no bother at all."

Steve turned to Katie. "Stay with Tyler," he said. "I'll take Penelope."

Katie hesitated a second. "You sure about that?"

A silent look passed between them, and Pen blinked back the unexpected hurt at witnessing such intimacy. There was a time when she and Steve had communicated with looks and touches. A time when they understood each other without needing to speak. Now Katie held that honor.

"Of course I'm sure," Steve assured her. "Don't worry, I'll take care of everything."

Katie smiled then. "I know you will, Steve. Thank you."

The familiarity of their look, of their silent conversation, was almost too much for Pen. On top of the tiredness and the despair, it cut straight through her and tears crowded her eyes.

Damn it, damn it, damn it. She couldn't let them see how much their relationship affected her. Couldn't let them see their forthcoming marriage was almost as horrendous as Tyler's accident. Dropping her head into her hand, she rubbed her eyes. On the surface it should look as though she were wiping away the fatigue. Only she need know she was also tackling the abject misery she experienced at the sight of Steve with his fiancée—with little success.

An unexpected hand on her elbow made her jump.

"Come with me, Pen," Steve said. "I'll take you to the apartment." His voice sounded strained. Not surprising, really. He was forcing himself to leave his fiancée so he could help her, the woman who had dumped him more times than she could count.

"That's quite okay," she said formally. "I'm perfectly able to get there myself."

"Of course you are." Now Steve spoke without any emotion at all. He shrugged. "But Tyler would kill me if he knew I'd let you leave here alone, or with Kate, in the middle of the night."

Reluctantly, she nodded in acquiescence and rose with his hand as he pulled her up. Steve was right. Tyler would give him what for, and the last thing she needed to do was complicate Tyler and Steve's friendship further.

He couldn't know it, but his touch burned her arm, sending wild messages pulsing through the rest of her body. She couldn't look Katie in the eye, so she leaned over and pressed her lips to Tyler's cheek, conscious of the regular rise and fall of his chest as he breathed.

"You get better now," she told him. "Enough of your crap. Wake up and get on with your life. You hear me?" Talking to Tyler, she didn't bother holding back the tears that sprang to her eyes again. "This time tomorrow, you had better be up. Got it?"

She swiped at her eyes, leaned in closer and whispered in his ear. "You have to be okay, Ty. Please. I can't do this alone. I need you. Now more than ever. Please, be okay."

Tyler didn't move.

Penelope straightened, took the tissue Katie held out to her and blew her nose. Then she nodded goodbye, not quite capable of speech. What could she say in this situation? What words were adequate? Her brother had returned to Sydney to win back Katie's love. He hadn't. Katie was still with Steve, the man who'd had Pen's heart since she was a girl.

Neither she nor Ty could blame either of them. They'd left Sydney. Left the people they loved behind. It might be killing her slowly, but in a bizarre kind of a way she was happy Steve had found someone else. It was just freakishly unfortunate that the woman he'd chosen to spend the rest of his life with was the only woman her brother had ever loved.

"Later, Kate," Steve said, and only when he squeezed her arm did Pen realize his hand was still on her elbow.

She turned around and glanced at his hand.

He yanked it away, fast, as if he too had only just realized he was touching her. Then he busied himself by picking up

Pen's suitcases, and the two of them walked silently through the deserted hospital corridors and into the parking lot, lost in their own thoughts. Hers centered around two things: the impossible, awful situation Tyler was in and the cold emptiness on her elbow where Steve's hand had been.

"You got a new car." She took in the sleek BMW with dulled surprise. What had she expected? He'd still be driving the ten—no, twelve-year-old Holden?

Steve nodded as he held the door open for her. "Over a year ago. It's not so new."

She ignored the iron fist tightening around her heart and internalized yet another change that had taken place in his life since she'd left him. As Steve placed her bags in the boot, she clipped in her seatbelt, knowing the drive home would be excruciating. Just the two of them, stuck together in the dark interior of the BMW. In another life they wouldn't have made it home before the privacy and the proximity had them grabbing at each other's clothes. Now, she was forced to sit primly in her seat with Steve next to her, close enough to touch, yet far away enough for him to be on another planet.

The silence stretched out between them, compounding the awkwardness. Talk had never been stilted before. In that other life they'd led, they hadn't been able to find enough time to say everything they wanted to say to each other. The days had seemed too short. Now the ten-minute car ride loomed endlessly ahead of them.

Finally, Steve cleared his throat. "It's a bit of a shocker seeing him like that."

"It's incomprehensible," she agreed, determined to act as naturally as possible—even if the circumstances were anything but. "I can't come to terms with the idea that Tyler might never recover from his injuries." That her older brother—the person she turned to for protection, for help, for insight and wisdom, for friendship and love—might never be the same. "It doesn't make sense. Things like this aren't supposed to happen to the people you love." Tyler was *supposed* to be okay. He was *supposed* to live a full and healthy life. His future wasn't meant to be all wrapped up in uncertainty again.

"I'd like to say you get used to it," Steve said in a rough voice. "But you don't."

"I want—" Her voice broke as the tears started up fresh. "I want him to be okay," she finished on a whisper. One of them was supposed to fulfill their dreams, and they both knew that person was Tyler. How could he be in this position? Her indestructible brother had sustained such serious injuries that he might never fully recover. What cruel joke was destiny playing on his life?

Steve answered somberly. "We all want him to be okay."

She swallowed and let the tears fall unobstructed. "Katie t-told me you've spent a lot of time at the hospital. She, uh, said you've only really been home to change clothes." That had been a fun discussion. Yep, a real blast discussing Steve with his fiancée. She hiccupped quietly.

"We both have." He sounded so detached. "We had to be with Tyler."

Although he answered her and talked to her, Pen sensed he didn't want to be here with her.

"Oh...I, er, I thought..." She let her words trail off, realizing what she'd been about to ask was none of her business.

"You thought what?" Steve prompted warily.

She sniffed through her tears. "I...thought you weren't speaking to Tyler."

He took a long time to answer. "I wasn't." He shrugged as if it didn't matter.

Pen wasn't fooled. The nonchalant gesture told her more than his words did. It mattered a great deal to him, but he wasn't about to share that with her. The thing about loving Steve since she was a kid was that Pen knew him. She knew every subtle nuance of his tone, every expression on his face. She'd spent so many years studying his every move, it was impossible not to understand the way his mind worked. So she knew now Steve was more than a little concerned about the way things had been between him and Tyler.

"And yet you still want to be by his side."

"We had a fight, Pen. Things got a bit tense. That's it. You think I wouldn't be here for my oldest friend?"

A bit tense? Tyler had told him he loved Katie, and Steve had belted him. A *bit* tense might be a *bit* of an understatement. "I'm glad you *are* here for him. He would be too, if he knew."

His face was momentarily lit up by another car's headlights, and Pen saw him grimace.

"He hated what he did to your friendship," she told him. "He wanted Katie back, but he never wanted to hurt you."

Steve's responding laugh was bitter, and Pen retreated into herself. What was the point in forcing a conversation with a man who did not want to talk to her?

They drove in silence. Deafening silence. Finally, Pen could take it no more. The tears had stopped for now, and she took a deep, silent breath and swallowed her pride. "I, uh, never congratulated you."

"For what?" He didn't look at her, concentrating on a red traffic light instead.

God, this was excruciating. Harder than she'd dreamed. "For your engagement."

He gave a little snort and pulled off as the light changed. "You're joking, right?"

What did he think? She'd have trouble behaving like a grown-up? She was too proud to wish her ex-boyfriend good luck with his new fiancée? "Not at all. Katie is lovely. I'm sure you'll be happy with her."

Pen closed her eyes against the hurt stabbing through her stomach. The important thing was that Steve should be happy. She wanted him to have a good marriage. Ideally, she'd have liked him to have a good marriage with her, but that was out of the question.

His next words had her eyes popping open in disbelief. "Katie and I broke up."

"*What?*"

"She called it off a couple of hours after I hit your brother."

Pen gaped at Steve. "But...but...I thought..."

"Yeah?" Steve prompted.

"Tyler told me Katie chose you." Halfway across the world, Pen had listened to her brother's drunken ramblings. Heard his sad lament of how he'd lost Katie to his ex-best friend. Even long-distance, she'd felt his devastation at the loss.

"Tyler was wrong." His voice was bland, his face in shadows.

"Oh my God!" Pen breathed, gobsmacked. "She chose Tyler."

"Yep."

"He doesn't know." She'd spoken to him a couple of hours before the accident. Tyler had been on his way to visit Katie and Steve, to wish them luck for their future together. He'd never made it to their medical practice. The four-wheel drive had stopped him a couple kilometers short of his destination.

"Nope."

"Oh God." She started to cry again. "He doesn't know." He'd been destroyed by Katie's choice. Lost. He'd thought everything

27

he'd put himself through for a chance at happiness with Katie was all for nothing—and he'd been wrong.

She hadn't chosen Steve. It had been Tyler all along, but before Katie had a chance to tell him, he'd been knocked clear off his bike.

Pen cried a little harder. "He's lying there fighting for his life, and he has no idea Katie's right there beside him, fighting with him."

Now it all made sense, Steve's stoic position holding up the wall, Katie's bedside devotion, her reluctance to leave Tyler's room even for a minute. The compulsive need to hold Tyler's hand or touch his face.

She dropped her head and sobbed. Through her tears, she registered Steve had pulled into a parking space beside the Medina. "It's not fair, Steve. He thought he was all alone. He thought he'd lost you and he'd lost Katie, but he was wrong."

Steve didn't comment, didn't stir.

The lump in her throat was back, making speech almost impossible. "You're both there for him, and...and...and he doesn't know." How could life be so cruel?

Steve sat rigid, staring at her.

Now she'd started crying in earnest, she couldn't stop. Too many emotions and too many memories rained down on her. She simply sat in the car and howled her eyes out.

Beside her, Steve shifted, moved, then froze again.

She sobbed. Tyler, her rock, her only stability in the tumultuous joke her life had become, was hurt.

She heard a bang as Steve smacked the steering wheel, and the next thing she knew, he'd unstrapped her seatbelt and pulled her onto his lap. The gear box nudged her thigh and the steering wheel pushed into her ribs, but she didn't care. She was back in Steve's arms.

It had been so long since she'd given in to the need to cry and even longer since she'd allowed herself the luxury of being held by Steve, she couldn't stop herself now. Not when the man she'd loved for longer than she remembered offered her the security of his physical and emotional strength.

She gave in to the iron fist squeezing her heart, put her head on Steve's shoulder and sobbed like a baby. She cried and she cried and she cried. She cried for her brother, who had no way of knowing how much he was loved. She cried for Katie, who sat at her true love's bedside, praying for him to regain consciousness. She cried for Steve, for the pain and the hurt that came from a broken engagement. And she cried for herself—for the innocent, happy past she could never have again and for the intolerable future looming ahead of her.

Eventually, when exhaustion overtook her, the sobs began to subside, replaced by irregular breathing and the odd hiccup, but she didn't move. She remained where she was, in the shelter of Steve's arms. He stroked her hair, running his hand over her head and then letting the strands of hair slip through his fingers before starting again.

Like he used to do when they'd sit together in comfortable silence, enjoying each other's company, sharing each other's space.

Lost in time for the shortest minute, Penelope felt safe, cushioned from reality by Steve's solid chest and steely arms. For an even briefer moment, before reality intruded, she let herself believe the Bonnard siblings could, and would, survive. She and Tyler would make it after all.

Of course, it wasn't true.

He held her. She was back in his arms and Steve was thrown by how good she felt there. How right. Damn, he'd fought it, rallied against it. Pen didn't want him. He shouldn't be holding her, but in the end he couldn't keep his distance. He'd never been able to. How could he just sit back and watch her torment? He had to offer her comfort.

Kate and he had never fit together this well, as though their bodies were made for each other. Pen's curves seemed to match his hollows, her softness the perfect foil to his sinew. How could he have forgotten?

Silent sobs still wracked her body every so often, but the worst of the storm was over. She lay spent, plastered against his chest. For the first time since he'd lost his best friend and his fiancée, Steve's heart began to beat again. Jaggedly, but at least it beat. At least he felt alive.

Her hair felt like spun silk between his fingers, and her slim body seemed frail as a child's nestled within his embrace. Except she wasn't a child. The enticing, round breasts pushing into his shirt were a tangible reminder of that fact. As were the sharp bones of her hips and the firm, feminine buttocks resting on his legs and brushing against his groin.

If her proximity hadn't felt so damn good, it would have been painful holding her this close. His body reacted on instinct, blood flowing to his groin.

Oh, Christ. An erection. Now. *Now?*

He fought it down, but knew he wouldn't stand a chance if she wriggled her butt one more time. Pen didn't need some lust-crazed, ex-boyfriend hankering after her with a raging hard-on.

Hell, he didn't need it either. He needed to push her off his lap and forget about her.

So why couldn't he? Why was the need to protect her and comfort her shadowing common sense, shadowing his anger and frustration and pain? Maybe he was doing it for Tyler. Maybe he was giving her what Tyler would have—had he been conscious.

A long time ago, before she'd kissed him and blown his world apart with her passion, she'd just been his friend's kid sister. His surrogate sister. Regardless of what had happened between them since then, a part of him would always view her as such. If Pen needed family now, he didn't really have a choice. For Tyler's sake, he'd have to be her family.

Or maybe he wouldn't... Pen chose that exact moment to sink a little deeper into his lap. While logic told him her actions were innocent, his body surged to life in an electrifying rush, leaving Steve winded and aroused. And not just a little perplexed.

He should have known, should have realized he stood no chance. From the second he'd pulled her onto his lap, he'd fought a losing battle. There was never any question of escaping unharmed. Pen need only breathe, and Steve responded. Even his experience with Kate hadn't dimmed his attraction to Pen. Her butt pressing into his thighs and groin was a savage reminder of their sensuous past. A past she'd tossed aside.

Before Pen had a chance to discover his predicament, Steve repositioned himself beneath her weight, gaining some much-needed space. Reluctant to let her go, however, even reminding himself of the pain she'd caused him, he kept his arms around her, ensuring her breasts still burrowed into his chest.

The movement must have jolted Pen, for she lifted her head from his shoulder and straightened her back.

"Oh, shit! Steve, I'm sorry." She wiped her eyes and then his shoulder, which was wet from her tears. "I...I didn't mean to lose it like that. I don't know what happened."

She was killing him. The hand on his shirt rubbed uselessly at the moisture, yet burned a hole through the cotton. He bit his cheek hard, determined not to groan out loud.

"And selfish of me too. What was I thinking?" Her hand stilled and she froze for a second before she hurriedly wiggled off his lap, over the gear shift—which did not look easy—and landed on the passenger seat. "Here I am crying for Tyler because Katie still loves him and I didn't even think about you." She turned to face him. "She...she left you."

Steve had trouble concentrating. His arms were empty, his lap free of its burden, and he did not like it one bit.

"She broke off the engagement," Pen said.

Okay. That did it. Brought his concentration back into sharp focus with a slam-dunk.

"Yeah, she called the wedding off." All of a sudden it wasn't so easy sustaining an erection.

"I'm so sorry, Steve." There was genuine sympathy in her voice.

Steve wasn't interested in sympathy. Especially not Penelope's. Pity about his broken engagement was the last thing he needed from the woman who'd destroyed his heart. "Don't be," he told her dispassionately.

"I know how you must feel," she commiserated.

He raised an eyebrow, even though he knew she couldn't see it. "You do?" Impossible. She didn't have a fucking clue.

"I understand the hurt and the pain of a broken relationship." Her voice caught.

His eyes had adjusted enough to the darkness to be able to see a tremor wrack her body. Another silent sob or something else?

Then she added as an afterthought, "Believe it or not."

Three days ago, he wouldn't have believed it. After she'd so callously cut him free from their relationship, he'd have had trouble believing she felt anything about it at all. But then three days ago, he hadn't known Pen had a fifty percent chance of inheriting a fatal disease.

Fuck, it hurt just to think about her risk of developing

Huntington's Disease—especially with Pen sitting right beside him, healthy and glowing with life and vitality. He pushed the thought aside and nodded. "Yeah, Pen. Broken relationships hurt like hell."

"You didn't deserve what you got."

"None of us did," he said. "Tyler doesn't deserve his injuries, Kate doesn't deserve to lose someone before she's even found him again, and, no, I don't need the pain of a screwed-up romance any more than you d—" He paused and checked his words. "Any more than you deserve to watch your brother suffer like this."

"You must have loved her very much."

Steve stared at her. Fuck, what did she expect him to say? What could he possibly say under the circumstances? How did he begin to explain what he and Kate had? He shrugged and said nothing, choosing to climb out of the car instead. He circled around it and opened Pen's door. "Let's go and get you checked in."

Steve offered her his hand, which she stared at for a full minute before accepting and stepping on to the pavement. He should have moved out of her way, given her more space, but for some reason, he couldn't. Didn't want to. He stood where he was, blocking her path. Wedging her between himself and the car so the length of her body was flush against his. His erection, which had been so ruthlessly squashed, came soaring back to life.

She looked up at him. "Steve?" Her voice trembled.

"Sunshine." Jesus, rational thought was impossible. He knew he shouldn't call her that. She wasn't his anymore, but she was so close, she consumed his senses. Her hair smelled like sun and honey, a remarkable achievement after a day spent on a plane and in a hospital room.

She caught her breath and then released it erratically. Her

hands fluttered at her sides—the way they always did when she was nervous.

He brought his fingers up to her cheek, touched the not-quite-dry trail of a tear and wiped it away. Then he did it again, this time to run his palm over her satiny skin.

"Wh-what are you doing?" Pen whispered.

"Remembering," Steve answered without thinking.

"You shouldn't." Her voice was soft.

"I have to." Touching her was a compulsion. He ran his thumb over her lips, felt a wisp of warm air escape from her mouth.

"You're still in love with Katie," she breathed.

"This isn't about Katie," he answered. It wasn't. Right here, right now was just about the two of them. Steve and Pen and the millions of unresolved issues between them.

"But—"

"Shh, Sunshine." He took advantage of her open mouth to dip the pad of his thumb inside. He should use her real name, but in the moment he couldn't think of her as Penelope. He thought of her as his own personal ray of light. In the moment, with her snug against him, although dawn was still several hours away, the sun shone again.

Well, almost.

"I...oh." Her teeth grazed the sensitive flesh of his thumb, and he bit back a groan. The need to kiss her was staggering. If he hadn't seen firsthand how exhausted and how emotionally overwrought she was, he'd have taken her lips right then. Molded his mouth to hers and reclaimed what once had been his. Once. A long time ago. Before he'd gotten engaged.

Steve dropped his arm and stepped aside, giving Pen the freedom to walk past him.

Chapter Three

Time seemed to blend into a confusion of jet lag and waiting. Penelope wasn't sure how late it was, or how long she'd been sitting at Tyler's bedside. She just knew several hours had passed since the neurosurgeon had been to see him.

"There's absolutely no change in his condition," she said out loud. She didn't care that she stated the obvious. The silence and the tension were taking their toll, and if someone didn't speak, she would surely go insane. "He hasn't moved. He hasn't coughed. He hasn't even taken an irregular breath. What good is stopping the sedative if he still isn't waking up?"

That morning, encouraged by what she'd called "Tyler's progress", Dr. Lavine had not just reduced the Hypnovel, she'd stopped it altogether.

"I thought by now he'd have at least stirred," Katie agreed. She sat in the same chair she'd occupied last night. Although she'd been home to shower, she didn't look very different from the day before. She was still anxious and pale, and her gaze was still plastered on Tyler's face, intent, hopeful and frustrated.

Now that Pen knew the truth about the status of Steve and Katie's engagement, she found she did not resent Katie as much as she had yesterday. That didn't mean it wasn't excruciating to be in the same room as her, especially with Steve there as well. Even if the relationship was over, they had still been engaged.

Too many times Pen thought about what they had been like as a couple. Whether the sex between them was as explosive as it had been between her and Steve. Unwanted images of Steve making love to Katie plagued her—and the ecstasy she pictured on his face as he came made her want to throw up.

"What good is it being a doctor if you can't do a fucking thing to help your best friend?" Steve snarled, more to himself than to either of them. Far from looking ecstatic, his expression was pained as he paced the length of the room obsessively. He'd been doing it for so long, Pen had memorized the number of steps it took him to cross the floor and back again—five and a half each way. Without looking at him, she also knew from the shuffle of feet and the momentary pause between footsteps, when he reached one wall, stopped, turned around and paced back to the other wall.

"You're not Tyler's doctor," Katie reminded him gently. "You're his friend."

"Was his friend," Steve said without breaking pace.

Katie turned to look at him, compassion written over her face. Damn, there it was again, that special understanding between Katie and Steve. Their engagement may not have survived, but that bond between them had.

"And you will be again, Steve," Katie reassured him. "When he wakes up, when you can talk to him, you can settle all of this."

It wasn't just compassion, Pen realized with a start. Tangled up in the look Katie gave Steve was a hint of desperation as well. A desperation Pen could not begin to fathom.

"*If* he wakes up," Steve growled, then as if realizing what he'd said, he stopped short in front of the wall and kicked it, hard. "*When* he wakes up, damn it!"

"Tyler will wake up," Pen said, more wishful than certain.

"He has to." The thought of him never regaining consciousness, or perhaps waking up but being...different was too appalling to consider. What if, instead of Ty looking after her, she'd be the one who had to take care of him? The breath caught in her throat. What if that happened? Who would look after Tyler in the long run? Who would take care of the brother who had always taken such good care of her? Katie?

"Soon," said Katie. "It will happen soon." Then she added, much softer, as if almost in prayer, "Please, God, let it be soon."

In that sentence, in that one, heartfelt plea, Pen could hear every one of Katie's reasons for breaking up with Steve. No matter what Steve and Katie shared, no matter how special their connection, Katie was in love with Tyler. Fully, wholly and completely in love with her brother.

The knowledge, however, did not make spending time with her easier. Nor did it lessen the impact of picturing Steve's face while he made love to Katie. Their engagement might be over, but it had existed, and Pen couldn't get over that fact easily. Not when every one of her fantasies for the last eighteen years had revolved around Steve being married to her.

Steve. He'd been there for her last night when she needed him. The comfort she'd gained from his embrace had been immeasurable.

As had the pleasure. Through her grief, she'd been aware of the way her body responded to his. The way her heart fluttered haphazardly and her limbs filled with a cozy warmth. The way heat strummed through her veins and her skin quivered beneath her clothes. The way her head tingled beneath his touch like it always had. If she were a hundred and five and Steve touched her, she knew she'd respond the same way.

If.

Pen took a deep breath. The atmosphere was heavy in the small room. Weighted with expectancy and disappointment. She felt stifled, experienced a prickling need to get outside and breathe fresh air. Instead, she filled her lungs with stale oxygen and forced herself to remain seated. How could she think about her own needs at a time like this?

"I have to get out of here." Steve's irritated voice mirrored her thoughts. His face was drawn, his lips pressed together. He clenched and unclenched his left hand. "I'm going to get some coffee. Kate? Would you like something?"

Katie pulled her attention away from Tyler. She glanced at Steve, then at the door, then back at Tyler. For a second, she looked undecided, as if measuring up the pull towards Steve against the urge to stay with Tyler, but then a look of rugged determination crossed her face, and she sat back in her chair. "I'd love a long black with an extra shot of coffee and two sugars."

Steve nodded and slid his gaze across the room until it came to rest on Penelope's face. The lines around his mouth tightened. His lips, usually full and soft, stretched thin. "Pen?"

Her cheeks grew warm under his stare, and she shifted in her seat. What were her choices? Stay with Katie while her brother slept and let the awkward silences draw out endlessly between them? Or go with Steve and risk letting him see the longing and the desire she felt for him, the urge to seek further comfort in his embrace?

She looked at her sleeping brother, heard his even breathing and was reminded once again she shouldn't leave him. If he woke up, she wanted to be there.

Then her foot began to tingle. It had been tucked away on the seat, beneath her butt for so long, she was getting pins and needles. Restlessness got the better of her, and she stood. "I think I'll come with you." And then, unsure about imposing herself on Steve yet again, she added, "If you don't mind?"

A hint of a smile touched his lips but was gone long before

it reached his eyes. "Let's go," he said and motioned with his head towards the door.

As Pen stood, uncertainty wracked her. Was it okay to go? What if Tyler woke up? What if he needed her?

Steve must have read the doubt in her expression. He held up his mobile phone to Katie, who nodded in response. Pen sighed. If anything happened, they were only a phone call away.

She didn't mean to do it, but as Steve held the door open for her, she inhaled his scent. The once-familiar aroma of spicy lemon and sexy male permeated her senses, blocking out the medicinal odor that pervaded the hospital. God, his smell. It had always driven her to distraction, and nothing had changed. She had to force her eyes to stay open. The lids threatened to droop in conjunction with the urge to melt against his chest, rest her nose in the hollow of his neck and breathe him in for the rest of the day.

Giving her head a little shake to clear it, she scooted out of the room. It didn't matter what Steve had said or done last night, didn't matter that he'd had an erection as he'd held her, he was no longer hers. He wasn't Katie's either, but that had nothing to do with Penelope's reason for leaving Steve in the first place. No matter how enticing the thought of slipping back into the old "Steve and Pen" routine was, it could not happen again.

"Coffee shop's this way," Steve directed as he fell into step beside her. "Christ, I was going stir-crazy in there."

She checked her watch. "It's been almost six hours since they stopped the meds."

Steve swore. "There should be some kind of a response by now."

Penelope stopped dead in her tracks and stared at him, aghast. He was a GP, and if he was worried, there was something to worry about. "Does this mean...?" She swallowed hard, too scared to ask her question. Or rather too scared to hear the answer. "Are you saying...?" Damn it. The words stuck in her throat.

"Hell, no," he answered quickly. "That's not what I'm saying at all. Look—" he shoved his hand through his wheat-colored hair, "—Kate was right. I'm not Tyler's doctor, I'm a friend." His voice was rough. "I'm not talking medically. I...I want to see a response, that's all."

She saw the weariness and strain in his sky-blue eyes. "I know how you feel." She sighed tiredly. "It's doing my head in."

He nodded. "Mine too. C'mon. Let's get that coffee."

They ordered food as well. Pen hadn't eaten since early morning, and her stomach had begun to protest.

"Do you think he can hear us?" she asked as she bit into her roast vegetable wrap.

"Honestly? I don't have a clue." He set his phone down on the table between them and shrugged. "It would be nice."

Pen stared at the silent phone. "He'd know what was happening. That Katie still—" she hesitated, checking her words, "—that Katie is with him."

Steve ate his food without answering.

"And you," she said. "If he knows you're here, then he knows you're not mad at him anymore."

He let the words hang in the air between them.

It was surreal sitting with Steve. The last time she'd seen him, two years ago, she'd been leaving for London. It had almost killed her to stand so near and not say a word. But she was too close to tears to risk a goodbye. If she'd opened her mouth, she would have blurted out the truth.

That would not have been fair. Not to Steve and not to her. So instead she'd remained stoic and icy. She'd ignored his silent petition to stay. She'd ignored everything that day, even the desolate weeping of her heart.

Of course she was paying the price now. Steve had erected his invisible barriers again. He treated her like a virtual stranger. "How have you been?" she asked him.

He looked at her, his gaze shuttered. "Okay, I guess."

She could hardly bear his distance. He didn't want to be with her. But circumstances had drawn them together, and the thought of spending this already dreadful time with Steve ignoring her drove her to act. She was determined to break the ice, to get him to talk. "Tell me about the practice," she invited.

He shrugged again. "Not much to tell. It's going well. Our patient list grows every day."

Maybe if the conversation wasn't so focused on him he'd unwind a little. "And how is your family?" She adored Steve's family. Always had—and she knew the feeling was reciprocal. Or it used to be, anyway, before she'd dumped Steve for the last time.

"They're good." He nodded, and to her relief his shoulders relaxed slightly. "Sam's in Tanzania with his girlfriend. They've just climbed Kilimanjaro."

"Sounds like something your brother would do." She smiled. "Is he a millionaire yet?" Sam had always promised to be one by the time he reached thirty. He was twenty-nine now.

Steve didn't try to hide his pride. "Several times over. He listed his company about eighteen months ago. Things went well, even taking into account the economic slump."

Fantastic news. At least someone's brother was living his dream. "I never expected anything less. Will you send him my love?"

Steve nodded. "He'll be happy to hear from you."

"And how are your parents?"

"Exactly the same." Her tactic was working. This time his

smile reached his eyes. "My father's still threatening to retire, yet happily going to work every day, and my mother's still threatening to leave him if he doesn't quit, yet dropping him at the office every morning at eight-thirty sharp."

Pen smiled. Hearing about them was bittersweet. From the minute she'd met Steve's folks, they'd made her feel like part of the family. They treated her like the daughter they'd never had. As much as she loved his domineering, headstrong mother, it was his father—the loving, laid-back man so much like his elder son—who especially held a place in her heart. His jovial smile and paternal kisses never failed to wrench a reaction from her. It didn't take a psychologist to work out why.

Steve was a lucky guy. He had a perfect family.

Pen had Tyler. The perfect brother—in an imperfect condition.

A look of cynical amusement flashed across Steve's face.

"What?" Pen asked.

"What, what?" Steve responded.

"What was that look all about?"

"What look?"

"The one that said you should laugh but it's not appropriate."

Steve shook his head. "It's nothing." But his mouth lifted on one side for the briefest time before he frowned.

"What?" she asked again.

"What, what?"

"Steve, quit stalling. What is that look all about?" Damn, it was too familiar. The half-finished sentences, the ability to read him so easily. After all this time things should have changed. She shouldn't still know him this well.

He stared at her for a long time. "Know what my father said when I told him I was getting married?"

Her stomach lurched. Oh, crap, maybe she didn't want to know after all. Even though his engagement was off, it hurt to think about it. She shook her head. "No?"

"He wanted to know when you'd gotten back to Sydney."

"You...mean he...?" She let her voice trail off.

"Yeah, Pen. That's what I mean."

Penelope internalized that piece of information. "Katie must have been thrilled about that," she said after a while.

"I never told her. Some things are better kept to yourself."

Now there was a comment Pen agreed with wholeheartedly. Just look at what she'd kept to herself all this time.

Steve gave a snort of unamused laughter. "Want to know what he said when I told him the engagement was off?"

She didn't answer.

"He wanted to know when you'd gotten back to Sydney."

"Steve. I—" Good grief, how was she supposed to respond?

"Don't worry about it. My mother gave him a couple of not-so-gentle nudges in his ribs. I didn't need to answer—either time."

Pen had two options. She could either cry because more than anything in the world she wanted to be the one Steve married, and she loved the fact his father had assumed Steve felt the same way. Or she could laugh at the typical Stan Sommers' lack of tact.

She chose to laugh. Only the sound caught on a lump in her throat and came out as a hiccup, which was quickly followed by her eyes filling with tears. Before she knew it, she was crying again.

"Shit, Pen, I'm sorry. I didn't mean to make you cry. I know you and my father had a special thing going between you. I thought you'd appreciate his...misunderstanding."

Pen couldn't speak. An overwhelming grief washed through

43

her, overshadowing logic and common sense. She couldn't think straight. All she could do was feel, and all she felt was sad. Damn sad.

Was this it then? Was this how it all started, with an inability to control her own emotions?

The unexpected thought shocked her so severely her breath caught in her throat, making her hiccup again. Panic clawed at her chest.

Irrational thought processes and lack of control.

Her breathing was all messed up. She hiccupped again and then again. Now? It was starting now? She was too young, wasn't she?

It wasn't supposed to happen like his. Tyler was supposed to be okay and healthy. He was supposed to help her through all of this. How could he if he was bloody unconscious? And how could she help him not be unconscious if she was in the process of losing her mind?

Was she actually losing her mind?

Her hands felt funny, warm, and she stared down at them. Steve held them, rubbing them rhythmically with his own, talking softly to her. "It's okay, Pen. It's all going to be okay."

It took a while for the meaning to sink in. She was overwrought and more than a little terrified. This was her second emotional outburst in less than twenty-four hours. Had she lost control completely? She, who'd learned to hold her emotions in such tight rein?

She looked at him wildly and hiccupped. "How can it be okay, Steve? I can't even help my own brother. How is it ever going to be okay?"

"You're not alone. Kate and I are here to help Tyler too." He laced his fingers through hers and caressed her thumbs with his. "I'm here to help you."

She shook her head. "Uh uh. You can't help me. You have to stay away from me." He didn't know. He didn't have a clue.

"I'm here for you, Sunshine."

"Damn it." She yanked her hands away from his, anger replacing the sorrow. "This isn't about me. It's about Tyler."

Unexpected outbursts of rage.

"Yeah, Pen. It's about Tyler. But it's about us also. It has been from the minute you arrived home." His gaze was steady, but his voice was uneven.

"There is no *us*," she snapped. "There hasn't been for a long time." Not since she went to live in London, and certainly not since Steve proposed to Katie.

"There will always be an us, Pen." This time he couldn't look at her. He stared over her shoulder. "As long as we live, there will be us."

"As long as we live?" She snorted out loud. "Hah, there's an ironic little twist." And then she bit her tongue because she'd already said way more than she'd meant to.

Lack of concentration?

"Look, be glad there is no you and me anymore, Steve. You have no obligation to be there for me."

Steve's gaze shot back to her face. "What is that supposed to mean?"

"Nothing. Okay? It means nothing." Shit, she needed to shut up. Now.

He sat a little straighter. "Pen, are you all right?"

She didn't answer, merely looked past him towards the gift shop opposite their table. What would she say anyway? *No, I'm not okay, and if my damned behavior is anything to go by, I don't think I'll ever be okay again.*

"Pen?"

She shook her head, ignoring his gentle probing.

"It's okay to be angry," he told her. "It's natural under these circumstances."

She looked at him, horrified. Oh God. Did he know? Her heart beat a little faster.

"I'm also angry. Furious actually," he told her matter-of-factly.

She stared at him.

"I'm pissed your dumbass brother did this to himself."

She nodded as she breathed a short sigh of relief. He was talking about the accident.

She too was incensed Tyler's life should get so messed up at the exact time it was getting back on track. She knew it was irrational to be cross with him, knew he was blameless for his present circumstances. Nevertheless, she was furious. But then Steve was too, so maybe it was natural and it wasn't symptomatic of anything else.

"I'm scared too, Pen."

She bit her lip. Felt the lump in her throat resurface. At least the hiccups had stopped. "You are?"

He nodded. "And more than a little upset."

Even though he was mad as hell at her, he still took time out to normalize the situation. Calm her down. Make her irrational behavior and thoughts seem usual under the unusual circumstances. It worked. If Steve experienced the same things she did, maybe she wasn't becoming symptomatic yet. Maybe she was reacting normally to an abnormal situation.

She took a deep breath, covered her face with her hands. "I'm sorry," she said at length. "You must think I'm some kind of lunatic."

He smiled. "Yeah, I do, but then I always have. Nothing's changed. Besides—" she heard something in his voice she couldn't identify, "—I always liked that you were a little crazy."

He took her hand again and held it gently in his own. "I also think you're in crisis now, and instead of apologizing for your behavior you should let it out."

Just like before, Steve was taking control of the situation, giving her comfort, encouraging her to voice her grief instead of brushing it aside. When her mother died at that terrible, terrible time of her life, Steve had been the one to hold her, comfort her, share her pain. He'd been the one to make it almost tolerable. Alone, she doubted she'd have gotten through it. With Steve she'd survived.

Now he was making sure she survived again.

How did he do it? After all this time, after all she'd put him through, how did he still manage to reel her in when she lost the plot? He'd always been able to lay her irrational fears to rest and add laughter to her tears. He'd injected reality into her fantasies, yet shown her magic in everyday life. When she'd let him, he'd anchored her firmly to the ground, yet pushed her to go the distance. Now he'd done it again—made her feel normal in a time that was anything but.

Was it any wonder she'd never stop loving him?

She took a sip of her half-finished coffee, which by now was lukewarm and bitter. In the midst of her chaos she'd forgotten to add sugar.

She owed him the truth. Never mind if some things were better kept to herself. All along she'd known it was damn unfair to leave without an explanation, to let Steve believe she didn't love him enough. The fear of his discovering her secret, however, had always been a more powerful deterrent than the justice of telling him had been a motivation. In her mind the worst possible outcome would be Steve knowing.

She'd debated the issue in her head endlessly, discussed it with Tyler to the nth degree. Every time her position had remained firm. Steve could not be told. The mortification that came with his comprehension of the situation would be worse than the hurt she caused him by retaining the truth.

Yet suddenly, sitting across from him, she knew she owed him an explanation. Knew she couldn't hide out any longer. No matter how much pain she'd caused him in the past, and God knew it wasn't a nominal amount, he still offered her strength and support in her time of need. He selflessly gave of himself to make her feel better. He deserved the truth. No matter how insufferable it might be for her.

For the entire duration of their on-again, off-again relationship, she'd never once explained her inability to commit. She'd simply let him believe she wasn't interested in a long-term romance. How many times had she broken up with him? Four? Five? The times when she'd gone to him for the pure physical release of making love and then left again didn't count as breaking up. They were simply times when she'd needed him so badly, she couldn't get through another day without touching him. He was her drug of choice and she was addicted.

Shortly after her mother died, the gritty truth of her reality had become too authentic to deny, and she'd walked away permanently. Her brother had gone with her. The move had been necessary. An addiction was an addiction, and she'd never have given Steve up if she lived close by. She had to be on another continent.

Now unforeseen circumstances had brought her back home, and she knew she had to tell him the truth at last. It was the right time to do it. They weren't ensconced in each other's lives anymore. They'd had two years apart and could both be objective about their relationship. Well, Steve could be at any rate. Since he'd been engaged to another woman it was highly unlikely he still thought about Pen quite as much as she thought about him.

Still, how could she ever, *ever* dredge up the courage to tell him?

"Steve?" Unable to look him in the face, she studied his T-shirt.

"Yeah?"

His shirt was navy, with a Mambo logo on it. Beneath it his chest rose and fell as he breathed. She couldn't make out the six-pack under the material, but she knew it was there, hard and appealing and sexy as hell. Last night, when she'd laid her head against the solid wall of muscle, she'd felt the calm of his masculine sturdiness and the predictability of her feminine response.

Even now, watching it, her heart trembled beneath her breast.

"Yeah, Pen?" he prompted.

Tremors ran down her spine. Nerves? Awareness? "I need to tell you something."

His chest stilled for the briefest time before resuming its steady motion.

"I have a secret."

Steve inhaled sharply, causing his shirt to stretch taut across his shoulders.

Her hands shook. "A terrible secret." She wanted to throw up. Didn't know if she could go on. She should have done this years ago. Should have told him the truth when she'd ended their relationship for the last time.

"Tell me about it." Steve's response was firm. There was no backing out now.

She tensed her shoulders, bracing herself for the gritty conversation. Before she said a word, the silence between them was pierced by a shrill ring.

Pen stared at the vibrating mobile phone with a kind of morbid fascination as the name "Kate" lit up the screen.

Chapter Four

Tyler's eyes moved slowly from person to person. He stared at Kate for the longest moment before swinging his gaze to Pen's face and then to Steve's.

Steve's heart banged. Fear and anticipation welled together. His friend was awake. He didn't have a chance to smile before Tyler swung his gaze back to Penelope. He looked at her, baffled.

"Pen?" he rasped

"Yeah, Ty. It's me."

He had to give it to her. Her voice was smooth and clear, even though she trembled beside him. Unable to stop himself, he placed a comforting hand on the small of her back and was rewarded by her leaning into it. The closeness they'd shared moments ago, however, was lost in the drama of Tyler's awakening. Whatever Pen had been about to tell him would have to wait, indefinitely.

While Steve was thrilled Ty was awake, he was not so happy he never got to hear Pen's secret. A secret he'd waited two and a half years to be told.

Tyler narrowed his eyes and frowned. Again he looked at Kate and then Steve. His face appeared perplexed.

"Pen?" he said as he focused back on her.

"I'm right here, Ty." She took his free hand, gently, Steve

noticed, so as not to jolt his injured arm. "How are you feeling?"

Tyler furrowed his eyebrows, concentrating. "Tired?"

"Then rest."

Tyler opened his mouth but then closed it, as if he'd lost whatever words he'd been about to voice.

Pen placed a hand on his cheek. "Don't try to talk now. Rest."

His gaze locked with Penelope's, and he nodded as his eyes drifted shut.

One nurse monitored his vitals while another checked his drip. Dr. Lavine wrote on his chart. Steve watched, frustrated and emotional, as Tyler slipped back into an exhausted sleep. His friend might have woken up, but he was confused and out of sorts.

Dr. Lavine replaced his chart and looked at the three of them. "We can't tell much yet. It'll take a couple of days for the drugs to wear off. Only then will we be able to assess his condition accurately."

"He doesn't know where he is," Pen said.

"No," the doctor agreed. "His thoughts are disorganized."

"Is it...is it indicative of something serious?" she asked.

"We won't know until he's fully conscious," Dr. Lavine told her candidly. "It might be from his injuries. It might be from the drugs. Time will tell."

Kate sighed. "He may have woken up, but the wait's not over."

Although he'd expected this, a second rush of frustration hit Steve square in the chest. At least, he consoled himself, Ty had recognized his sister.

Tyler woke again about an hour later, complaining of a dry mouth. He fell straight back to sleep after a sip of water.

The third time he awoke, Pen had stepped out of the room,

and Kate was asleep in her chair. Steve watched as Tyler opened his eyes and settled his gaze on Kate. Steve didn't say a word, didn't disturb him. He watched as Tyler took in Kate's face.

Tyler was conscious for maybe five minutes, and in all that time he did not look away from Kate. Whatever else went on in his head, whatever else he thought or tried to work out, one thing was blatantly evident. Tyler loved Kate. The accident had done nothing to change that fact.

There was a time Steve had looked at a woman the same way Tyler looked at Kate. A time when he couldn't keep his eyes off Penelope. Didn't try. Across the room or at his side, Pen had drawn his gaze, and he'd known, each time he looked at her, the depth of his love had shone from his face. He couldn't suppress it. He'd simply loved her, and he wanted her to know it every time she glanced his way.

Never, in all the time he'd been with Kate, had he ever looked at her in the same manner. When he was with her he felt affection, fondness, warmth, and yes, love too. But he had never been intensely, deeply in love with her. Not the way Tyler was. Not the way Steve had once loved Pen.

He wondered what Pen saw now when she looked at him.

Kate stirred and stretched, and her eyes, when she opened them, immediately sought out Tyler. Then she yawned, frowned and looked at Steve. "Any change?"

Steve shrugged. "He woke up again but not for long."

Kate's shoulders drooped.

Shit, it hurt to watch her watch Tyler, but still, he hated to see her so unhappy. "He couldn't look away from you."

"I..." She nodded. "Thank you. I needed to hear that." A small smile tugged at her lips and was gone.

"He loves you, Kate."

She took Tyler's hand. "I love him too."

Steve nodded and then frowned. Pain churned in his gut. Kate loved Tyler—not him. The rejection bit at him sharply, but he forced himself to see reason. The hurt had more to do with being rebuffed than with losing his soul mate. Kate was not his soul mate. She never had been, and they'd both known it.

They sat silently for a minute before Kate said quietly, "It's all fucked up, isn't it?"

Steve jerked his head up.

"This whole goddamned situation." She gestured at the room around her. "It's all fucked up."

Steve stared at her, unsure what to say or how to respond.

"If Tyler and Penelope had never gotten on that damn plane in the first place, we wouldn't be here. If they'd just trusted us a little, put their faith in us, we wouldn't be acting like lost farts now."

Lost fart. Yep, that neatly summed up how he felt. He opened his mouth to agree then closed it again, not quite ready to admit it to Kate.

"See?" Kate grimaced. "That's exactly what I mean. You can't talk to me. Can't even say what you think. Since Penelope arrived, you've hardly said two words to me."

True. They'd been getting along a lot better before. Tensions had been easing between them. And then Pen arrived.

The fact was, he didn't know how to act towards Kate with Pen there. Just like he didn't know how to behave towards Pen with Kate there. For fuck's sake, how was he supposed to act? It wasn't natural. These were freakish circumstances, spending every minute of every day with the woman he'd loved more than life and the woman he'd planned to marry. Neither of them wanted to be with him, and here he was, stuck with both of them. *Both of them.* Was it any fucking wonder he didn't know what to do?

"Talk to me, Steve. Don't you pull away. Please. We were getting close again. We were becoming friends. I can't bear the idea of you locking me out now."

"What do you want me to say, Kate? You want me to tell you this is easy for me?" He clenched his jaw. "I can't because it's not. It's just fucking not. Okay?"

Kate sat up and leaned towards Steve. "That's my whole point. It can't possibly be easy. Jesus, I'm in hell. You must be going out of your mind." She paused to draw in a deep breath. "At least I know Tyler loves me. If there's nothing else keeping me sane, that fact is. I...I can only imagine how you must be feeling right now."

Unloved? Unwanted? Is that what she was getting at? Steve eyed her angrily, willing her to shut up. He did not need her reminding him of his humiliation.

"I can't pussyfoot around this anymore. Whatever else we've been, you're my best friend. You held me up when I couldn't hold myself up. Let me be that for you now. Let me help you. Please."

He couldn't prevent the snort that slipped out. "What are you going to save me from? Penelope?"

She didn't return his sarcasm, just asked gently, "Do you need saving from Penelope?"

He didn't know what the fuck he needed. "Don't go there. I can't deal with this with you."

She wouldn't let it go. "Then who can you deal with it with? Who else can you turn to?"

He jumped up. "I don't need to turn to anyone. I'm good with just me."

"You still love her," she said.

"What?" He lifted his eyebrows menacingly.

Kate wasn't deterred. "You still love her."

"Do not go there, Katelyn," he warned.

"You told me so. Two days ago. You told me we would never have worked out because you still love her. And don't give me any crap about feeding me a line. We both know it was true."

Yes, he'd said that. When it was safe to confess it. When Pen was thousands of miles away. Not when she was roaming somewhere outside the door of this room, a real-life woman and not just a fantasy borne of years of missing her.

"She's here now, and you look like hell. You need someone to talk to about it."

He almost laughed out loud at the invitation. "And you, my ex-fiancée, would be the right person to talk to?"

"Don't think of me as your ex-anything. I'm your best friend. Like I used to be before we got engaged."

"You're being naïve." Too much had passed between them. How could he think of Kate as anything but his ex-fiancée?

"Is that so terrible? I...desperately want to be close with you again, to share our lives like we used to. I want to be able to help you when you need me, and I want to turn to you when I need a shoulder. Is that so objectionable?"

He didn't answer. Didn't want to.

It didn't shut her up. "Is it? Do we have to go on punishing each other because we couldn't make our relationship work?" Her face was red, her voice hoarse. "We're being punished enough. Tyler—" She choked on his name. "Tyler is injured. I don't know if he's going to come through this okay. He might...he might..." She shook her head, her eyes awash with tears. "You know what I'm saying."

He pursed his lips but didn't respond. Yes, for God's sake. He knew exactly what she was saying.

"It's just as hard for you with Pen. I don't know if Tyler will be mentally okay, and you don't know if Pen has the

Huntington's gene. It's all just fucked up."

Steve glowered at her. He never lost his temper with Kate, never, but he was on the verge now. She was talking about issues that were already slicing his gut in half. Sitting like lead weights in his chest. Without confronting them he'd be okay. If he had to face them head-on, like Kate was insisting, he'd lose the plot altogether.

"Katelyn, I am going to ask you once, nicely, not to say another word. You're upset, I get that, but I don't want to deal with it now, and I don't want to deal with it with you. I am trying, *trying* to hold onto my cool, but it's going fast. So do me a favor, and please, just quit while you're ahead."

Kate shook her head. "You don't lose your cool with me. That's why I'm the right person to talk to."

"Back off," he bit out, the last thread of his temper unraveling.

"It's not me you're angry with."

He sprang to his feet. "Fuck, Kate, enough already."

"The only person you ever get this wound up about is Pen."

"Don't talk to me about Penelope."

Kate stood too. "I have to talk about her. You love her, and it's killing you that she's here."

"What the fuck is wrong with you?" he snapped. "It's not enough that you dumped me? That you kicked me out the second Tyler got home? No? You have to go and remind me about every other fucking failed relationship in my life too? Does it make you feel better, *sweet Katie*?" He spat out the name. "Does it ease the guilt in your life? I hope so, because it's not doing a fucking thing for me."

"Sweet Katie? You're calling me by Tyler's pet name again?" She looked at Tyler, fast asleep and oblivious of the tension around him. "What is that, Steve? Your way of punishing me for breaking the engagement?"

"Punishing you?" He snorted. "Kate, babe, you're the one who's throwing every single one of my failures in my face. Who do you think is being punished here?"

"You see our relationship as a failure?" She gawked at him. "You're a bloody idiot then. I'm going to say this real slow and clear so you understand me." She pointed at him. "You *never* failed me. You saved me. Every day since I met you, you saved me. You gave me our medical practice, you gave me your friendship, and you gave me your security. Christ, you even gave me up so I could be with Tyler. Without you I would be a quarter of the woman I am today. You *made* me. And I don't care what you think, I love you. I always will." She shook her head. "Not in the same way I love Tyler or you love Pen. But I love you—in the exact same way you love me."

She paused to take a breath, and Steve got the distinct impression that had she been standing closer to him, she would have thumped him in frustration.

"If you stop seeing what happened between us as a failure and start looking at it as a time when we needed each other and were there for each other, then maybe you'd see now how good we are for each other."

She stopped then, looked him dead in the eye and nodded. "You and I were never meant to be lovers, but we were supposed to be best friends. You can be as angry as you want with me. That's okay. But damn it, I won't let you go. I won't let you push me away. You're my best friend and you always will be." She grimaced and stuck her nose in the air. "Deal with it."

It was his turn to gawk. "You're supposed to be intimidated by my temper," he said eventually, when he couldn't think of anything else to say. He couldn't exactly yell at her after that.

"You're supposed to be my best friend."

He tried to stare her down. "I'm too pissed off to be a friend right now."

She kept her gaze level with his. "You're allowed to be pissed off after what I did. You're just not allowed to ignore me or skirt issues."

"I told you, there are *issues* I don't want to discuss right now."

"Keeping them to yourself won't make them go away. Won't make Pen go away. She's here, and you need to talk to someone about her."

"What do you think talking is going to do? Help me accept that she might have an incurable disease? Yep, a good old chat is sure to put me at peace with that thought."

"She left you because she knew she might inherit an incurable disease. That has to have an impact on you. Has to make you feel something."

"It makes me feel like shit. Okay? Is that what you want to hear?"

Her eyes filled with tears. "It made me feel like shit too. Tyler left me for the same reason."

"Tyler came back for you."

Kate's face fell. "Oh God. That's what it's all about. Isn't it?" She collapsed onto her seat.

Steve couldn't stand still anymore. He resumed his obsessive pacing of the room. "That's what what's all about?" he asked irritably.

"No wonder you're so angry with me." She shook her head as though the truth should have dawned on her days ago.

Steve paused, looked at Kate, then carried on pacing.

"Just after we broke up, you found out about the Huntington's." Her voice was soft, sad. "You realized Tyler came back for me, but Pen never came back for you." She pushed her chair back, walked to him and stood in front of him, forcing him to stand still. "It was another slap in the face. And just after I'd left you. Christ, you must be devastated." A tear slipped out of her eye.

"Don't pity me, Kate."

She shook her head. "My pity is reserved for people I don't respect. I love and respect you more than anyone else. I respect your strength and your courage and your ability to hold your head up high when your heart must be breaking. You have to deal with Tyler and me and Pen and the Huntington's all at the same time. You have to, and you do, and you do it all without flinching. No matter what is going on in that heart of yours, you just face the day and every damn obstacle it throws in your way with steely determination. I don't pity you. I envy you."

Without waiting for him to respond, she stood up on tiptoes, wrapped her arms around his neck and pulled him close. The embrace she offered was void of sexual overtones. It was simply an embrace of warmth and friendship and support, and unable to stop himself, Steve leaned into her. Christ, he needed the closeness now, needed to feel like he wasn't facing the world alone and unwanted by everyone he gave a damn about. His arms went around her waist, and the two of them held each other. Steve felt the wet warmth of her tears against his neck, and his own eyes watered.

"I'm not strong, babe," he said in her ear. "I feel like shit."

"I do too." Kate held him tighter, and his anger with her began to slip away.

Once again he was reminded that marrying her would have been a mistake. If it were Pen holding him this tight, his body would be enduring all sorts of physical torture. His muscles would be straining to get closer, his dick would be hard as a rock, and his balls would be yelling for release. With Kate he just felt oddly reassured.

"Have you had a chance to speak to her?" she asked him.

She wouldn't let the Pen thing go. Stubborn as a pit bull she was, but maybe, just maybe, he didn't actually want her to let it go. Maybe he did need to talk to Kate about Penelope. "A little," he said cagily.

"Does she know you still love her?"

"Don't ask that, Kate." He wasn't angry any longer, but he refused to confront this particular issue with her. The question was way too profound. It demanded too much introspection, and he wasn't ready to look at himself that deeply just yet. "Don't ask, because I cannot answer you."

"Okay." She let it go. "Does she know you know about the Huntington's?"

That question was fair game. Kate was too entrenched in the problem to be denied the answer. Steve shook his head. "No."

Kate drew back to look at him but did not move her arms. "It's my fault you feel like shit." Guilt darkened her expression. "If I'd never opened my big mouth and told you about her risk of inheriting Huntington's in the first place, you wouldn't be caught up in all of this."

Of course he'd be caught up in all of this. Pen was back in Sydney because her brother, his best friend, had almost been killed in a motorcycle accident. Where else would he be but caught up in it?

"It's no one's fault," he told her. "I needed to know." He sighed. "At least now I understand why she ran." Although it offered no solace whatsoever, and it did not make up for the fact that she never came back to fight for him, it did give him some insight into Pen's decision to end their relationship once and for all. It even gave him insight into why she'd not been able to make a permanent commitment in the first place.

"Does it seem real yet?" Kate asked in a quiet voice.

Real? "No, it still seems like a fucking nightmare." Steve

grimaced. "Pen's nightmare." He prayed to God that like her brother she'd been spared, but until he actually spoke to her, until she confided her secret to him, he had no way of knowing one way or the other.

All he had was the icy cold fear in the pit of his stomach. "What if Pen *were* to develop Huntington's Disease?" he asked Kate. It was a very real possibility. "Christ, she could die. It would kill her."

"Not right away," Kate reminded him.

"No," he agreed, and his stomach filled with dread. Death wouldn't come straight away. It would come years after the genetic disease had robbed her of her sanity and peace of mind.

Kate hugged him a little tighter. "They—"

Whatever she'd intended to say was lost as the door opened and Pen walked back into the room. She took one look at Kate and Steve locked in each other's arms and froze.

Kate pulled back, but not before she'd given Steve one more reassuring squeeze. Then she stepped away and moved closer to Tyler.

The look on Pen's face made Steve feel like he'd been caught in a flagrantly illicit act. Kate must have felt the same because she looked from Steve to Pen to the window facing the corridor outside.

"I, uh, need some fresh air," she told no one in particular. "I'm going to take a walk. Please—" she looked at Tyler, "—phone me if he wakes up." Before she left, she turned back to Steve. In her eyes he read sadness, frustration and empathy. He read affection too. The one thing he did not see was pity.

With Tyler asleep and Kate gone, it was just the two of them. Pen studiously avoided his gaze, looking everywhere but at him. He stared straight at her, wondering if they'd ever get to finish their conversation. Christ, he wanted to. He suspected she'd been about to bring up her risk of inheriting Huntington's Disease. Or he hoped she had, anyway. He hoped she'd finally have the courage and the trust in him to share the truth.

Pen shifted awkwardly in the chair Kate had vacated. She looked as though she wanted to be anywhere but where she was. Not surprising, really—she'd walked in on her ex-boyfriend embracing his ex-fiancée, Pen's brother's lover. Jesus, he also wanted to be anywhere but here.

Or did he? Here at least he was with Pen again. Here he and Kate had begun to sort out their differences. For a moment there, before Pen had interrupted them, he and Kate had recaptured their bond, their friendship.

How had it made Penelope feel? What would she say if she knew they were hugging because of her? Because her arrival back in Sydney had him going out of his mind?

What would she say if she'd heard Kate asking him if Pen was aware he still loved her?

Fuck, that was a question he hadn't even asked himself. He was too terrified of the answer. Breathing became difficult. Did he still love her? Did he?

"Tyler woke up while you were gone," he said, guessing she would want to be told.

She lifted her face. "He did?" Hope shone in her eyes.

Christ, she was so beautiful it hurt to look at her. The pain was a physical ache in his chest. A burning, stinging, throbbing ache, and it wasn't about to relent anytime soon. He hurt because she hadn't come back to fight for him, and he hurt because there was a good chance her incredible mind might be cut down by a devastating illness. That her humor and quick wit might be destroyed by an errant gene. That her body, her perfect body, might lose all ability to control itself and its own actions.

He nodded. "For a couple of minutes. But he didn't say anything. Just stared at Kate before falling back to sleep."

"There was no change?" The brief flash of excitement receded.

"I'm sorry," he said with a shake of his head. Tension rolled through his stomach. Shit, even in a hospital room, in the middle of a crisis, he responded to her. His body tightened as awareness washed over him. It was subtle, an acknowledgement of her scent, of the soft lilt of her voice. His heart beat a little faster and blood pooled in his groin.

For fuck's sake. Another erection? Jesus, what was going on with him?

Does she know you still love her?

Kate's question echoed in his head over and over. Did Pen know he still loved her? Because he did love her. God help him, he always had, and the way she made him feel, he suspected he always would.

"Pen—"

"I'm sorry," she interrupted him.

That threw him. "For what?"

"For, uh, walking in on you and Katie."

He raised an eyebrow, refusing to show emotion. "Why are you apologizing?"

"Because I disturbed you." She blushed.

She made it sound as if she'd disturbed them having sex. "What exactly did you think you walked in on?" Steve asked.

She eyed him irritably. "I'm not an idiot, Steve. I'll knock next time. Give you fair warning."

She wasn't blushing. The red that stained her cheeks was anger.

"Fair warning about what?" What did she think? That Kate had dumped him for Tyler, and now that Tyler's health was in jeopardy they were having an affair? He almost laughed. Almost. "We don't need you to warn us."

"Get your affairs sorted out, Steven," she snapped. "Quickly. If Tyler's okay, I don't want you and Katie hanging about, flaunting yourselves in front of him."

"You think Kate and I were flaunting ourselves, eh? A couple minutes after your brother regained consciousness?"

"It doesn't matter what I think," Pen said defensively. "It matters what my brother would think."

She's jealous.

The realization hit Steve hard and made him smile. And then not smile. Pen wasn't jealous. If she were, she would have taken the test to discover whether or not she carried the gene—like Tyler had—and then come back and fought for him.

He shrugged off the pain, or tried to anyway. "Kate and I are over. Whatever you thought you saw, you're wrong. We hugged. That's it."

Pen eyed him suspiciously.

"I learned the hard way, Sunshine. Secret relationships cause problems." He didn't need to mention Kate and Tyler's secret relationship. Pen knew exactly what he was talking about. "They always end up hurting someone. If Kate and I were involved again, you'd know about it. We're not. End of story."

Pen nodded and lowered her eyes. "I apologize. I jumped to conclusions and it wasn't fair. It's just…" Her voice trailed off.

"Just what?" he prompted.

She bit her lip. "I…saw the way you were holding her. The way she was holding you. You looked…close."

Steve shrugged. "We are close." Then he corrected himself. "We were close. Once. We're trying to get there again, that's all."

That wasn't all. His conversation with Kate had been huge. *Huge.* She'd gone a long way to make him feel okay about the two of them and about their relationship. A long way to make him see she hadn't rejected him, she'd rejected a physical relationship between them. And she was right. He and Kate weren't supposed to be involved physically. Their relationship was close, but it was platonic, and it should have stayed that way. Kate had just set it back on its correct course.

Pen sighed. "Do you think we should get Ty some flowers?" she asked. "The room looks kind of empty."

Steve wasn't interested in flowers, and he suspected Ty wouldn't be either. "Forget about the flowers. They're not important." He wanted to talk about her. About the conversation she'd begun in the coffee shop and never got to finish. "You never got to share your secret earlier, Pen," he said softly.

Her shoulders drooped.

"Tell me about it now," he invited in his gentlest tone.

She stared at the door and said nothing.

"Kate's not coming back for a while. It's just the two of us." He looked at the bed. "And Tyler."

Her brother didn't stir. He'd slept through Steve and Katie's argument, and he was sleeping through Steve and Pen's.

Pen wriggled on her seat. Her hands fluttered by her sides.

"You said you needed to tell me, Sunshine. I'm here and I'm listening. What is it?"

Pen pressed her fingers into her eyes and frowned. "You... I... There is something you need to know." She swallowed and lowered her hand. "You have a right to know. I... It's..." Her voice trailed off, and she looked around, hopeless. "The time...the place." She shook her head. "I'm sorry, Steve. It's not right."

On her face he saw reluctance and hesitancy. He ached to hold her, to take her pain and her uncertainty away. He wished he could say he was surprised by his need, but he wasn't. When Pen was around he always ached to hold her. "Will the time ever be right?" He strongly suspected not.

"Probably not." She inhaled and gave him a weak smile. "But that doesn't matter. You have a right to know, and I will tell you." Her lower lip trembled. "Not now. Please?"

He nodded and gripped the handles of the chair to stop himself from going over to her. "Okay. Not now." Christ, he wanted to pull her up and press the sweet curves of her body against him. If he could have held her, comforted and consoled her, he would have, but he didn't. That wasn't what Pen wanted.

Relief washed through her eyes. "Soon. I promise." She opened her mouth but then shut it again. Offering him another feeble smile, she turned to face Tyler.

Steve continued to look at her. He couldn't help himself. He looked at her like he used to. If she caught him staring, he knew she'd see it. See the love that he couldn't deny anymore.

The emotion crushed his chest, compressing his lungs. He yearned to rediscover her body, to kiss every inch of her exposed flesh, from nose to toes, but Pen didn't want him. She may once have been powerfully attracted to him, but she'd never loved him. If she had, she would have returned to Sydney when Tyler did. After he and Kate got engaged. Her brother had loved Kate enough to face his fears. Tyler had undergone predictive testing to determine whether or not he carried the gene for Huntington's Disease. He'd come back to Sydney to fight for the one he loved.

Penelope had not.

Chapter Five

Tyler was still asleep when Steve drove Pen back to the apartment that night. Once again, Katie chose to remain at the hospital, and neither Pen nor Steve voiced any objection. It was Katie's right to be there and to have some time alone with Tyler.

Like the night before, the trip home was silent, both of them lost in their own thoughts. Even as they made a quick stop at the supermarket to stock up on some essentials for her, they didn't speak much. On Pen's part, she was still thrown by what she'd seen in Tyler's room. Still upset by the fierce jealousy she'd experienced seeing Steve holding Katie. She believed him, though. She honestly trusted him when he told her there was no longer anything between him and Katie but friendship. It didn't stop the green-eyed monster from rearing its head, and it didn't stop her from wishing she'd been the one in Steve's arms.

Since their talk in Tyler's room Steve had withdrawn into himself. Several times she'd caught him staring at her, his expression... No. She wouldn't go there. She wouldn't contemplate what she'd seen in his eyes. She should never have brought up the blasted truth. She should have shut the hell up and let Steve carry on thinking whatever it was he thought about her.

But no, she had to go and open up the can of worms. After keeping her mouth zipped for years and years, she had to blurt out she had a secret. What was she thinking? What could she possibly achieve by telling Steve? All she'd get was pity and perhaps revulsion—although she had no doubt he'd hide that well.

This time, when Pen climbed out of the car, Steve did not block her way. Thank God. He wasn't going to come inside, so she wouldn't have to confront the truth. At least not tonight.

Her relief was short-lived. Steve opened his door and followed her through the lobby and into the lift. He didn't give her a chance to object. The door to her apartment clicked softly behind them by the time Penelope voiced her thoughts.

"I think it's better if you leave," she told him as he took the groceries and began to pack them into the kitchenette. The apartment hadn't seemed so tiny last night, but with Steve here, it seemed full to capacity. Full of her and him and the double bed standing empty behind her. "I'm exhausted."

She didn't mean to stare, but his back was towards her as he stacked boxes and food on the shelves, and well, damn, his ass looked unbelievable in his jeans. In another life, she would have walked up behind him, pressed her pelvis against his butt and run her hands across the width of his shoulders.

In another life, he would have turned to face her, lowered his lips to hers and molded his hips to the shape of her groin. In another life they would have lasted less than a minute before clothes were torn from their bodies and tossed all over the kitchenette.

In this life, no matter how much she longed to follow through on her thoughts, she didn't. Lust for him settled in her belly like a hive of swarming, stinging bees.

"Better for whom?" he asked. He turned two mugs right way up and opened a jar of instant coffee. While she spoke, he poured water into the kettle and switched it on to boil.

"For both of us," she answered quietly. "It's been a long

day, an emotional rollercoaster, and I want to get some sleep. Perhaps we could talk tomorrow?" She knew if he stayed, he would push her for an answer. Insist she tell him her secret, and she wasn't sure she had the strength to face it.

"Perhaps," he agreed. "I know you're worn out."

"You look pretty tired yourself."

He added sugar to one mug. "I'm beat." Again, the expression she did not dare read was in his eyes. This time it was accompanied by a stiffening of his shoulders.

Then go home. Please.

"But I can't leave, Pen. Not yet."

Her hands fluttered at her sides. "Why not?"

A muscle twitched in his cheek as the expression deepened. "As if you need to ask."

Damn it, she didn't need to. She knew exactly why he was there. "Steve—"

"Tyler and Kate are at the hospital. It's you and me. Alone. There is no one else here, no one to disturb us."

She shook her head. "Uh uh."

"The time is right, Sunshine."

No. No, no, no. The time could never be right to tell him.

Steve leaned back against the counter. "Talk to me, Pen."

The persistent buzz of desire in her belly grew louder as he crossed his left foot over his right, causing a fold in his jeans right around the zip area. Her gaze settled there for an instant before she wrenched it away. Too late. Her brain had enough time to process what it had seen—his jean-framed cock—and her heart rate picked up, tripling in speed.

Heat zinged in her breasts and she longed for that other life, when nothing on earth would have stopped her from stepping forward and cupping her hand over him. From feeling his cock jump and grow beneath her palm.

The kettle whistled behind him. He ignored it.

She swallowed hard. "I can't, Steve." Even as she groped in her mind for a suitable excuse, she itched to hold him. To forget about Katie and her role in Steve's life as his fiancée. To forget about her own reality. To throw caution to the wind and pick up where she'd left off two and a half years ago—naked, in his arms. Damn it. She couldn't. For the very same reason she couldn't tell him the truth. "I can't," she said again.

"Why not?"

Because I never want you to find out what is to become of me, she screamed in silence. "Because I'm tired, and you're tired, and my head's still in the hospital, and I can't focus on anything else right now other than Tyler."

Steve swung his arm back suddenly, banging his fist on the counter, startling her. He swore out loud. "Is being alone with me that difficult for you, Pen? Do you despise the idea of it so much you'd rather make excuses about Tyler than have me stay with you?"

Her jaw dropped open.

"I'm sorry you find me so repulsive. There were occasions when you wanted to be with me. When you wanted to talk to me." The look in his eyes had turned cold, distant. "Time has obviously changed that."

He pushed away from the counter and stalked to the door. "I won't bother you anymore. The pressure's off. Keep your secret to yourself. It's none of my business anyway."

She would have interrupted him, corrected his misguided thoughts, but shocked by his outburst, words failed her. She hadn't seen this coming, not for one second. How was that possible? What had she missed?

"Goodbye, Pen," he said. "Have a nice life." His hand was on the door handle.

"Steve...wait!" She had no thought or plan in her head

other than to stop him. She couldn't let him leave like this.

He turned to face her, nodded. "Yes, I know. We'll still see each other at the hospital. I promise to be civil to you. I won't make it any harder than it already is."

For a second his grim expression broke. Pain and hurt flashed through his eyes, so intense they almost stopped Pen's heart. Then they were gone and there was nothing but cold detachment on his face.

Oh God. She clapped her hand over her mouth so she wouldn't groan out loud. In a moment of absolute clarity she realized Steve's despair had nothing to do with Kate and their recent break-up. Here, now, it was her fault. He was hurting because of her. By confessing she'd had a secret earlier, she'd opened doors that should have remained shut. Then when she'd tried to close them, she'd locked Steve out again, reinforcing their separation.

It wasn't Katie standing in the way of Steve's happiness. It was her.

She couldn't stand it. Couldn't bear the idea of him hurting. She had to make it better, any way she could.

"You don't know what you're talking about," she said fretfully.

His eyes were shuttered. "I've had enough practice getting to know when you don't want me around. I'm an expert by now." He shrugged and opened the door. "Like I said, I'm sorry I intruded on your space."

"Damn it, Sommers, shut up for a minute and let me talk."

He shook his head. "That's okay, Pen. I'm through trying to get you to talk."

Pure desperation led her to strike out with her foot and kick the door closed. Anything to get him to stay.

Steve's face was guarded. He didn't speak.

"You've got it all wrong, Sommers. You don't understand." Time had changed nothing. *Nothing.* Of course she still wanted to spend time with him. Talk to him. *Of course.*

He leaned back against the door and crossed one foot in front of the other. Like before. Then he hitched his thumbs through his belt loops too. "What don't I understand?"

The movement drew her gaze downwards, and this time it wasn't so easy tearing it away. She stared at his groin, forgetting what she wanted to say. A low-grade ache started up between her legs. A tingling sensation she couldn't ignore. She bit her lip.

"Penelope?"

Lift your eyes, woman. Look into his face.

God knew she wanted to, like she wanted to tell him why he'd got it all wrong, but for the life of her she couldn't move. She couldn't put two words together. All she could do was stare at his cock as memories of that other life suffused her. Memories of how she'd loved him—and how he'd loved her.

"Fuck, Penelope," he rasped. "What are you doing?"

He didn't move, but beneath her gaze the soft denim of his jeans shifted and pulled tight across his groin. She didn't suppress her groan this time. It had nothing to do with the pain she caused him and everything to do with his growing erection.

"You're killing me, lady." It was the timbre of his voice that finally broke the spell, the deep longing in his words that propelled her into motion.

"You don't understand, Steve," she said one more time, before she launched herself into his arms and clamped her mouth to his.

She was only human. One human, fallible woman, and he was her drug. Her addiction. Fuck, she shouldn't be doing this. She should be walking the hell away, or better yet, slamming the door behind him, confirming his beliefs. But damn it, she couldn't. Not again.

Steve absorbed her weight without flinching. If anything, he froze, holding his body hard and tense—like an elastic band pulled taut. He didn't respond to the urgency of her kiss. His lips, usually soft and warm and welcoming, were clenched together in two thin lines, and his shoulders, usually curved protectively around her form, were stiff and unyielding.

Ah, but his cock. His jean-framed cock. It spoke volumes. Full and erect, it did not hide what the rest of his body strove so hard to cover. His desire. The ache in her groin deepened, and she ground her hips into his, rubbing her clit against his erection. She dragged her right hand up the solid muscle of his thigh while she buried her left one in his blond hair—his thick, silky, blond hair. And then she opened her mouth and touched her tongue to his lips.

Steve gave an agonized cry and closed his arms around her, pressing her closer. His lips moved softly, sensuously against hers, drawing her teasing tongue into his mouth. The muscles in his leg tightened beneath her fingers as her hand trailed from the outer seam of his jeans around to his inner thigh. She felt the restrained power in the flex of his movement.

He pressed her even closer, so close it was hard to breathe, and intensified the kiss. Breathless, she couldn't wait to run her hands over his erection. Revel in the knowledge that she'd been the one to put it there.

She, not Katie.

Shit, she shouldn't be here. Shouldn't be doing this, but she couldn't stop. Touching Steve like this was tearing her world apart. She was breaking all of her own rules. The worst thing she could do was give in to her hunger for him. She'd struggled for so long to put physical distance between herself and the man she loved, and now she was back in the exact place she shouldn't be. In his arms.

This was self-destruction. This was an addict pretending she could have a taste of her drug without plunging head-first back into the sordid world of addiction.

Yet even as her mind fought her actions, her hand moved higher, seeking out the hard ridge behind his zip. Even as she told herself to step away, she continued her frenzied assault on his mouth. God, he tasted incredible. Like man and sex and forbidden pleasures. He didn't seem to mind the force she used to kiss him. In fact, he responded in kind, returning her kiss with an unrestrained zeal of his own.

His lips stole her breath and his tongue stole her resolve. Fire swept through her veins, lighting every molecule in her body. Would there ever be a day when she didn't respond like this to Steve? When her body didn't ignite when they kissed? Would there ever be a day when she could stand in a room with him, alone, and not want to touch him?

Not in this lifetime.

She dragged her hand over his erection, then pressed her palm flat against the front of his jeans and stroked. Her insides turned to jelly. He was aroused and excited, and she was the one who'd done this to him. *Not Katie.* After all this time, there was still a part of her that couldn't quite believe he was as attracted to her as she was to him, still couldn't quite believe he saw her as a woman and not as his friend's little sister.

Steve murmured nonsensically and jerked into her hand. At the same time, he cupped her butt through her jeans. Goose bumps followed his touch, and she shivered as she felt an answering tug between her legs. She instinctively arched her back, inviting further exploration.

His fingers curled around the curve of a butt cheek and squeezed, kneading, caressing, and he moaned deep in her mouth. As she dipped her own hand below the waistband of his jeans, he used his free one to push her T-shirt up, exposing her bra. Her practical cotton bra. Before, when she'd seduced him, she'd made sure to wear her sexy lingerie, her silk and lace. Today she wore cotton. Today she hadn't planned on this.

Steve didn't seem to notice. His mouth hadn't left hers. His eyes were closed, tight, the lines around them pulled into a mask of desire, confusion and pain. She let her own eyes drift shut. She didn't want to see his ambivalence, didn't want him reinforcing her poor judgment. Now she wanted...Steve.

Cool air blew against her bare nipples as he unclipped her bra and pushed it aside, causing an almost painful sensation over the tightened buds.

She knew she should pull away. She was doing the very thing she'd fled to London to avoid—making love to the man she'd loved almost her whole life. But her body betrayed her mind, demanding fulfillment and pleasure. Demanding satisfaction. Refusing to acknowledge the logic her head dictated.

Why was she surprised?

By now she should be accustomed to her body's betrayal.

She freed his button, pulled at his fly and finally, finally held his hot, hard erection in her hand. The satisfaction was so thrilling, she didn't give the betrayal another thought. He groaned her name and bent her backwards, making her arch her back and thrust her breasts upward.

Without releasing her butt, he leaned over her and took a nipple in his mouth. The impression of his warm, wet tongue on her cool, tight skin blew her mind. She cried out as he ran his tongue over the areola before tugging at the nipple with his teeth.

Her legs trembled, and her knees turned to mush.

It *was* over with Katie. It had to be. She knew Steve too well. No way on earth would he kiss her like this, hold her like this, if Katie featured in any part of his head. When Steve gave himself, he gave everything, and she had him all to herself now.

All of him. Every last inch, body and soul.

The expression she'd seen on his face earlier? Of course she knew what it was. She'd recognized it immediately but had been to terrified to think about it. Too nervous to acknowledge what it meant. She still didn't want to acknowledge it, because that would mean there was still something between her and Steve. Something more than just sex, and she didn't want that to be the case.

She just wanted sex. That was all. Pure, unadulterated sex. With Steve. Only with Steve.

She wrapped her fingers around the length of his cock and slowly drew them up and then down again, taking his heavy panting as a sign he liked what she did. Oh, sweet Lord, she liked it too.

The hand on her rear moved, trailing around her hips, until he stroked the front of her jeans. He slid a finger down, touched her hypersensitive clit through the heavy material, made her shudder and then ran the same finger lower.

She let out a throaty cry.

"Pen," he responded, as if in physical pain.

She understood. The need was so powerful it hurt. It had always been like this between them. Always.

Steve switched breasts, paying careful attention to the as yet untouched one. While his mouth tortured and tantalized, his finger sought and found. He tugged at her zip and button and then pushed her jeans over her hips, leaving only her practical cotton panties on. His breathing deepened and almost stopped when he dipped his hand inside the panties and found her wet and swollen. He muttered incoherently against her breast.

As he slid a finger over her engorged clit, he sucked a nipple into his mouth, making her gasp in pleasure. He knew. He remembered how to touch her. Where to touch her and when. The finger moved lower, found her slick folds and slid between them. Penelope began to shake, so aroused she feared she'd lose it right there. His finger worked magic, slipping in and out, in and out. She pumped him a little more firmly, in time with his movements, but she couldn't concentrate, couldn't focus. The pleasure was too intense.

"How could you ever think I find you repulsive?" she asked on a sob. "I can't keep my hands off you." She'd been a fool to think she could.

He stilled completely. Even his breath seemed suspended in midair.

She trembled uncontrollably. "Please, Steve. I need you. Now!"

He let out a savage cry and backed her against the wall. Then he ripped off her panties. Her shirt and bra followed the rest of her clothes. In one smooth movement, he pinned her hands above her head and kissed her. Devoured her mouth as he rubbed his chest against her excruciatingly sensitive breasts. Each motion was torture. Painful, exquisite torture.

He pulled away and looked her dead in the eye. "Are you sure?" he growled.

"Yes, goddamn it!" A little taste wasn't enough. She wanted more. Craved more. "Do it. *Now.*"

He shoved his hand in his pocket and hauled out his wallet. Then he yanked out a condom and tore the packet open.

As caught up as she was in the moment, a flash of jealousy ripped through her. Steve had condoms in his wallet. He only kept condoms in his wallet when he was involved with someone. Those condoms were meant for Katie. Not for her.

She repressed the attack of jealousy. She couldn't handle it. Not now, not when her body demanded satisfaction and the man who could give it to her, generously, was preparing to fuck her. Her, not Katie.

She watched the nimble movements of his hands as he sheathed himself. His jeans were unbuttoned, his dick sticking out. Hell, even in the awkwardness of his half-dressed state he looked sexy as sin. Her stomach lurched as he rolled the condom down his hard shaft.

His gaze swept over her body, then lifted to meet hers. Hunger raged like a furnace in his eyes, and when he spoke his voice was thick and raw. He stepped closer. "You know once we get started there is no going back."

It was a warning, a chance for her to back out. She should take it. She should put on her clothes and kick him the hell out of the room. Get him as far away from here as she possibly could.

But her body was a frenzied vortex of need. "Fire it up, Steve," she begged, grabbing his T-shirt with both hands and hauling him closer. The once familiar invitation slipped from her mouth as naturally as the first time she'd said it. And the second, and all the other times they'd made love. It was their cue, their catch phrase, and once it was spoken there was no going back.

There was no awkward fumbling, no misplaced body parts. Their coming together was as instinctive as breathing. Pen braced her hands on his shoulders as he bent his legs. When he straightened, she wrapped her own legs around his waist, lowered herself onto him, and just like that, he slid inside her.

Her body stretched to take his size and immediately adjusted to his width. Her inner walls recognized him instantly. The nerves embedded in them did a happy dance to see him again, and, completely unexpectedly, Pen climaxed. Tingles of ecstasy showered over her, and she cried out as her body clamped down around his cock.

Steve swore out loud and was moving in her before the first waves of pleasure had receded.

Oh God, he was going to make her come again. He never could let her ride out one orgasm. No, he had to push and push until the agony and the pleasure became too much to bear, until she had no choice but to writhe again in the glory of another climax.

Perhaps it was the lead-up of stress from the past few days; perhaps it was the simple joy in being reunited. Whatever it was, it didn't take long. Less than a minute and she was coming again, only this time the sensations were much stronger. This time she shouted out as her muscles contracted and relaxed, shouted until she heard Steve call her name and felt his own shuddering release deep within her traitorous body.

Even as they collapsed together on the floor, Pen knew she'd blown it. She'd given in to her cravings, and the addiction was back. Once with Steve would never, ever be enough. He was her drug of choice, and a single fix would not satisfy her.

Chapter Six

Steve picked her up and settled her on the bed. He dumped his clothes on the floor in a haphazard pile. Then he lay down next to her, on his side, and traced his fingers over her cheekbone, down to her mouth and around the outline of her lips. She couldn't move, couldn't respond. She simply lay breathless beneath his touch, her heart still pounding in the aftermath of their passion.

His soft caresses were hypnotic. They moved from her face, down to her neck and swept over her breasts and her belly. Pen closed her eyes as Steve chased the movement of his hands with his mouth. Feather-light kisses landed on her sensitized skin, sending goose bumps breezing down her spine. Slowly, languidly, she gave herself over to the inviting call of his lips, her body arching against his mouth.

He dipped his head lower and kissed her. Intimately.

This soon after sex, the sensation his mouth evoked as it made love to her was excruciating. His lips were both firm and tender and his tongue merciless as it stroked her clit and her folds with deadly precision.

As the exquisite vibrations rippled through her, her eyes filled with tears. It had been a long time since she'd been treated to such tender, carnal ministrations. An eon since anyone had kindled such desire or worshipped her so sensuously. Only Steve had the ability to incite this much yearning and bestow this much rapture.

It felt so good, she curved her back into the mattress and pressed her hips up to his mouth, needing more. Clutching handfuls of sheet, she let the tears fall down her face. Christ, she'd missed him. Longed for him. Staying away had been insufferable.

His mouth seduced and delighted. It felt unbelievable pressed against her like that. Intensely, deliciously unbelievable. Time stood still. The world danced around her. She was alone with him again. Alone with him and his tempestuous mouth. It teased, it tantalized, it tormented, and when he licked her engorged bud again, it tipped her over the edge. She exploded in a million shards of pleasure.

When the world finally stopped spinning and the last pulses of excitement ebbed away, Steve sat at her side. His fingers laced through hers. He'd switched on the bedside lamp and soft light filled the room.

Blue eyes bore into her, seeing past her secrets, right through to her soul. Silent questions were reflected in their depths.

A full minute elapsed, but she couldn't speak, couldn't bring herself to say anything.

"It's time, Pen," he said quietly.

She stared at him, trapped. The lethargy of her post-orgasmic body sapped her of the energy to argue.

"Talk to me," he said with a little more assertion to his voice.

No. Please, not yet. She wanted to writhe in ecstasy for a little longer, hide behind her denial for...well, forever.

His shoulders tensed. "No more hiding. No more secrets. You left me for two and a half years, and I need to understand why."

Her mouth was dry as a desert and she licked her lips. Still the words would not come.

He withdrew his hands, putting distance between them. She understood. As hard as he tried to reach her, to talk to her, she blocked him. Her silence spurned him. After what they'd shared they should be as close as lovers. But they weren't. Pen was shutting him out.

Wordlessly, she shook her head.

His response was immediate. He stood, and the grim expression that had shadowed his face yesterday slipped back into place. Steve might have given her three sweet, erotic orgasms, but in less than a minute a gaping river opened up between them.

"Fuck." Steve spat the word out. "Nothing's changed, has it? Not one fucking thing."

His eyes were raging infernos of anger—and rejection. He was mad, and he was hurt, and it was her fault.

"You don't give a fucking inch, Pen. You give nothing. Am I supposed to be happy you don't find me physically repulsive? Am I supposed to celebrate the fact you decided to fuck me? Again? That's all I am to you, isn't it? One giant dick. Someone to bring you off when you're horny."

She gaped at him, shocked. In all their time together he'd never spoken so brutally to her.

"Well, it's over, lady. I've had enough of you fucking me around. Go find some other idiot to screw over."

This was a good thing. She wanted Steve to hate her. If he hated her, he'd leave her. He wouldn't hang around to watch her god-awful demise. She pushed herself into a sitting position. "I don't want another idiot. I only want you."

Shit. That's not what she meant to say.

He snorted. "For what? Another orgasm? Forget it."

"No, damn it. I won't forget it. It's never just been about sex with you, Steve, and you know it."

"The only thing I know is as soon as we do the deed, you leave. Every single time. I'm through, Pen. I'm not interested anymore."

Obviously their time apart and his engagement *had* helped him gain some distance. He'd never called an end to things before. That had always been Pen's role.

"What do you want from me?" she asked. "Do you want to hear the truth? Do you want to know why I leave every time? Why I went to live in London?"

"Of course I want to know," Steve yelled. "It's the only thing I've wanted to know about you for years."

She backed down. "The truth is not easy."

He looked up at the ceiling, counted to three out loud. When he finally looked at her again, his face was calmer, his voice quieter. "Your silence is harder."

Darn, how'd he do that? How'd he always manage to get his temper back under control? "Silence hides the secrets. It hides the things too awful to confront."

"You think I'd rather confront your silence? You think I'd rather make up excuses for you than know the truth? Right now, all I know is you can't bear to be in a room with me longer than it takes for you to climax."

"It is not about sex."

"It's always been about sex, Pen. You won't let it be about anything else. I tried—" His voice broke. "I tried so damn hard to love you, to make you stay, but time and again, you left. You fucked me and then you left. Of course it's about sex for you. Tonight is no bloody different."

"I can't let it be anything more, don't you see?"

"How could I possibly see? You've never shown me.

Anything." He shoved his hand through his hair. "What was so terrible you had to hide it in London?"

There was no more dodging. No more hiding. The time had come. She had to tell him the truth. Her throat felt thick, and she began to tremble. "Some things are easier not to know," she warned him again.

He froze. "I'm not interested in easy, Pen. I need the truth."

She hesitated. "It's hard, Steve. I need to find the words. The right way to tell you." Her pulse raced. Air seemed trapped in her lungs.

He nodded, sensing her capitulation. She was finally going to tell him, and he knew it. "Take your time." He walked to the wall, leaned against it, crossed one foot over the other and folded his arms below his chest.

Penelope was momentarily thrown. Steve stood with the grace of a dancer and the confidence of a lover. He was breathtaking. The hard planes of his chest and the extraordinary length of his muscular legs were highlighted by his trim hips and steely arms. The man was built. It was no wonder, with everything else going on in her life, she was still addicted to him.

Minutes passed.

"What was so terrible?" he prompted.

Her trembling increased tenfold. "Not was," she corrected at last. "Is."

He furrowed his brow. "What *is* so terrible?"

She was cold. Freezing. And exposed. She pulled the sheet over her nude body. Then she clasped it around her breasts and began to speak in a faltering voice. "When I was twelve, my father died."

Steve nodded. "You came to live in Sydney right after that."

"He was sick for a long time. Years." She had to tell him

from the beginning, so he'd understand.

"You never spoke about him. Or his illness." Steve's voice was back to normal. Kind, compassionate. The anger was gone.

"It was too...complicated." It was still too complicated.

"Complicated?"

"What he went through...was...was...horrible. The disease ravaged him, both mentally and physically." She swallowed. "It ravaged the whole family."

Steve stepped forward, but she held up a shaky hand. She didn't want him touching her now, because if he did, she'd fall apart, and there'd be no way she'd ever finish her story.

He stepped back.

"I was three when he was diagnosed. He was forty-two. I didn't understand what it meant or what was happening. All I knew was my father began to act strange." She picked at imaginary threads on the sheet. "He never improved. His behavior only got more and more bizarre." How could she compress a lifetime of illness into a few explanatory sentences? "It was tough living with him. Virtually impossible. He forgot things, became inexplicably angry, stopped making sense. He used to jerk uncontrollably."

Pen swallowed down her bitterness. Oh, what a legacy her father had bequeathed her.

"My mother couldn't manage on her own, not with two young children, so we had a nursing aide who used to help look after him and us. But even then we weren't coping. One day, when I was about ten, I got home from school and he wasn't there. My mother had admitted him into a home." The words were tumbling out now. Fast. "He stayed there for two years until he got a cold. It happened quite quickly after that. The cold persisted. It went to his chest. He developed pneumonia and couldn't shake it off. He died three weeks later."

"He died from pneumonia?" Steve asked.

"Yes." She nodded. "But he lived with Huntington's Disease."

There. She'd said it. It was out in the open. She knew no further explanation was necessary. Steve was a doctor. He'd heard about Huntington's.

It was impossible to look at him. She didn't want to see his face as he acknowledged the tragedy of the situation. She waited for him to gasp in horror, or to reel at the injustice, or to be struck speechless by the news. To react in some way which highlighted how thrown he was by her disclosure.

His response shocked her.

"I know, Pen," he said softly.

"What?" She gaped at him in utter incredulity. "Tyler told you?" Never. She didn't believe it. Tyler would never reveal her secrets. Ever. Not to Steve. He knew how much her privacy meant. Knew how much their secret had cost her. There was not a chance in hell Tyler would have told him.

"No. Not Tyler." Steve shook his head. "It was Kate. She inadvertently let it slip after the accident. She thought I already knew."

Katie. Of course. She must have assumed Tyler had told Steve when he got back from London.

The question was, how much did Katie know, and how much had she told Steve?

As though reading her mind, he answered. "Kate never mentioned you. She was lamenting the irony of the accident, that life could be so cruel as to almost kill Tyler after he learned he didn't have the gene."

"It is incomprehensible. He finally had the chance to live a full life, and then this went and happened." Pen gave him a sad smile. "Life can be a real bitch."

"It can," Steve agreed. "Is that why you left Sydney? So you wouldn't need to tell me or anyone else about the Huntington's?"

She nodded. "I never wanted you to know. I wanted to leave with my pride and my dignity intact. So when you thought about me, you thought about the healthy, normal Penelope. Not some rotting caricature of my former self."

To her astonishment, he smacked the wall behind him. "Damn it, Pen, how could you do that?"

"Do what?" She stared at him with wide eyes.

"Leave me. Abandon us. Without so much as an explanation." His voice was tortured. "I deserved better. *We* deserved better."

"I had to go, Steve. I couldn't stay. The prospect of you watching me slowly lose my mind was unthinkable."

"That is bullshit." His voice was still anguished. But there was something else in his tone now too. Resentment.

"Excuse me?" She gawked at him.

"What? You think I can't be angry with you? You think because you might have some dreaded disease I have to tiptoe around you?"

"You're angry I *might* have some disease?" This wasn't how she'd expected the conversation to pan out.

The color drained from his face. "No. I'm gutted you might have some terrible disease." He raked his fingers through his hair. "I'm pissed off I had to find out about it from my ex-fiancée."

"I'm not exactly thrilled by that either," she bit back.

"This isn't about Kate. This is about you and me. I loved you, damn it. You weren't just a warm body when I was feeling horny. A convenient sex partner." He stabbed his chest with his finger. "*I* loved you!"

"Exactly! That's why *I* had to go." Pen stabbed at her own

chest. "That's why *I* never stayed all those times. You loved me. And that just wasn't fair to you."

"Who the hell are you to decide what was fair to me or not?" His eyes snapped with rage and suppressed emotion.

"Who am I?" She answered with a bitter laugh "You mean apart from the other person involved in our relationship?"

"Relationship?" It was his turn to laugh cynically. "A relationship is based on trust, sweetheart. Honesty. Something we were obviously lacking. What we had was sex. You wanted it, you took it, you left. It was my bad luck to fall in love with you in the process."

"You think I didn't love you?" She was horrified. She'd had to leave him, to save him from the complications of the disease. Surely he understood that, especially now he knew about the Huntington's? Surely he knew she loved him?

His face was cold and his voice calmer, making her feel more distant from him now than she had felt living in London, thousands of kilometers away. "See, that was my mistake. I did think you loved me. I was convinced of it."

"I did," she whispered. "How could you doubt that?"

"What's that old saying about the proof of the pudding?" His smile was empty. "I got my proof, after I found out about the Huntington's. It made me realize what a fool I'd been. It didn't make me love you any less, mind you." His expression was haunted. "Or make the news of the disease any easier to accept." He shook his head slowly, as though clearing his thoughts, and anger snapped back to life in his eyes. "You never loved me, did you, Pen? I was Mr. Convenient. The sucker who took you back no matter how many times you left."

"Steven! Oh God, no. That was never, ever the case." How could he think that?

"It didn't occur to me at first," he said. "I guess I was too shocked. After I'd had a while to think about it though, I put two and two together. That's when I realized you'd never loved me." He shook his head. "It hurt like hell. It hurt almost as much as the thought of your getting sick." His voice was quieter now. "It still hurts."

What was he saying? How could he ever deduce that she did not love him?

Steve lurched away from the wall. He grabbed his jeans and boxers and shoved his legs into them. "I'm sorry about the disease, Pen." His voice was calmer and very sad. "I am terribly sorry."

This was going all wrong. There was some major misinterpretation somewhere. Her confession was never meant to end up like this. Steve was supposed to understand why she'd left him. That she went because she loved him, not because she didn't. He was supposed to kiss her on the forehead and give her his blessing to leave. To wish her the best of luck for her future.

Instead, he was pulling on his T-shirt. And his shoes.

Oh God. He was leaving her. He was walking away.

She cried out as he headed for the door. "Steve, wait! Please. I don't understand." She threw the covers off, jumped out of bed and grabbed his arm. "How could you ever conclude I never loved you?"

He didn't turn around, but he didn't pull away either. "That's easy. I got engaged to Kate."

"Huh?" What did his blasted engagement have to do with this?

Steve turned slowly. "Your brother came back, Penelope. He wouldn't let Kate marry another man. He came back and he fought for her."

It was all starting to make sense in a surreal, sickening kind of a way. Her heart began to bleed. "I didn't fight for you."

"You didn't try." His tone was flat.

"I couldn't. The Huntington's..." She dropped his arm. It was suddenly too heavy to hold.

He shrugged. "Tyler took the test. He loved Katie enough to find out if he had the gene."

With that, Penelope's legs gave out beneath her, and she slid numbly to the floor. "You think I didn't love you enough to take the test?"

Steve looked down at her. Through her watery eyes, she made out the hurt in his face and the rejection in his stance. The humiliation in the nodding of his head. "That, sweetheart, is exactly what I think."

"Oh, Steve, you don't get it, do you?" Her heart felt empty now, all bled out. "I didn't need to take the test when you and Katie got engaged." She closed her eyes. "I'd already taken it. Two and a half years ago."

Chapter Seven

Her words smashed into Steve's chest, their impact knocking him off balance. He collapsed to his knees.

"Oh, Jesus, Pen..." Bile rose in his throat.

She might have answered, but he couldn't hear. Blood roared in his ears, blocking out everything but the sound of his violently thumping heart.

He hadn't allowed himself to consider it. Hadn't let himself move past her risk of inheriting the disease. That possibility was bad enough. The actuality of having the gene was too abhorrent to contemplate. Easier to lose his temper. Easier to focus his anger on Pen's silence than her actual status.

Because if Pen had the gene, it meant she *would* develop Huntington's. Pen *would* become symptomatic. Not might. Would.

He swore. In his mind? Out loud? He wasn't sure.

She'd taken the test after all. Not now. She'd gone through the whole rigmarole while they were still together. Before she'd gone to London. His head hurt. Hell, a million cannons exploded under his skull, blinding him with pain. Pen had taken the test and then left him.

"Pen?" His throat felt raw.

"I have the gene, Steve."

"No!" Another cannon exploded.

"Yes."

"You can't." His voice was hoarse. Razor blades cut at his throat.

"I can. And I do. That's why I left you. Not because I didn't love you, but because I did. I couldn't let you watch me rot."

This time a cannon exploded in his chest. Was that how she perceived her future—as a time to rot?

"There's very little dignity in the disease. In the way it destroys the body and the mind. I've seen it firsthand," Pen said. "I chose to save my dignity while I still could." Her voice was flat.

He floundered, speechless. Of all the scenarios he'd cooked up in his head about why Pen had left, this was the only one he couldn't have faced. Concluding she didn't love him was a damn sight more acceptable than finding out she carried the gene. Of course he'd never allowed himself to picture this possibility. It was too awful, too horrible to contemplate. Pen, his sunshine, the only woman who'd ever lit up his life, was going to develop Huntington's.

It was no longer a matter of risk or possibility. It was a certainty. Pen was going to become very, very sick

"Admit, it." She straddled him and tickled his waist. "When I walk into the room, your whole day lights up."

He tucked his elbows against his sides, managing to trap her hands under his bare arms, and laughed. "Yeah, what can I say, you're my own personal ray of sunshine."

"I make your day brighter."

He snorted in response.

She dug a trapped finger in his waist, catching him at a weak point so he convulsed beneath her. "Go on, say it. I make your day brighter."

He guffawed and said it. "You make my day brighter."

Another prod of the terrible finger. "Like you mean it." Her eyes danced, lighting her face with humor.

"I mean it," he told her and rolled his eyes comically.

"Say: Without me, your life would be dull," she prompted.

"Without me, your life would be dull," he replied dutifully.

She attacked with her other hand, using the only finger she could free from under his arm. "You know what I mean," she warned.

"Yeah, Sunshine," he said as a warm wave of love washed over him. "I know what you mean. And it's true. Without you, there is no light in my life."

Pen had the Huntington's gene. Slowly but surely, his little ray of sunshine would lose her spark, her light. She was going to get sick. Very, very sick. Her mind would slowly deteriorate until her thoughts no longer made sense, her memories eluded her and her ability to control her emotions became defunct. Her actions would grow clumsy and her body overwhelmed by a multitude of involuntary movements. That same body that glowed now in the prime of health would eventually have difficulty performing such mundane tasks as talking and swallowing. Her body, like her father's, would lose the ability and the strength to fight even a common cold.

And by the time that happened it would be a warped kind of a blessing.

Steve's stomach twisted in agony. If the pain of knowing Pen had left him for London had been bad, this was insurmountable. Her absence he could deal with. Her disease he could not.

He slumped against the wall. "You sure about this?" Of course she was sure. Geneticists did not randomly assign positive Huntington's status to patients.

"I'm sure, Steve. I will develop Huntington's."

He nodded. Just nodded because words could not begin to convey his thoughts.

After an immeasurable length of time had passed, and the certainty of Pen's situation had lodged like a bullet in his chest, he simply opened his arms to her.

"Come here, Sunshine," he said, feeling moisture on his cheek.

She bit her lip, studied his face, then slowly closed the distance between them. As she crawled into his lap and curled herself into a ball, he wrapped his arms around her and held her tight. He held her until dawn spilled through the blinds and across the carpet, and Pen slept with her head tucked against his chest.

Chapter Eight

Pen picked at her fruit salad and yogurt but didn't taste a thing. She watched Steve through gritty eyes. He chewed on his toasted Turkish, silent and miserable. Despair and desolation marked his face. At least she could cover up her red blotches and puffy eyes with make-up.

Steve's gaze flickered around the tiny restaurant before stopping to rest on her. "You know, a month ago I would have spent the night at Kate's place," he said dispassionately. "I would have woken up safe in the knowledge that my future and the future of my fiancée was secure."

She closed her eyes, not wanting to hear about his life with Katie.

"Instead, I'm sitting in a coffee shop, looking at a woman who sacrificed our relationship to protect me from her future."

She opened one eye and watched him tiredly. Where was he going with this?

"I don't want a future with Kate, Sunshine. Not anymore." Her heart lurched. "And I don't want to be protected by you."

"Steve—"

"Marry me, Pen."

"*What?*"

"You heard me. Let's get married."

She stared at him, openmouthed.

"I've spent the whole night considering this. It's our only choice. The only way I can think of to make the next ten-odd years bearable—for both of us."

She tossed aside his proposal with a bitter laugh. "You must be crazy." The last thing she wanted was to marry him. No, correction. She wanted that more than anything. The last thing she wanted was for him to be around as she slowly lost her mind.

"Probably, yes. I still think we should do it."

She looked around, feeling out of place and out of sorts, as though she'd just been sucked into the twilight zone. "I'm going back to London, Steve."

"You don't have to. You can stay here."

"No, I can't." She spoke, but her emotions were disconnected from her words. She was more a casual observer than a participant. *Disassociation.* It was a tactic she'd employed before, several times. Every time she'd walked away from him in the past. Easier to make it surreal than to confront reality head-on.

"As soon as Tyler...when we know what's happening with Tyler, I'm going back." Even removed from her words, that one hurt. "If...if need be..." She cleared her throat. "If need be, I'll make any plans that have to made from London."

"Tyler doesn't want to be in London. He came home. You can too. For good." His voice echoed as though coming through a cloud. A cloud that protected her, kept her safe from Steve and his idealistic, impracticable rantings about marriage.

"My life is in England now."

"What life, Pen? What have you got there that you have to go back for?"

"My job, for one." She couldn't just leave the school. She had obligations.

Steve nodded. "Tyler told me you were teaching again."

She frowned. "You discussed me with my brother?" Damn it, hadn't she told Tyler not to mention her to him?

"Of course we discussed you." He looked uncomfortable, and she wondered what exactly they had discussed. "He also told me that it wasn't really the school you liked, it was the kids."

"Tyler talks too much." She sighed to herself, exasperated. How could she pretend she wanted to be in London—more than she wanted to be with Steve—if Tyler had told him all her secrets? She shrugged and let the cloud carry her further away. "He's right. I do like the kids. I have a responsibility to them and I won't let them down."

"What else do you have there, Pen? Besides the students. Have you made friends?"

"Some."

"Some?"

"Enough." Okay, none. Acquaintances, maybe, but not friends. People who staved off the loneliness but didn't get too close. She couldn't afford for anyone to get too close.

"You're seeing someone." It wasn't a question.

She exhaled slowly. *Oh, Tyler, another secret?* "Yes, I am," she confessed, and then a jolt went through her body. In her haste to get to Sydney, she'd forgotten all about Jeremy. She hadn't even phoned to tell him she was coming here or why. Crap, she'd have to email him later when she had a chance.

Steve frowned. "You're involved with someone else, yet last night you slept with me."

Her protective cloud began to evaporate. Now Steve would think she was the one keeping an affair to herself, which was so not the truth. As much as she liked Jeremy, the thing that appealed to her the most was his complete disinterest in commitment. Just like her. "It's not serious. We date now and again, that's all."

Bugger. The minute she confessed the truth she knew she shouldn't have. She should have made it seem like she was more serious about Jeremy. Should have let Steve think she was interested in him. That way Steve would know there was no chance for a future for them, and he'd forget all about his marriage scheme.

Damn, she preferred floating in the twilight zone to facing reality.

"Okay, then." Steve nodded, accepting her explanation. "So what you're telling me about your life in London is that you have some friends and a guy you're dating casually. Right?"

"Right."

"Sounds like a thrill a minute."

She bristled. What was his case, anyway? "What do you want to hear, Steve?"

His blue eyes darkened. "I want to hear that you're happy. That you've made a life for yourself there and you have people you can lean on, depend on." He pursed his lips. "And if you can't tell me that, then I want to hear you say yes, you'll marry me, so that I can make you happy. So that you can depend on me."

She took a deep breath and said evenly, "I have the gene. I don't want anyone to lean on, least of all you. I have to do this by myself." Her heart squeezed painfully in her chest. That wasn't even close to the truth. Leaning on Steve would be like a little piece of heaven. A selfish piece of heaven she refused to allow herself.

"No, you need to do this with someone who loves you. Someone who can take care of you when the time comes. Someone like me."

Her heart missed a beat. There it was again. The look in his eyes. The one that confirmed the words he'd just uttered. The look that made her feel warm and protected and whole. Complete. It always had. "You love me?"

He blinked and sank back into his seat. "Yeah, Sunshine." He nodded, "I never stopped."

Shit. Shit, shit, shit. This shouldn't be happening. Things weren't supposed to go this way. She was supposed to keep Steve at arm's length, not fall super crazy in love with him all over again. "Well, stop. Now," she ordered.

He laughed cynically. "I tried to. Remember? The whole Steve-and-Kate-are-getting-married thing? Guess what? It didn't work."

"Then find someone else," she snapped, suddenly at the end of her tether. "I'm off limits." It was all too much for her. Not only had she gone against every morsel of common sense she'd ever possessed by sleeping with him, she now sat discussing marriage with the man she'd vowed never to touch again. Her behavior was stupid and damaging and would only end up hurting both of them. She had to quit while she still could, before Steve convinced her that marriage might actually be a good idea.

"You weren't off limits last night," he told her in a low, edgy voice.

"I am today. And every other day after this." She pushed her chair back and stood. "Last night we were both over-emotional. We got carried away. I am sorry for that. It won't happen again."

"Oh, but it will. It will happen often. Every night if I can help it. It's part of being married."

"Let me spell this out for you." She leaned forward, placing her hands on the table. "I'll make it real easy. We. Are. Not. Getting. Married."

"Yes, Sunshine. We are."

Stubborn dickhead. "Really?" She shaped her mouth into an O. "In which reality? The one where I go home when Tyler is discharged, or the one where you suffer from psychotic delusions?"

Steve stood too and, like her, placed both hands on the table. Then he leaned forward until their noses almost touched. "The one where we stop wasting what little time we have to be together and start taking advantage of every moment we have left."

"Ah, I get it now," she said sarcastically. "It's the pity proposal. The one where you feel sorry for me because I'm going to get sick, and you want to make me as happy as possible in the ten-odd good years I have left." Typical Sommers behavior. Galloping in on his white horse to save her in her final hours of need.

Irritation flickered across his face. "No, it's the proposal where you get to say yes, and we both get to be happy for the first time in over two years."

"Yeah, Steve. That's right. I can see how happy the thought of marrying me is making you right now." His face was haggard, his eyes bloodshot and his shoulders so tense she practically saw the knots forming in them.

"You deal with the night I dealt with last night and see how damned happy you look," he snapped.

"I've been dealing with it my whole life. Last night was no different."

"Last night we got to deal with it together."

She spluttered. "Honey, you didn't deal with a damn thing." She'd had years to come to terms with the illness. She knew what she was in store for, and it was no bed of roses. Unless of course you counted only the thorns. Steve didn't have a clue. He could not begin to comprehend the ins and outs of living with the disease on a daily basis—and she would never allow him the displeasure of finding out.

"Ah." His eyes narrowed. "So spending a night coming to terms with the fact you will develop Huntington's was all about avoidance, was it?"

"Please, you spent the night on the floor with me in your arms." It had felt good. Bloody marvelous actually, but that was as far as she'd allow it to go.

He stalked around the table, grabbed her shoulders and turned her to face him. "Then you'll know when I held you I had no intention of letting you go."

She looked around. People were staring. "Good intentions won't change destiny. You'll have to let me go sometime. Whether you like it or not."

"I don't like it, damn it!" he ground out. "Not one bit. I'm not prepared to give up what time we do have because you're too proud to let me see you succumb to some godforsaken illness."

Too proud? She almost laughed. Her pride and dignity were the only things she had left to hold on to. She wouldn't die with them, mind you. The disease would suck them both away long before death saved her. But now, while she still had the ability to make her own decisions, she chose to uphold her pride and her dignity.

"And I'm not prepared to marry you because you're too weak to say goodbye." She shrugged out of his grasp. Public displays of disaffection had never been her thing.

"Trust me, Pen." He smiled derisively as he took out his wallet and threw some money on the table. "One thing I've grown strong at is saying goodbye to you. I've had a lot of practice. Hell, I can do it with my eyes closed."

He had done it with his eyes closed, and she had the grace to blush at the memories. She'd left him, more than once, in the middle of the night. Waited until she was sure he was asleep before creeping around the room and dressing in silence. The guilt had been too much, knowing she'd gone to him because she couldn't keep away, yet fully aware she needed to stop seeking him out when her cravings became irrepressible.

One time, after a night of hot passion, assuming he was asleep, she'd tiptoed towards the door. The time had been too intense, too magical. They'd made love and they'd laughed and they'd spoken and they'd made love. Again and again. Pen had known if she didn't get out of there she'd never leave. Never be able to pull herself away from his adoring, safe arms.

He'd surprised her by speaking. *"G'bye, Pen. Once again."* He hadn't even opened his eyes, just rolled over and ignored her departure.

She'd fled from his unit, pausing only once she'd closed the front door to reply. *"Goodbye, Steve. I love you."* Three months had passed before she'd sought him out again.

"Doesn't count," she told him now. "You knew I'd be back."

"Hoped," he corrected. "And for the record, I did not know you'd be back this time."

"Well, brace yourself, buster. It's not for long. Soon as Tyler is out of hospital, I am gone again." And to make her point, she walked out of the café.

He caught up with her almost immediately. "Uh uh, Pen." His eyes glittered. "Not this time. This time we do it my way. This time you don't get to leave. Not unless we've set a couple of ground rules first."

"Ground rules?" She raised an eyebrow. He wanted to set rules now? Hah! Didn't he know there were no rules as far as the disease went?

"Yeah, Sunshine. Ground rules. Like exactly how long you'll be gone before you come back. Oh, and for the record? Rule number one: You will be back."

"There are no rules here. When...if..." Goddamn it. *"When*

Ty is better I am going back to London. Alone and for good. Deal with it." The sooner he accepted that, the better for both of them.

He shook his head. "You know, Pen, you might have some rose-tinted view of the dignity of doing this by yourself, but I have some real tainted hindsight of doing it alone. I think I can say, with some authority, we're better together. Both of us. No matter what we have to face."

Shit. He would not take no for an answer. "You know what you are? A bullheaded, stubborn piece of—" Out of the corner of her eye she noticed a taxi. She raised her hand to signal to it. There was no point in standing here continuing this ridiculous conversation. She wasn't staying in Sydney. She was going back to London, and she sure as hell would not marry Steve. No matter how much her traitorous body demanded otherwise. No matter how much she still tingled from last night's lovemaking. No matter how damned addicted she was, her future did not involve being railroaded into a marriage with the one man she could not bear to have around while she wasted away.

When Steve thought of her, she wanted him to remember the feisty, healthy lover she was now and had been a few years ago. He should remember the wondrous nights, when they'd had so much to tell each other neither of them was prepared to waste time sleeping. And the early summer mornings surfing at dawn, chasing the perfect wave and watching the sun break through the shackles of night. And the wintry Sunday afternoons, wrapped together in a single blanket watching DVDs. The candlelit baths they shared, the stolen weekends away. And the love. The whole, healthy love of two whole, healthy people.

She did not want him to picture the distorted joke she would become.

Right now, it would be difficult for Steve to picture her as the shell of the person she was destined to turn into. He was making rash decisions and rash demands. He needed a little space and perhaps a little time in order to come to terms with her future.

She had no doubt whatsoever that when he finally did accept it, he'd be sagging in relief about her refusal to marry him.

"I'll take you to the hospital," Steve growled as the taxi pulled up beside her and she opened the door.

"No, thank you. Today I'm going alone." Because, she thought, if I drive with you you'll probably convince me to marry you on the way and that would be a bad, bad idea.

"Running again, Pen?" Steve challenged.

"Visiting my brother," she shot back, but couldn't deny the prickly sensation in the back of her neck. Déjà vu. Steve was right. She was running again, but it was all for a good cause. Her future was unsalvageable. Steve's was not. Steve had the rest of his life to live, and she would not stand in his way.

"I'm sure your brother will be touched when he learns how much you use him as an excuse."

"This conversation is over."

"Perhaps. But we're not."

She ducked into the cab, desperate to put up barriers between them. She needed Steve to back off. For his sake and hers. "Fuck you, Sommers." She slammed the door shut.

Of course he refused to let it go. He had to have the last damned word. "Keep saying the name, sweetheart," he said through the open window. "It's going to be yours soon."

Chapter Nine

If the atmosphere in Tyler's ICU room had simmered before, now the tension practically boiled over.

Katie was back in her regular chair, trying to force Tyler to wake up by strength of will alone. Penelope could almost see the waves of determination flowing from her resolute face. As far as Katie was concerned, the rest of the world did not exist. It was just her and Tyler.

For the first time since she'd arrived, Pen found she bore Katie no ill will. She did not even feel threatened by her. For the first time, she saw Katie as a woman deeply in love with her brother and not as Steve's lover, fiancée or even ex-fiancée. She couldn't help the niggle of resentment that still plagued her, though. It was tough to feel absolutely no negativity about a woman who had slept with the man she loved.

Thankfully, the Katie issue had receded significantly in Pen's mind, because another was expanding at a rapid rate. Steve did not even pretend to look at Tyler. His gaze was fixed on her, his focus unwavering. While he may have appeared to lean indifferently against the wall, Pen knew better. The bricks gave him no support whatsoever. His rigid body was held together like a tight coil. He did not allow himself the luxury of reclining. Uh uh. He was too worked up, too agitated. His mouth was set in grim lines and his eyes were hard.

Pen glared right back at him. If it were anyone else, or any other time, she would have shifted uneasily on her seat. The intensity of emotion on his face was frightening. But she didn't care. She was too damn furious. What kind of arrogant ass made the assumption she would marry him? Had he not listened to one word she'd said, or was he the world's stupidest man?

Her story wasn't particularly difficult to understand. She had the gene, and she needed to be alone. Period. She didn't want Steven Sommers in her life or in her future. Not like this. She needed the space and the dignity to succumb to her illness alone. Away from the pitying eyes of the man she loved.

But, oh, no. Rather than respect her wishes, Mr. I-must-save-the-world-and-be-a-hero felt compelled to save her from herself. Compelled to share her horrible fate. Mr. Hero felt compelled to marry her.

Idiot! This was her life. Her real life. This wasn't a storybook with a happily ever after. She didn't get to have the happily ever after, and if Steve insisted on marrying her, he wouldn't get it either, no matter what he thought. The years they might have together before she succumbed to the illness would be fraught with fear of the future, and when she did become sick Steve would kick himself for making such a dumb decision. He would spend the last ten or fifteen years of her life regretting his impulsivity.

It wasn't worth it. For either of them. She wouldn't be able to bear the guilt of afflicting her genetic weakness on him, and he'd live his life knowing he'd made the biggest mistake possible.

He didn't get it. What kind of fairytale did he think this was? The last thing she wanted was for him to be around when her life crumbled. When her body twitched and jerked involuntarily and her memory lapsed. When her mood swings swung out of control and her personality changed.

Pride was a big thing for Penelope. It was about the only

thing she had left to hold on to. The only thing she could manipulate—well, for the next few years anyway. By Steve asserting his will to marry her, he deprived her of her one last stronghold. He took away her self-respect.

Tough. She wouldn't let it happen. Let him lay down as many ground rules as he liked. She hoped they worked well for him, because they meant nothing to her. Not a thing. Not one tiny, niny little thing. Their tryst last night had been another temporary lapse in judgment. End of story. When Tyler woke up properly—he *had to* wake up properly—she was going back to London. Alone.

Steve must have read something in her expression, because he lunged forward and took two menacing steps towards her.

But whatever he was about to do or say was interrupted by the door opening.

Stan and Joyce Sommers walked into the room, sending Pen's already tumultuous emotions rocketing all over the place.

A shutter fell over Steve's face, blanketing his aggravation. "Mom. Dad," he greeted them in a remarkably relaxed voice.

"Steve," his mother said as her was gaze drawn to the bed. "I know you told us you'd phone when Tyler wakes up, but we couldn't keep away. We needed to see him."

"She needed to feed him is what she means," Steve's father said as he placed a huge basket on the floor, his gaze also glued to Tyler. "I warned her to wait, warned her that men in comas don't eat, but your mother felt compelled to cook him a four-course meal and bring it to the hospital anyway."

Joyce *tut-tutted* under her breath. "For heaven's sake, Stan. The boy hasn't eaten for a week. He has to be starving."

Stan gestured at Tyler with both hands. "He's asleep."

"I mean when he wakes up."

"So bring him some chicken soup."

"He needs more than chicken soup."

Pen snorted in amusement. Some things never changed.

"What he needs—" Stan stopped midsentence. "Penelope!" His face lit up, and before she knew it, he'd enveloped her in a hug. An all-encompassing, loving, paternal hug. When he released her, it was into Joyce's waiting arms.

"Welcome home, honey," Steve's mother said as she held her tight. "We hoped you'd come back soon."

Pen was wrapped in a cocoon of love and acceptance. Though why Steve's parents should love her so unconditionally escaped her. She'd put their son through hell. Wait 'til they found out about the latest humdinger she'd handed him last night. They'd be seriously thrilled.

Not!

She nodded at the bed lest they think she'd returned for Steve. "I had to come back," she said. "To be with Tyler."

"Of course you did," Joyce agreed. "Family needs to stick together in tough times."

Pen nodded. This she knew to be the truth, and she was more than a little grateful for Tyler's support over the last two and a half years.

"Tyler's not the only one who could do with a good meal," Joyce observed as she looked Pen over. "You're skin and bones, young lady. Don't they feed you in London?" She shook her head. "Still beautiful, but skin and bones. Never mind. A few good dinners back at our place, and we'll get you eating properly again."

Joyce didn't wait for a response. She bustled over to Katie and hugged her. "You listen to me," she told her. "He's going to pull through. Your Tyler is going to be fine." She let Katie go. "He may not be my son, but a mother can sense these things." She put her hand over her heart. "In here."

Stan put his arm around Pen's shoulders in a fatherly manner, and Pen gratefully accepted his support. More than that, she immersed herself in it.

"Thank you, Joyce," Katie said as her eyes filled with tears, leaving Pen to wonder if this was the first time she'd seen Steve's parents since breaking off the engagement. Whether it was or not, Pen had to applaud Joyce's behavior. She showed no animosity towards Katie whatsoever. If anything, she demonstrated her full support of Katie's decision to be with Tyler.

Steve's mother leaned over Tyler and placed a gentle kiss on his forehead. When she lifted her head, she took a moment to study the three other younger adults. Then she swung into Joyce Mode.

"Stan, take out the cheesecake. Steve, go down to the coffee shop and get us all something hot to drink. Ladies? Chins up. From what the nurses tell me, Tyler is doing far better than expected. It's time to get rid of this oppressive atmosphere. Tyler is going to gain full consciousness soon, and when he does, it's going to be to smiling, happy faces. Got it?"

Stan winked at Pen, then walked over to the basket, bent down and took out a large dish. Steve touched a finger to his forehead in silent signal to his mother and headed out the door, while Katie lifted her shoulders a little higher.

The corners of Pen's mouth lifted. For the first time since receiving the news in London she felt a glimmer of optimism. For the first time she believed Tyler might actually pull through. Maybe it was Steve's parents' reassuring presence, or maybe it was Joyce's upbeat attitude. Whatever it was, something in the room changed and Pen knew she wasn't the only one aware of it. When Stan and Joyce arrived they brought hope with them.

✧

"You're in a better mood," Steve commented as he drove her back to the hotel that night. For a good few minutes she'd pondered catching a cab again but knew in the end if she did she'd appear childish.

"I've started to think more positively about Tyler," she told him. She was still mad as hell with Steve, but something had clicked in her today, and she had a feeling inside she couldn't deny. A good feeling about Tyler's outcome. Could be wishful thinking, but for now it didn't matter. It made her happy, and under the circumstances, it was hard to cling to her anger.

Steve smiled. "My mum does have an uncanny knack of making you believe the best, doesn't she?"

"Your mum is the best."

"Yeah, she is." He kept his eyes focused on the road. "She'd make a good mother-in-law too."

"The best," Pen agreed as her heart beat crazily against her ribs. Once upon a time, she'd dreamed about Joyce being her mother-in-law. Before real life had set in and destroyed her fairytale fantasies. "Doesn't mean I'm going to marry you."

"Nope," Steve agreed without missing a beat. "You're going to marry me because you love me. Not because I have a fantastic mother."

Good grief, the man was tiresome. Still, she couldn't find it inside to get angry. "Tyler seemed restless today."

"Changing the subject isn't going to change the outcome. You're still going to marry me."

Yes—or not. "He was thrashing around a lot." His sleep had been disturbed as a result, making him wake up often. He'd spoken a little while conscious; however, most of what he'd said was nonsense. Dr. Lavine had insisted it was still too early to tell if there was permanent damage.

"Sooner rather than later," Steve persevered with the marriage talk.

In his dreams, she thought. *And mine.* "Is that a side effect of the drug wearing off?" She knew it was, but if she could get Steve to talk about Tyler, he wouldn't be so frigging persistent about a wedding that could never take place.

"I was thinking in a couple of weeks. While it's still summer, and we can have an outdoor ceremony. Maybe even get married on the beach."

Her breath caught. Had they ever discussed it? How did he know when she'd pictured them together, making their vows to each other, it was on the beach with a flaming sunset behind them filling the sky with a wondrous, luminous light?

"Dr. Lavine said she hoped to see a change soon." Her voice was reedy and she cleared her throat, hating herself for showing weakness. "Tomorrow even." She needn't tell him. He'd been in the room with her. Apart from nipping out for coffees, Steve had been with her the whole day. He'd been the one who'd asked Dr. Lavine all the questions and explained all her answers to Pen.

"Know what I'm going to do when we get back to your apartment?" Steve asked.

She looked at him suspiciously. Had he changed the subject? "What?"

He lowered his voice dramatically. "I'm going to kiss you."

Her breath caught in her throat.

"Like I've been wanting to do the whole day."

Ack. She couldn't help it. Her heart beat a little faster. "You are *not* going to kiss me because you are *not* coming in."

"And then I'm going to rip off your shirt and ravage your naked breasts." He had the audacity to lick his lips.

She placed a hand on her chest, in part to prevent him from gaining access and in part because her heart beat so loudly she feared he might hear it. "'This is officially the last time I let you drive me home," she told him through gritted teeth.

"Your bra has been peeking through your shirt, driving me nuts. I can't stop looking at the black lace." As proof, he shot a sideways glance at her chest and groaned.

Her breasts grew heavy. "Tomorrow, I catch a taxi." Damn it. Why hadn't she chosen the practical cotton again?

"Every time I look at you I get an erection. Just thinking about you in that bra makes me hard." He shifted in his seat.

Her nipples tightened beneath the lacy material. "Well, I'd hate to keep you away from something that excites you so much. I'll be sure to pass the bra on to you once I've washed it."

"Keep the bra, Sunshine. I want the breasts."

Against her will, Pen's breath turned ragged. She wanted him to have the breasts. Altogether too much. "Perhaps tomorrow when we get to the hospital Tyler will be fully alert."

"Perhaps," Steve replied. Then his voice deepened. "Perhaps you're not wearing panties."

Pen clamped her mouth shut. Of course she was wearing panties, but she wasn't about to tell him that.

"God, I loved it when you walked around without. It got me so hot."

Okay, so she used to do it a lot, but only when she was with Steve and only because she knew what it did to him.

"Know what else gets me hot?"

Pen held her breath. His voice was so sinfully sexy it sent shivers down her spine.

"The thought of tying you up."

She drew her back up straight. "Steve..."

"Tying you to the bed," he amended.

As if that made any difference.

"I'd strip off your clothes first." His voice dropped a notch. "To see if you were wearing underwear," he clarified, "and then I'd tie you to the bed."

"You are not tying me to the bed," Pen told him in her stuffiest tone.

He carried on as if she hadn't spoken. "If you were wearing panties, I'd remove them *before* wrapping the scarves around your ankles."

"There will be no scarves around my ankles." Pen flexed her toes and then pointed them as though testing the confines of his imaginary knots. God, how many times had she turned down his suggestion of a little light bondage?

More than she could count. And yet he still hadn't let go of that fantasy.

"Your bra will have to go too. I couldn't tie your wrists to the headboard if you're still wearing it. It'll just get in the way."

Oh, crap. Against her will lust tugged between her legs. "Forget about it, Steve. It's not going to happen."

How could she explain that no matter how appealing the physical side of bondage might be, it was the psychological control she could never relinquish? In a few years' time, she'd have no choice but to give it up. While she had the capacity to act on her own accord, she would. She would be in control of every event in her life—including sex with Steve.

Something in her tone must have supported her convictions, because Steve relented. "Okay, no scarves. But I'm still going to kiss you when we get up to your apartment."

"Did you forget already? You're not coming up to my apartment." She turned to look pointedly out of the window as he pulled into the Medina Apartments parking lot and turned the car off.

Steve leaned in close. "Are you wearing panties?" he whispered in her ear.

Holy crap! His smoky voice reverberated through her belly, making her tingle—everywhere.

She grabbed the handle and pushed the door open. "Thank you for the lift," she gasped. "See you in the morning." As she scrambled out of the car she quickly said, "Uh, don't worry about me tomorrow. I'll make my own way to the hospital." With that, she slammed the door, raced to the lift and as quickly as possible, made her way to her apartment. With the door securely locked behind her, she collapsed against the wall, panting.

Oh God. Her heart hammered against her chest and her hands shook, her body desperately craving a fix.

Steve infuriated her. He drove her nuts. He was the most stubborn, obnoxious, presumptuous man ever, and yet she still hungered for his body and his touch. Like an addict. She clenched her fists and howled in frustration—then nearly jumped out of her skin as the securely locked door opened beside her.

She stared in horror as Steve stepped inside. "How...?"

"Key," he offered helpfully and held it up to show her. "The receptionist gave me an extra one when you checked in. You didn't notice?"

"What...?" Shit, what was he doing here?

"Weren't you listening?" He set the key on the table and stepped closer, trapping her against the wall. "I told you in the car. When we get back to your apartment, I'm going to kiss you."

"You can't." Could he?

"Oh, but I can." He pressed his hands against the wall on either side of her head and dipped his face towards hers. "And I will."

And he did. His lips claimed hers. In seconds, he was devouring her. Enticing her. Exciting her.

Penelope reacted on instinct, in the same way any fuming woman in her situation would. She lifted her rage-filled arms and threw them around his neck, kissing him right back. Ravenously. It didn't matter how hard she'd rallied against him in the car or how much she'd refused to take his verbal seduction seriously. The instant he touched her, any idea of resistance melted away.

When he did as he'd promised and ripped off her shirt, Pen didn't flinch. On the contrary, she yanked off her bra and pushed his head down to her aching, swollen breasts. As his lips touched her burning skin she couldn't suppress the moan that burst from her throat. He suckled her tight nipples, his predatory mouth lighting fires all over her body.

The five o'clock shadow on his chin grazed her sensitive flesh, the light burn triggering a sweet, urgent ache. "Steve," she gasped, "please..."

He raised his head from her breast, stared at her through midnight blue eyes. Eyes darkened by desire. "Please what?"

"Please." She couldn't talk. Couldn't think.

"Tell me, Pen." He nibbled her lower lip. "Are you wearing panties?" His hands covered her breasts, kneading them.

"Oh." Her head fell back.

"Are you?" Fingers pinched lightly at the taut nipples, the erotic pain shooting through her in tiny bullets of pleasure.

"Yes," she managed to whisper.

He sucked gently on her lip, running his tongue along the inside. "Do you want to be wearing panties?"

"No." That wasn't a whisper. It was a heartfelt plea. She didn't want to be wearing anything. She wanted to be naked. With Steve.

She'd barely drawn breath when she found herself in his arms as he carried her to the bed. Her mouth was on his neck, feeding on the salty skin of his jaw line. Her hands were in his hair and her breasts were pressed against the steely muscle of his chest.

Pen was a fool and she knew it. She was weak and in need of a hit and could not resist what Steve offered. While in theory she'd told herself repeatedly she would not make love to him again, in practice it was a whole other story. A whole other story of sleek, rugged sinew, of hard male muscle and of sensual, sexy man.

He set her down on the mattress and tugged his T-shirt off. As his washboard abs came into view, Pen wanted more. She wanted to see all of him. When, still standing, he leaned over to kiss her, her hands went to his waist and fought with the buttons on his jeans. The task was tough—his tongue did crazy things to her, scattering her concentration, but the end result was worth it. She freed his erection from the tight confines of his pants and held it in her hands as he groaned.

The taste of his salty skin lingered and she wanted more. With Steve she always wanted more. She pushed his jeans over his hips then pulled away to watch him shrug them off. She could not wait to dip her head down and wrap her lips around the tip of his penis.

When she did, Steve muttered something unintelligible. She went to work making love to him, sucking and kissing and licking in ways she knew would drive him to distraction. His musky scent filled her nose and his masculine taste exploded on her tongue. His cock swelled and thickened as she caressed. The skin of his toned butt filled one hand, while round, soft testicles nestled in the other.

For someone who knew the smallest morsel of Steve would only serve to fan the flames of her addiction, she was being given a sensory overload—and she only wanted more.

"I thought," Steve rasped, "you were *not* going to kiss me."

"I wasn't." Her answer was muffled.

"Well." Steve shuddered and pulled away from her. "I'm glad we've got that sorted out."

He drew her up until they stood face to face. "You said I couldn't tie you up either."

"You can't, and it's not negotiable."

Steve blinked. Once. "But kissing is?"

"Kissing is."

He took her mouth with his. Negotiations on this topic weren't necessary. While his lips beguiled, his hands undressed. Her jeans landed in a pile on top of his.

"You are wearing panties," he acknowledged as he slipped a finger beneath the silky material.

"I won't be if you take them off." His finger felt shockingly cool in the heat of her slick folds. She shivered as he ran it over her lips once before dipping it inside. Deep, deep inside. The pleasure was so sharp her inner walls clamped around him.

He dropped to his knees and pushed her until she sat on the edge of the bed. Still he did not remove her panties. Instead he withdrew his finger and lowered his head to her lap. Through the silk and lace he kissed her, running his tongue slowly over her throbbing clit. He kissed her until she was a shivering wreck on the bed. Until she was panting and sobbing.

"Fire it up, Steve," she begged, and finally, finally her panties were discarded.

He moved away for a second, grabbed his wallet and put it down again, and then he was back, fired up and ready to go.

Pen scooted up the bed, making space for him between her legs, and Steve settled there, right where he belonged, with the tip of his erection torturously close to her aching center. Her body trembled with longing, her hunger so insatiable she had to swallow down a cry.

"You told me you weren't going to kiss me," Steve said again as he lowered his face to hers and kissed her chastely.

"We've been through this already," she answered and deepened the kiss. As her tongue invaded his mouth, he nudged his erection stingily between her lower lips. In response, she wrapped her legs around his waist, inviting him in further.

Sweet heaven, if he didn't take her now, she would not be held accountable for her actions.

"Steve," she moaned. "Please."

"Please what?" Beads of sweat formed on his brow.

"Please." She ground her hips against him, trying to increase the depth of penetration. "Make love to me."

He squeezed his eyes shut, as though in pain, and then opened them again. "You told me you weren't going to marry me either."

Oh, please. Not that again. Not now. "I'm not." Again she ground her hips into his. The ache between her legs grew worse, the longing brutal. "I'm going to use you for sex."

"The thing is, you changed your mind about the kissing." He gave her another inch, and she accepted it greedily.

"You should know by now, Steve, when it comes to kissing you, I always change my mind." She spread her legs wider and planted her hands on his buttocks. She ached to have him deeper, throbbed at the emptiness.

"And you," he panted, "should know by now, you're going to change your mind about the marriage thing also."

She shook her head and pushed at his butt. "No, I'm not."

His punishment was harsh. He withdrew from her completely, and she cried out in indignation. "Goddamn you, Sommers."

"It's all about give and take, Pen," he said smugly. "You

kiss me, I don't tie you up. You marry me, I don't pester you about it anymore."

She pushed viciously at his shoulders, using all her weight and strength to roll him over. The second he was on his back, she straddled him. God help her, he'd gotten her into this situation. He was going to see it through to the end. Punishment be damned.

She took his cock in her hand and pumped it. "You can throw around your threats of marriage as much as you want," she gasped, winded from their struggle and from the strength of her desire. "I don't care. What I do care about—" she pumped a little harder, "—is that you can kiss me and remove my panties and then deny me what I want."

"Talking about denial..." Steve's words trailed off as she massaged his balls.

She trailed her hand up his shaft and changed her tactics. "You want it too. Admit it." She ran a finger over the smooth flesh below his testicles. "You want to be inside me as much as I want you there."

Steve squeezed his eyes shut, groaned and grew an inch in her palm.

"You can talk about marriage to your heart's content, but this is what you want." She shifted and used her hand to guide him inside her. Not giving him a chance to object, she engulfed him completely, finally getting what her aching body demanded. He filled her, stretched her and delighted her.

Before she knew what happened, he'd flipped her over so she was on her back again. This time, he stayed lodged inside her. Deep inside.

"You bet I want this." His voice was gravelly. He stretched her arms above her head and pinned them against the bed with his left hand. Then he withdrew his penis slowly before thrusting into her and making them both moan. "I want this every day of our lives. You, me, this. Every." He withdrew and thrust again. "Single." Another thrust. "Day."

With her upper body trapped in place by his firm grip, she ground her hips up to meet his. "You have today," she challenged him. "Make it count."

He did, shifting slightly so he could lean down and draw his hot, wet tongue over her nipple. The move changed his angle of penetration so the next time he drove into her a million lights flashed behind her eyes.

"More," she demanded, and he rocked into her again. And again and again, until the lights weren't just exploding in her head. They were flashing in her breasts and her belly and between her legs. He kept going and going, intensifying the rapture, escalating the tension, until she could take it no more. The lights exploded and she came, crying out her pleasure, calling Steve's name.

He stilled suddenly inside her wildly bucking body and then released his own orgasm with a force that matched hers.

In the dazed aftermath of their lovemaking, Steve released her arms and collapsed on top of her.

"We have every day," he corrected.

She was too thunderstruck to argue.

Chapter Ten

Penelope must have dozed off. She awoke slowly, languidly, with a delicious warmth seeping through her veins.

Steve.

He was kissing her, his mouth brushing her lips lightly. Then her nose. And her cheek and her forehead. Then back to her mouth.

She sighed, stretched and let her lips drift apart, tilting her head to meet his. The edginess and greed that had marked their earlier lovemaking was gone. This was a gentle embrace, tender and sweet. Their tongues met, their teeth nibbled and their lips clung. Time passed. Time stood still. They kissed. And when they finally broke apart, Steve fell back with a low rumble in his chest.

"Mmm. Nice."

"Mmm," Pen agreed. "Very." It was dark outside. She had no idea of the time.

"Hungry?" Steve asked.

As if on cue, her stomach rumbled. "Starving, actually." She hadn't had much of an appetite of late, but right now she was ravenous. "What's the time?"

"Three-thirty." Steve sat up slowly and offered her his hand. "Come with me. I'll make you something to eat."

She let him pull her up. "You will?"

"Nothing fancy. Scrambled eggs okay?"

"Mmm. With toast." She yawned, dropped her head on his shoulder and silently marveled at its size. "You really gonna cook?"

He ran his hand through her hair. "I'll make you a deal."

"I'm not marrying you," she said quickly. "Even if you cook breakfast every day for the next year." His hand felt so good in her hair, tickling her scalp, she couldn't muster up the energy to get annoyed.

"You're jumping to conclusions," he chastised. "I'll cook all the food and even make the coffee...no wait, tea?"

"Tea," she agreed. "If?"

"If you promise not to put any clothes on the whole time."

Pen pretended to contemplate the idea. Her problem around Steve was not keeping her clothes off. It was keeping them on. "What about you?"

"What about me?"

"What'll you be wearing?"

He chuckled. "Not a damn thing."

Pen grinned in satisfaction. "Okay."

"Okay, what?"

"Okay, you've got a deal."

He turned his face, kissed her until her knees trembled, then hopped off the bed. "Two servings of eggs coming up," he announced and opened the tiny fridge.

Pen took a few minutes to freshen up before joining him in the kitchenette. As she brushed her teeth and threw water over her face, she accepted the inevitable. When she and Steve were together, they could not be apart. It was that simple. Whatever attraction she felt for him, his attraction for her ran just as deep. They could not be alone in the same room and not touch. Kiss. Make love.

Perhaps she was being too hard on herself, demanding she stop whatever was happening between them. If Tyler made a complete recovery, she would return to London. Even if he didn't, she'd go back. She'd take Tyler with her, with Katie's blessing of course, and arrange care for him there. But once she left, she'd never see Steve again. Ever.

This time, now, was her and Steve's last chance to be together. Once she left for London again, she would not come back. At least, thousands of miles away, she had some measure of control over her hunger for him. Inches apart, it was impossible, and for now she was going to stop trying.

She'd consider this her last party. A farewell party—and Steve was the only guest invited. While in Sydney, when she was not tied up in Tyler's life, she would celebrate her own. She would celebrate Steve. Every last inch of him. For as long as he agreed to let it continue.

She would not do so under the pretence of giving into his request and marrying him. She'd set up well-defined boundaries. While she was in Sydney, they could sleep together, enjoy each other, find comfort and solace in each other's arms. Thereafter, there would be no ties and no commitments. In fact, once she left for London, there would be nothing. No affair, no communication. Nothing.

There would be no more Steve and Penelope. There would be Steve and there would be Pen, but there would never again be the two of them.

Satisfied with her decision, she dried her face and headed out of the bathroom. Before taking a seat at the small table, she walked up behind Steve, pressed her front to his back and nuzzled his neck. He murmured his encouragement wordlessly.

Watching Steve cook in the nude, she decided as she leaned back in her chair, was one of life's little pleasures. Muscle rippled up his arm as he whisked the eggs, and his butt cheeks tensed appealingly as he reached for the salt and pepper.

When the eggs were bubbling on the stove, Pen spoke. "This is a good look for you." Her voice was throatier than she'd intended, but then her body was more alert than it should be for this time of the morning. A few of the side effects of Steve's bare butt.

"What is?" he asked as he stirred the pan.

"Barefoot and naked in the kitchen."

He looked over his shoulder, focused on her breasts and took a deep breath. "Looks better on you." He stepped from one foot to the other and his gaze darkened.

Pen raised an eyebrow and suppressed a grin. "Something going on I should know about?"

He eyed her devilishly for a moment longer before turning back to the eggs. "Matter of fact, there is. Come here and I'll show you."

Unable to resist, she walked up behind him and snuggled into his back again, delighting in the delicious contact between his warm flesh and her breasts. "What am I looking at?"

"You're not looking." He caught her hand, pulled it forward and curled it around his straining erection.

"Hmm," Pen said thoughtfully as she palmed him, "I never knew cooking turned you on."

"Oh, yeah." He turned off the stove and shared the eggs between two plates. "There's nothing like the smell of raw yolk to get me hot and bothered."

The toaster popped, spitting up two slices of freshly grilled bread.

"Want to grab the toast?" he asked.

"I would," she said regretfully. "But my hand's full." She squeezed him gently for emphasis.

"Do that again, and your hand will be full of—"

"I'll get the toast," she volunteered with a laugh and let go of him.

The atmosphere was easy and relaxed. It had been a while since Pen had simply shrugged off her anxiety, and it felt good. Very good.

Too good, perhaps, because after flirting shamelessly, Pen let her guard down. "Question," she said.

"Yeah?"

"Last night...the condom."

Steve raised an eyebrow.

"You had it in your wallet?"

"Mm hmm," he said around a mouthful of toast.

"Uh...?" How did she ask this tactfully?

He swallowed. "Yeah?"

"How many condoms do you keep in there?"

"A couple." He laughed devilishly. "I confess. I put a few more in yesterday morning."

"Oh. A few more?" He had? "A little presumptuous don't you think?"

"More like a little hopeful." He wound his fingers through hers. "It was presumptuous to bring condoms into the kitchenette with me."

She spluttered. "You didn't."

"Oh, but I did." He pointed his fork at the counter. "They're right there. Next to the butter."

"They?"

He grinned. "Okay. Maybe that's a little presumptuous."

She grinned right back. His thumb caressed the top of her hand, sending sharp prickles of lust shooting through her. "Maybe. Maybe not." She took a bite of egg, chewed, swallowed. "Steve?"

"Yeah?"

"Were they meant for Katie?"

He almost dropped his fork. "What?"

"It's a simple question. You had condoms in your wallet before. You two were engaged. I wanted to know if they were meant for her." Simple? There was not one single thing simple about her question, and they both knew it.

He put the fork down as a slow, stunned expression spread across his face. "You're jealous."

Of course she was. "Not jealous," she lied. "Curious." But perhaps withdrawing her hand from his was a little too telling.

Steve's gaze trained on her face. "Not curious. You are jealous."

She would not answer.

"You hate the fact Kate and I were lovers, don't you?"

She flicked her gaze past Steve and focused instead on a spot on the wall behind him. *Lovers.* Did he have to use that word?

"You're wondering about us. About our sex life." He shook his head in amazement.

Pen bristled. "She's your fiancée. It's hard not to wonder."

"Ex-fiancée," Steve corrected. "Don't, Sunshine." His voice was soft. "Don't wonder about me and Kate. What we had has nothing to do with you and me. Nothing. It never did, it never will."

"You were engaged to her," Penelope pointed out. Oh, Jesus. She had no right to act like this. She had no claim over him. She'd wanted him to find someone else and get married. What kind of a hypocrite was she, moping over his ex-lover?

"*Were*," he agreed. "Not anymore."

She frowned.

"Pen." Steve took her hand again and refused to let it go. He cradled it in his, gently, sweetly. "Kate and I were lovers. Now we're not. And we're not because of you and because of Tyler. I don't love Kate, not the way I love you." He shrugged. "I never did. Kate knew that, and you need to know it too. Especially if you're going to marry me."

And just like that, the last of Pen's resentment towards Katie evaporated. In that moment she knew Katie was no longer her enemy. She never had been. She was just another victim of the horrible realities of Huntington's Disease.

An enormous weight lifted off her shoulders. Perhaps now, her and Katie's relationship would change. They'd always gotten on well before, in the times when Pen had hung out with the circle of three—her brother, Steve and Katie. Perhaps now they could be friends again. Friends and maybe even sisters-in-law— *if* all went well with Tyler.

As for her relationship with Steve, well that was another story. She knew she'd best set him straight—again. "I told you. I'm not going to marry you. I'm just using you for sex."

He grinned, and his eyes filled with mischief. "So there is a chance we might get to use both those condoms over there?"

It was the wicked glee in his face that did it. Warmth seeped between her legs. She grinned backed. "There's a chance."

His grin widened and he winked.

Oh, sheesh. One wink and she'd turned all squishy and wet. One blasted wink and she was ready to use both condoms. She winked back. Desire built in her, repressing her appetite for food, but she refused to act on her impulses yet.

"Jokes aside, I can't marry you."

"I wasn't joking when I asked you." His eyes were serious now, compelling. She couldn't look away.

She nodded. "I know, and I wasn't joking when I made love

to you. I seriously cannot keep my hands off you when you're around. I want to touch you..." She hesitated, blushed. "Well, grope you, actually. Throw you down and make wild, animal love to you."

He grinned. "I kind of counted on that."

"Laugh if you want. Even now, watching you eat breakfast, I'm getting seriously turned on." Her breasts tightened, and her breathing shallowed. "I want you," she finished on a whisper. "Bad."

Steve groaned. His eyes dilated as color rose in his cheeks. "Pen—"

"I can't...won't marry you." Her belly responded to the naked lust in his eyes by lurching. "But if you'll let me, I'd like...love to be your lover again." She swallowed. "For now. For a little bit. Until Tyler's...out of hospital and I have to go back to London."

"No." His body was motionless, his expression unfathomable.

She pressed on, desperate to make him understand she was giving herself to him one last time. Without any ties. "I cannot, will not, ask any more of you. I love you." She shrugged. "I always have—no matter what you might think. All I want is one last chance to be happy with you. One last chance to love you, to make love to you, so when I leave, I'll have these memories to tide me over. Until the end. That's all I ask. All I want."

"But that is not all I want." His voice was calm; his eyes were not. "I want it all. With you. Marriage, children, the whole bang shoot."

"I'm sorry." She was. She was heartbroken. "This is all I have to give."

"No, it's not. You have years—"

She stood. Cut him off. "I want you. I want you to take me in your arms and fuck me. And I want you to do it now. Not next week. Or next year. Now, while we still can. While I still have the time and the know-how to enjoy it."

"Pen..."

"I can't force you. I'll understand if you don't want to." She walked around the table and he turned to face her. "But if you do, I'm here. We could see it as a...farewell gift to each other, a final goodbye. We could part knowing the full truth. Maybe after that we'll be able to move on."

"I don't want to move on. I want you for as long as I can have you."

"You can have me for now."

"Sunshine..."

"Steve..."

"It's not enough."

"It'll have to be."

"I want more."

"You can take as much as you want. Take it now."

"I don't just want now."

Pen took a deep breath, squeezed her eyes shut and nodded. The conversation had done nothing to reduce her hunger for him. It still buzzed through her belly, nipping at her breasts and her groin. She still ached to feel him inside her, moving, sliding, loving her. But now was not enough for Steve. He couldn't cope with a definitive length of time. She understood. Hell, she couldn't cope either, but she had no choice.

"It's okay," she said as she opened her eyes to look at him. "I understand." She sighed heavily. "It was selfish of me to ask, to expect you to play by my rules again. I'm sorry. I should never have put you in this position." She wished she didn't feel the iron clamp tightening over her heart or the tears burning the back of her throat, but she wasn't surprised by the pain. She'd felt it before. Every time she'd walked away from her addiction.

She smiled, kind of, and turned from Steve. Before she'd taken two steps away, he spoke.

"Where are you going?"

"To shower and get dressed. I...it's hardly appropriate to stand here like this anymore." Besides, a shower would drown out the sound of her tears. Her eyes had already filled and she kept her back to him so he wouldn't see her cry.

"Uh uh. No way. We had a deal." The heaviness in his tone had lifted. It was light and teasing and utterly unexpected.

Her breath caught. "Under the circumstances, I hardly think..."

"I made you eggs, sweetheart. And tea. Even though you may not have polished off every last crumb on your plate, you ate enough that I can comfortably say dressing now would be reneging on your side of the bargain."

She shook her head. "I can't do it," she whispered. "I can't pretend to be strong enough to sit here naked, to see you naked and not act on it."

"Who's asking you to pretend?" A chair scraped against the floor. "Act however you want."

This time it was his front touching her back, sending a million tiny prickles skittering up her spine. A livewire couldn't have increased the electricity sparking between them.

He wrapped his arms around her, bent her neck forward so her hair fell over her shoulder and leaned in to nibble on the exposed flesh. His erection, thick and pulsing, nestled in the cleft of her butt, and desire, wanton and unchecked, washed through her.

She blinked back her tears. "I can't marry you, Steve." She had to say it again, had to ensure he understood.

"Hush, Pen. No more talk about marriage." He guided her to the kitchen counter, slowly, torturously, as with each step his hard cock brushed against her butt, sending darts of desire whistling through her body. When they reached it, he pressed against her back, bending her forward, bending with her.

Her heated breasts touched cold granite, sending icy shivers scuttling over her bare skin, and she moaned. She didn't want to wait another second. She needed him inside her, touching, moving, filling her. Needed him to satisfy the emptiness that threatened to overwhelm her.

"Fire it up, Steve," she begged as she ground back against his erection. "Please." She didn't need foreplay or stimulation. She was wet and she was ready and if he didn't fuck her soon, she'd weep in sheer frustration.

The condoms were right in front of her, beside the butter, as Steve had said. She tore one open and shoved it in his hand, a hand that brushed the side of her breast, causing her nipple to swell against the icy, smooth granite.

He made a sound, a mixture between a laugh and a groan, and pulled away from her for an instant, and then he was back and his erection no longer nestled in her butt. It touched her intimately between the legs, requesting permission to enter.

She widened her stance, braced herself on the counter and pushed backwards. Permission granted, he slid into her, filling her, giving her what she most wanted, and the tears were back, threatening to spill from her eyes at the intensity of the pleasure. Nobody made her feel this way. Nobody but Steve.

Behind her, he sighed her name, gripped her hips and pulled her closer, sheathing himself deeper. She cried out once and then again as he pulled out and thrust back in. The pressure that sat in Pen's chest, weighing heavily on her heart, broke its hold and headed south. Between them the tension built and grew, the consuming urgency pushing them harder and faster. Their bodies joined, fusing together to become one. Pleasure blossomed, starting deep within her inner walls and branching out, encompassing her belly and her breasts and every other tingling part of her. And him. He groaned and lengthened within her, probing deeper than she thought possible, igniting flames that could not be doused.

Fire burned between them, searing, licking and scorching.

When his hand left her hip and crept into the cleft of her ass, massaging and teasing, she couldn't contain the pleasure that shot through her, couldn't hold it back. She didn't want to. The tremors began low down and moved like lightning, increasing in strength and speed until full-blown shudders tore through her. She convulsed around his blazing shaft, the onslaught of rapture transporting her to another galaxy.

Only the sound and feel of Steve's release pulled her back to the present, where the thrill and the excitement of his gratification prolonged the glory of her own.

It took several minutes before Penelope's breathing returned to normal and before Steve, who had slumped deliciously over her back, lifted his weight off of her. It took a few more minutes until she had the energy or the strength to stand on her two shaky legs.

When at last she had the presence of mind to tackle the task of cleaning the breakfast plates, she stood at the sink, dreamily running warm water over the teacups. Steve sat at the table, and a warm quiver settled in her stomach.

He watched her, she knew. Hadn't taken his gaze off her, and her body responded to the knowledge by tightening all over. Would she ever be able to get enough of him?

How could she cram a lifetime of pleasure with Steve into a few days?

The thought left her empty, bereft. She didn't want a few days with him. She wanted a lifetime. She wanted forever, but that was something she did not have. She had today. She could give him herself. Her body. Totally and completely. It was his to do with as he wished. Whatever he did, she knew it would be as significant and meaningful for her as for him.

The thought of what he might do left her floundering, struggling for air. Steve made a throaty sound as she clenched her buttocks together, fighting her building desire. She eyed the second condom, licked her lips and beat down the thought. After what they'd shared, there was no way Steve would be ready. The idea had taken root, however, and she had to clamp her thighs together as the flesh between them began to pulse.

"Fuck, Pen." Steve rasped. Before she was able to respond, she found herself being twirled around and lifted onto the countertop. The condom she'd eyed seconds before was whipped away, and then she was wrapping her legs around his waist as he pulled her forward and thrust into her.

It was more frenzied this time, more intense—if possible—and when it was over, instead of them drifting apart again, Steve held her for a very long time. With her legs around his waist and his arm around her neck, they leaned into each other. Embracing. Cherishing.

They may not have forever, Pen knew, but they had now, and she was going to make it count.

Chapter Eleven

They were laughing and wiping down the countertops when Steve's phone rang. He answered after the first ring, his heart hammering. Although a few rays of sun painted the horizon pink, day had not set in yet, which made it too early for anyone to be phoning socially.

"Hello?"

"It's Katie."

His breath caught in his throat. "Is everything all right?"

Her voice echoed through the phone. "Everything's better than all right, Steve. Everything's perfect. Tyler's back!"

They made it to the hospital in record time. Kate met them outside his door with a huge grin. "He woke up." She laughed and hugged them both. "I was asleep and he woke up and he was fine."

"Completely fine?" Pen asked in awe.

"Completely fine," Kate told them.

"Confusion?" Steve asked, automatically assuming his professional persona.

"None. He's thinking and talking lucidly. As clear as any of us." She shook her head. "Although he has no recollection of the accident. He doesn't remember anything about it."

Post traumatic amnesia, Steve thought, associated with the time immediately preceding, and including, the accident. A common occurrence after an MVA. In all likelihood, he'd never gain back those memories. "Movement?" he asked.

"Full movement," Kate confirmed. "He even sat up briefly."

"Experiencing any pain?"

"A lot, but the medication is taking care of it."

Steve stopped short. He couldn't think of anything else to ask. Suddenly, he couldn't be Dr. Sommers anymore. He was too emotional. He was just Steve, and the truth had begun to dawn on him. Tyler was awake, and although he had sustained a head injury, he was not displaying symptoms of permanent brain damage.

Tyler was going to make a full recovery. There would be no long-term consequences or repercussions. Tyler was going to be fine. *Fine.* His best mate had made it. He'd pulled through, and he was going to be fine.

A grin of exultation split his face, and if he hadn't been standing in ICU, he would have lifted Katie and Pen up, twirled them both around and whooped with unadulterated joy.

Tyler was going to be fine.

Beside him, Pen had a big, goofy expression on her face. "Can we see him?"

Kate's smile faltered for a second. "I hate to tell you this, but he's sleeping. It will take a while for the Hypnovel to work its way out of his system. He's going to be pretty tired for the next few days."

Pen groaned in frustration. "I'm going in. Asleep or not, I want to see my brother." She walked into the room.

Steve turned to follow, but Kate touched his arm, holding him back. When Pen was seated beside the bed, out of earshot, Kate spoke. "I need to tell you something."

Steve's stomach dropped. What hadn't Kate wanted to mention in front of Pen?

Kate must have seen the concern on his face because she rushed to reassure him. "No, it's not what you think. Tyler is fine. He will make a full recovery. It's something else."

"What?"

"We spoke this morning, Ty and I."

He nodded. "I'm glad. You've waited a long time to speak to him." Two long, painful and worry-filled weeks.

"Yeah." She nodded. "Actually, he spoke before I had a chance to say anything. He told me something I know you'd want to know."

Steve raised an eyebrow. What was it?

"Tyler was on his way to see us at the practice when he had the accident."

That took him by surprise. "He was?"

She nodded. "He was coming to wish you and I luck for our future together. He...he wanted us to be happy."

Steve's jaw went slack. "Christ, that must have just about killed him." Then he realized how sickeningly and unintentionally close to the truth his words were, and amended them. "It must have ripped his heart out. He thought he'd lost you, yet he was big enough to come and wish you well." Fuck, that was admirable. "He loved you enough that he was willing to give you up if it meant you would be happy." Steve was not that admirable. He refused to give Pen up again—even if it was what she wanted.

"He wanted you to be happy too, Steve. It wasn't just about me. It was about both of us."

Steve swallowed down a hard lump in his throat. "He did it again," he said in a voice thick with emotion. "He proved to us that no matter what he had to endure, we came first. Just like he didn't want to subject us to Huntington's Disease, he refused to stand in the way of our happiness." He frowned to himself. "I hit him, and he still refused to stand in our way. He still proved himself to be a friend."

Kate smiled. "The best friend. Yours and mine."

"Did you set him straight about us?" Steve wanted to know.

"I did." Her smile turned shy. "That was the other thing I thought you should know. I told him we called off our engagement."

"Did you tell him why?"

"Yeah. I told him he was the man I wanted to share my future with, not you."

Steve checked his chest for any leftover feelings of rejection or hurt. There weren't any. Just honest-to-goodness happiness and hope for his friends. He was glad Katie had finally gotten to share her heart with Tyler. "How did he respond?"

Her eyes twinkled with tears and with joy, and her smile grew wider "How do you think? He grinned a lot and then he fell asleep." Katie laughed. A full, uninhibited, carefree laugh, and Steve couldn't help it. He laughed with her.

"You look cheerful this morning," Katie commented.

"As do you."

"I am. For obvious reasons. How about you?"

How about him? Good question. Was he happy? How could he not be, after the morning he'd had? It had started with two mind-blowing orgasms and only improved with the news of Tyler's recovery.

On the other hand, how could he be truly happy when he knew Pen had the gene? He neatly sidestepped the question. "I'm happy for you. And for Tyler."

"My question wasn't about me or Tyler. It was about you."

"I'm sorry." He shook his head. "Can you not ask me right now?"

"Of course." She squeezed his arm. "I didn't mean to pry."

He placed his hand over hers. "You're not prying, babe. You're asking because you care and I appreciate it. Nope, I more than appreciate it. I like it. A lot." He did. It felt good knowing she cared. Damn good. "I just don't know the answer to your question is all." He sighed. "I seriously don't know the answer."

"Well, hey, if you need someone to talk to about it, I'm here, you know that?"

He nodded. Twenty-four hours ago he hadn't been sure, but now he knew for certain. "Same goes for me, babe. If you need to talk, I mean. I'm here."

A smile broke out on her face. "We're going to make it, aren't we? You and I are going to be friends again."

He smiled back. "You know what? I reckon we are." His smile broadened. "It feels good."

"Doesn't it?" The smile reached her eyes at the same time her tears did. Then she looked thunderstruck. "Oh my God, we're whole again." Her voice told him she could barely believe it. She could barely fathom her own luck. "I-I have you back. I have you *both* back." She sniffed loudly as the tears spilled over. "B-b-both of you. Tyler's awake, and...and you're my...friend again. I-I have you both..." She could hardly talk. "The...the circle's almost complete." The tears took over. She began to shake. "We're almost a circle of three again."

Goddamn, his own eyes filled as well. He felt Katie's overwhelming joy and relief, and he was happy for her. So happy for her. At least one of them was getting everything they had hoped for. Personally, he'd have preferred a new and improved circle, a circle of four. One that encompassed Pen as well, but for now he'd settle for the three of them. He still had time to increase the numbers.

This time it was Steve who wrapped his arms around Kate, Steve who offered his warmth, friendship and support, and Kate took it all, eagerly. Damn, it felt good. Right. This was how it was supposed to be between him and Kate. Good. Close. Friends.

Steve knew if Pen looked out the window at that moment and saw them together, she would also see it. She'd see two people hugging, celebrating their friendship and Tyler's awakening, and the thought made him smile. It was obvious he and Kate were always meant to be friends.

When they drew apart, he left an arm around her shoulders and led her into Tyler's room. Indeed it felt good to smile in the ICU. It felt better than good. It felt bloody brilliant.

Steve and Katie were describing their recent skydiving experience over leftover cheesecake when Tyler woke up. It was only when Pen heard a derisive snort beside her that she noticed his scornful eyes appraising them.

"No fair. I'm allowed a couple sips of water every few hours and you get to eat cake."

She screeched. "You're awake."

"Well, I wouldn't be if you'd spoken a bit softer. Can't a man get a decent night's sleep here?" His voice was gruffer than usual, but it was about the sweetest thing Pen had ever heard.

"You can and you will. Tonight. But it's midmorning now and it's about time you opened your eyes." She hugged him—awkwardly, considering his state, but hugged him nevertheless. "How do you feel?"

Tyler grimaced as he shifted to sit a little higher. "Like I've been hit by a bus."

"A four-wheel drive, not a bus," Pen corrected helpfully. "You don't do things in half measures, do you?"

"Neither do you." He cleared his throat. "You came all the

way to Sydney because I broke my arm?"

"Yeah." Pen rolled her eyes. "The coma and accident were incidental. I came to make sure they'd put the cast on properly."

"Bandage, not cast." He raised his arm, then dropped it with a huff. "I'm glad you're here." His voice softened significantly.

"I'm glad I'm here too." Pen's smile grew. Her brother truly was okay. He was sitting up in his hospital bed, bantering with her. *Oh, thank you, Lord. Thank you!*

At the same minute she felt Steve move to stand beside her, she watched Tyler's eyes narrow with caution. He lifted a shaky right arm as though to protect his face.

"You going to hit me again?" he asked his best friend.

"It all depends," Steve answered. "There anything else you haven't told me that I should know?"

Tyler's eyes flickered to Pen and shadowed over. She looked at her brother before shaking her head infinitesimally. Tyler blinked, then turned to Katie and stared at her for a long time. "Just one thing," he said, his gaze never wavering.

"Yeah?" Steve asked.

"I'm not giving her up." He stared at Katie as though he couldn't get enough of her. "I thought I could." He shrugged. "I was wrong."

"Just as well." Steve nodded. "Because if you leave her again, I'll beat the crap out of you. Again."

Tyler grinned but still held Katie's gaze. "Believe me, mate. I'm not going anywhere."

"Believe me, mate. I'm damn happy to hear that."

"Believe *me*," Katie intervened. "I'm even happier."

Katie and Tyler shared a smile. An intimate, personal smile that excluded the rest of the world. If Pen hadn't been so relieved and so excited her brother had woken up, she might have considered giving the lovebirds some time alone together. But she hadn't seen *and* spoken to Tyler at the same time in a month, and she wasn't quite ready to leave the room yet.

She knew Ty and Steve had a lot of talking to do as well, but there would be time to do that. Loads of time for Tyler to catch up with his friend, like there would be loads of time for him to catch up with his lover.

His time with his sister, however, was limited. Tyler was conscious. He was going to be fine. Which meant Pen could start planning her trip home. Yes, she'd enjoy her stay while she was here—even more now Tyler was conscious, but the clock was ticking. Her days were numbered.

Her time with Steve was almost over before it had even begun. Probably just as well. As it was, the detox was going to be unbearable. Perhaps the less time she spent with him, the easier it would be.

Or perhaps not. Whenever she left the agony would be excruciating, and she knew it. She trembled at the thought. Almost immediately, a warm body pressed against her. Steve had shifted slightly, silently absorbing her emotion.

Tyler spoke, breaking into her reverie. "Any chance I can have a slice of cheesecake?"

"Of course," Katie answered. "In a few days' time, when you've slowly been reintroduced to solids and your stomach can handle all the cream, sugar and fat."

"I'm starving," Tyler moaned. "I could eat a whole damn bakery, shelves and all. Never mind a simple slice of cake."

"No worries, mate," Steve volunteered. "I'll organize some food for you."

Tyler looked at him gratefully. "Thank you."

"Back in a minute." Steve headed for the door.

"Steak and chips," Ty called after him. "Medium rare with pepper sauce."

Steve snorted and exchanged an amused look with Katie. "I'll do my best," he promised and left the room.

When he returned he held a small tray with a bowl of jello and a slice of bread. Tyler stared at the food in disgust, but when it became clear neither Steve nor Katie would allow him anything more, he ate it reluctantly, all the while questioning them about the details of the last few days.

"And the other driver? How is he?" he asked after Katie had laid bare the facts.

"Fine," Katie answered bitterly. "Suffered a few scrapes and bruises, that's all. His blood alcohol level was way above normal."

"He didn't get off scot-free," Steve added. "He's facing a possible jail sentence. Up to eighteen months."

Pen was surprised. She'd been so involved in Steve and Tyler she hadn't thought to ask.

"He is?" From Katie's expression, she was equally surprised. "I never knew that.

"Yeah." Steve nodded. "The police were here on Tuesday, hoping to interview Tyler. I spoke with them instead."

"The bastard deserves eighteen years, never mind months." Katie's face contorted. "After what he did to you—"

"Hush, my sweet." Tyler's voice was smooth. "I'm okay." He took her hand. "I'm okay. You don't have to worry anymore."

"I know you are. But when I think of what could've happened..." Her voice broke.

"It didn't." Tyler spoke only to her.

Steve touched Pen's arm. She turned to look at him.

"I nearly lost you. Before I even had you," Katie told Tyler.

Steve quietly stood and signaled with his head towards the

door.

"You didn't lose me, sweet Katie. I'm right here, and I'm not going anywhere."

Words weren't necessary. Pen followed Steve silently out of the room. Tyler and Katie's conversation was personal. She and Steve had no business being there.

As Steve closed the door behind them, Pen swallowed hard against the lump in her throat. Katie and Tyler had trudged a lengthy, tough trail to reach this point. But finally, they were here, at the start of their lives together, the beginning of their future. There were no obstacles between them anymore.

Steve and Pen had reached the final chapter in their relationship. The last kiss goodbye. In a few days, she would forever close the book on their history, leaving him to trail her own lonely path into her own gloomy future.

She closed her eyes against the pain, bit back the sob that threatened to burst from her chest. This was not the time to show her grief. Tyler was whole again, and she would celebrate his return to life. Just as she would celebrate her final days with Steve. Tomorrow she could grieve. For today, she would be happy.

Steve sat alone beside Tyler's bed. A few days had past since Tyler awoke, but he was still exhausted and as a result, napping frequently—like now. The women had taken the downtime to get some air. It was a little odd watching Pen and Kate walk off together, but it was nice too. The women seemed to have relaxed significantly in each other's company.

The obsessive need to remain in the room in the hope there might be some change in Tyler's condition was gone. All three visitors felt free to come and go as they pleased, but still chose to spend the majority of the days with Tyler. Kate still spent nights there too.

Even if he'd wanted to, Steve couldn't have left. If Pen was at the hospital, he would be too. He was damn well going to make himself a constant in her life. He was going to make himself indispensable, so even if she did decide to pack up and return to London, she'd soon realize she couldn't live without him. Just like he couldn't live without her.

"You slept with her, didn't you?" The voice startled him out of his thoughts.

He looked at Tyler, whose clear, insightful eyes were staring straight at him. Silently, Steve thanked the powers that be. This scenario could have worked out so differently. Tyler's eyes could have been clouded with confusion. Or worse. Blank.

Then the question struck home, and he sighed. He couldn't fuck around with the truth. Not with an issue this big. They needed to have it out about Kate. If they didn't, she'd always remain an obstacle between them, standing in the way of their friendship. "I'm not going to lie about it. She was my fiancée. Of course we slept together."

Tyler grimaced. "I was talking about Pen."

"Oh." Steve nodded. "Ah," he added with a sheepish grin.

"But since you've brought it up, you may as well know. If you do ever sleep with Katie again, I will hunt you down and kill you," Tyler promised.

Steve snorted. "No worries there, mate. Kate's not interested in anyone but you." Then he added with a sardonic smile, "But I'll consider myself forewarned anyway."

"Getting back to my original point..." Tyler narrowed his eyes. "You slept with my sister."

He shrugged but didn't deny it. "You slept with my fiancée." One thing about the two of them, now that things were out in the open, there was no more bullshit. The conversation cut straight to the chase.

"I love her, Steve," Tyler said, and his expression softened. "I always have."

"Apparently," he answered dryly.

Ty smiled, but it didn't reach his eyes. "It killed me, mate, challenging you for Katie. You've got to know that. I hated what I was doing to our friendship."

"You wouldn't have had to do anything if you'd clued me in from the beginning," Steve said. "If you'd told me then about the two of you, none of the rest of this shit would have happened."

"You're right." Tyler frowned. "I should have said something." But he made no excuses for not doing so, no apologies, and Steve respected his silence. He still guarded Pen's secret.

"I understand why you didn't."

Tyler jerked. "You do?"

His gut twisted. "Yeah. I do. And I almost wish I didn't."

"You spoke to Pen?"

He nodded. "She told me everything." The agony of her full confession walloped him once again, making breathing difficult.

Tyler said nothing. He lay back, looking thoughtful.

"You're surprised," Steve gauged from his response.

"Pen's kept her secret a long time. She was determined you not find out."

"You know what her problem is? What your problem is?" Steve asked. He forced the anger and bitterness from his voice. "You Bonnards are too damn proud. You should have trusted us in the first place. Kate and me. What did you think? We would have rejected you because of the disease?"

"No, mate." Tyler shook his head tiredly. "Worse. We reckoned you'd have stood by us."

"So you left, in case, God forbid, we would have seen you deteriorate sometime in the distant future."

"Don't judge us for our decisions, Sommers. Until you've walked in our footsteps, seen what we've seen, you can't possibly know how bad it gets."

"I'm a doctor, Ty. So is Kate. We've seen enough illness to hazard a guess as to how bad it gets. Doesn't mean we're going to run from it."

Tyler pinned him with a penetrating look. "You'd stand by Pen? Knowing what's in store for her?"

"What kind of an asshole do you think I am?" Talk about suspending judgment. Did Tyler think he'd run because Pen was going to get sick? "Of course I'd stand by her. If she'd bloody well let me."

His face was unreadable. "Does she know that?"

"I've mentioned it once or twice." Or a million times.

"It's not what she wants," her brother replied carefully.

"So I hear." He grimaced. "She thinks it'll be easier to face her future alone. Like you."

"We didn't think it would be easier, mate. Not for one second. It's a more dignified option."

Steve swore out loud and jumped out of his chair. Damn Bonnards. Bloody determined to do things their way. Alone. Didn't they know they had friends to lean on, people who loved them? Did they think they had to be perfect in order to be acceptable? "Bullshit. It's all bullshit," Steve told Tyler.

Tyler chuckled as he watched him pace across the floor. "You did sleep with her."

Steve refused to answer. He kicked the leg of the chair instead. He'd have preferred to kick the wheel of the bed, but that would have jolted the bed, and in turn, Ty's arm. Pissed off as Steve was, Ty had suffered enough already.

"She always was the only one who could wind you up like this," he said with a smile. Then he was serious again. "I was right all along, wasn't I?"

"'Bout what?" Steve asked grumpily, not ready to tackle the sleeping with his sister question.

"About Pen," Ty said simply. "You still love her."

This time he toed the chair, the fight draining out of him. "Yeah, mate," he said, because if anyone knew how he felt about Pen, it was Tyler. "I always have."

Tyler nodded. "What about Katie?"

"I love her too." He looked at his friend. "But I'm not in love with her. We're pals, nothing else." He sighed. "It's a good thing you came home when you did. Kate and I? We'd never have worked." It felt good to speak about this with Tyler. "Besides—" he grinned, "—I was history the minute you got off the plane. I should have realized sooner there was something between you."

"You couldn't have," Tyler was quick to assure him. "I went to extremes to hide it. For Pen's sake."

"Yeah, for Pen's sake," Steve said sarcastically. "It's definitely in her best interest to go through this alone, rather than with a man who loves her at her side."

"She's a proud woman. She doesn't want to face the humiliation of deteriorating in front of you."

"Who does she have, Ty? If you're in Sydney with Kate, and she's on the other side of the world, who the hell does she have? How can you support her decision to be alone through this...this fucking disease?"

"I don't support her decision," Tyler said in a clear voice. "But I do understand it, and I respect it." He sat up, his face contorting at the sudden movement. "Do you think I want her to be alone, without anyone to turn to or to lean on? Christ, man, she's my sister. I want her to be happy, and when she can't be happy anymore, I want her to be cared for and looked after." He took a deep breath and calmed down a little. "I didn't come back to Sydney for my sake alone, mate. I came back for her sake as well."

"Yeah?" Steve asked angrily. "How do you figure? How does leaving her in London help her?"

"I came home banking on the fact you still loved her. If I couldn't get over Katie after all that time apart, I realized you probably hadn't worked Pen out of your system either."

"I hadn't," Steve admitted. He'd refused to acknowledge it to anyone, himself included. "Still, what's that got to do with anything?"

"You're like me, mate. You fight for what you want."

Steve grunted. "If I'd fought for what I wanted, I'd have been in London a long time ago."

"Nope," Tyler contradicted him. "You thought Pen didn't want you, so you fought for a second chance at happiness. With Katie."

"What's your point?" Steve asked.

"My point is, if you knew Pen still had feelings for you, you'd fight for her." He paused, raised an eyebrow. "Right?"

Steve almost laughed out loud. Tyler was right. Of course he'd fight for Pen. He was fighting. Damn, he was giving it everything he had. Pity the person he fought the hardest was the woman in question.

"Right," he said without embellishing.

"I would never have told you about the Huntington's, Steve, not without Pen's permission. But I would have let you know she still had feelings for you. Even if she hated me for doing it." His eyes shadowed. "She's my sister, and I can't do anything to save her from her future, but I'll be damned if I don't do anything and everything in my power to make it better. To make her life the best it can possibly be." He took a deep, shuddering breath. "And you, my friend, are the best. Especially where Pen is concerned."

Steve stood a little straighter, carrying on his shoulders the massive responsibility and gift Tyler had bestowed upon him. The man had just entrusted him with his sister's care and wellbeing.

His eyes burned as his throat choked up. Fuck, he was going to cry. He turned around quickly, resumed his pacing and swallowed down hard on the emotion welling in his chest. Finally, he leaned his forehead against the windowpane, using the cold glass to dampen the force of his feelings.

When he had some control, albeit not very much, he spoke. "I'll fight for her, Ty," he said hoarsely. He turned around and looked at his friend. "I swear I'll fight for her."

Tyler sank back against his pillows. "I banked on that." He closed his eyes. "But if I know my sister, she's going to be a bitch of an opponent."

"You're not fucking kidding," Steve growled. Then he added in a lighter tone, "She's one stubborn lady."

Ty smiled morosely. "It's in the genes."

Steve frowned. "Here's what I don't get, Bonnard. Why are you so okay with encouraging me to be with Pen—even knowing she's going to develop Huntington's—when you wouldn't let Kate anywhere near you when you thought you might inherit the gene? A bit hypocritical, don't you think?"

Tyler frowned back. "You don't mince words, do you?"

"The time for word mincing has passed. Long ago."

Tyler shrugged, then clenched his jaws together and swore in pain. "I watched my father suffer. For years. I watched what my mother went through, and I never wanted to subject Katie to that. Ever."

Steve shook his head. "Yet it's okay for me to go through

it?"

"I'm not being a selfish prick about this, Steve. It's easy to see things objectively when I'm not involved. You and Pen belong together. You deserve to be happy for as long as you can. And then she deserves a man who can continue to love her and care for her even when she's not all there."

"You think I'm stronger than Kate? That I could cope, but she couldn't?"

"Mate, I think Katie would cope with the fallout from a nuclear explosion. That was never the issue. For me, in the end, it was a matter of pride. I never wanted to lose my dignity in front of the woman I loved."

"You and your bloody sister. Putting your fucking pride and dignity before your happiness."

"What can I say?" Tyler pursed his lips. "It's a Bonnard thing. It's in the genes."

Chapter Twelve

Pen placed her fork on her plate and sat back with a sigh.

"Don't tell me you've had enough? You've hardly eaten anything," Joyce Sommers said in horror.

"Leave the girl alone," Stan argued. "She's had two helpings of everything."

But who's counting, Steve thought.

"Two helpings of everything don't help if you haven't eaten for a year," Joyce told Stan in all seriousness.

Steve looked at Pen and grinned as he too replaced his fork after consuming an enormous serving of roast beef and potatoes. She grinned back.

"At least have a little more pumpkin," Joyce coaxed.

"Honestly, I couldn't eat another thing," Pen insisted. "I'm stuffed. The last time I ate such an enormous meal was..." She stumbled on her words. "Well, was the last time I had dinner here."

Stan patted Pen's hand reassuringly.

Joyce *harrumphed.* "How about some salad, then? It's not very filling. You'll hardly even notice it."

"You're feeding the wrong Bonnard, Joyce," Pen told her. "It's Tyler who'd happily put away the mountain of food you're offering."

Joyce frowned at Steve. "Well, I don't have a choice now, do I? Steven won't let me bring any more food to the hospital."

"Joyce, let the hospital look after Tyler," Stan chastised.

"Mom, Tyler's only just regained consciousness. If he eats anything heavy it'll make him sick," Steve explained for the twentieth time that evening.

"He needs to get his strength back," Joyce insisted.

"And he will. With the right food," Steve argued, although he fought a losing battle. Joyce believed the world's problems could all be solved with a good meal.

"Why don't I help you with the dishes?" Pen interrupted and stood with her plate in hand.

Joyce gave her a delighted smile, and the two women made short work of the table. Before Stan could help himself to extra peas, his wife had whisked the dishes away.

Joyce had long since stopped refusing Pen's help. After Pen's first dinner at the Sommers' home, she'd simply allowed her into her kitchen.

Steve followed them out of the dining room to help stack the dishwasher and smiled as he watched his mother and lover work together like they always had, chatting and cleaning like old friends. No, like mother and daughter. Steve frowned. Damn it, they could be mother and daughter—if Pen wasn't so fucking adamant she had to handle things alone.

She glanced at him over Joyce's shoulder, and his heart nearly stopped beating. Her eyes were soft, happy, as if she was in the one place she wanted to be. The look on her face tugged at his heart and pulled at his emotions, and he knew then no matter what became of her, Pen would always be the only woman he loved this profoundly.

Their eyes caught and held, and his mother's voice faded into the background. All he saw or heard or focused on was Penelope.

Pen looked curiously at him before her lips curved into a wicked smile. She winked behind Joyce's back. Then she tilted her neck and asked, "What was that noise?"

Noise? The only thing he heard was blood roaring in his ears.

"What noise?" his mother asked.

Dirty glass in hand, Pen listened carefully. "That mewling sound outside."

Steve narrowed his eyes. Pen was up to something. She had her mischievous smile on, the one that said *you can't stop me even if you tried*. "I don't hear anything." But then every one of his senses was focused on Pen, so even if a hooter blared behind him, he wouldn't be aware of it.

"Listen."

The three of them stood in silence, listening. Or rather, Joyce and Pen listened. Steve watched Pen, bemused.

Joyce shrugged. "You're imagining things, Penelope." She handed Steve a rinsed plate to put in the dishwasher.

He nearly dropped it and had to duck to avoid his mother's pointed, accusatory glance. His mind raced. "There's nothing out there, Pen."

"Of course there is," Pen argued emphatically. She looked outside through the open kitchen door. "It is mewling. Did you get a cat?" she asked Joyce.

"No. Stan's allergic. Cats make him sneeze for a week."

"You hear that scratching sound?" Pen asked.

Damned if she didn't have a glint in her eye. Steve shook his head, as did his mother.

"Give me a second. I'm going to see what's happening." With another wink in his direction, Pen walked outside.

She was barely out of earshot when his mother handed him another dish. "If you don't marry her, I am going to take a belt

153

to your backside," she promised.

Again Steve almost dropped the plate, but this time he made a quick recovery. "I think DOCS would object, Mom." The Department of Community Services had pretty strict policies about child abuse nowadays.

Joyce continued as though Steve hadn't spoken. "We were fine when you told us about Kate, Steven. None of us thought you loved her, but we were willing to accept her if that was what you wanted. I'm not willing to accept that you're going to let Penelope get away again. That one you love."

Oh, Christ. A lecture. From his mother. About the women he should and shouldn't marry. Arguing with her was pointless. Joyce was in full-blown Mother Mode and she wouldn't hear him even if he did object.

"I'm not sure why you let her go in the first place. It wasn't my business to ask. But I'm telling you now, I want grandbabies. I'm not getting any younger, you know, and if you want me to baby-sit, you better hurry up and have those children already."

Steve chuckled to himself. He had to laugh. If he told his mother the truth about Pen, he doubted he'd ever be able to smile again. Joyce probably wouldn't be able to smile either. "I think dad's ready for dessert," he said.

"Your father's always ready for dessert. Now you get your butt out that door, and you go and ask Penelope to marry you."

"Is there ice cream in the freezer?" He'd have crawled after Pen if he thought for one second she'd say yes.

His mother looked at him as if he'd grown another head. "Of course there's ice cream in the freezer. And pecan pie in the oven, now—"

"It is a cat!" Steve and Joyce turned in unison at Pen's voice. "A tiny kitten, and she's stuck in the tree."

"Pen," Steve said reasonably, glad of the distraction from

the lecture, "cats don't get stuck in trees. They climb down them as easily as they climb up them. It's what cats do." At least he could reason with her. His mother was beyond logic.

Or so he thought. "Not this one," Pen insisted. "I think she's stuck. She's too little to get down."

Joyce gave Steve a not-so-gentle nudge. "Don't stand there. Go and help save that poor stranded kitten."

"Please?" Pen batted her eyelashes at him, drawing attention to the devilish gleam in her eyes. Steve gave up on logic. She was up to something and he wanted to know what it was.

He threw his hands in the air. "C'mon then," he said with an exaggerated sigh of resignation. "Let's go rescue the cat."

"Ask her!" His mother's whispered order followed him out the kitchen door.

"It's back here, on the other side of the gum tree," Pen said as she made her way across the dark, silent garden.

She vanished behind the trunk of the massive tree. Its branches stretched out, monopolizing at least half the yard. Of course a cat would climb the tree. It was kitty heaven.

"Okay, Sunshine," he said as he rounded the trunk. "Where is it?"

She leaned against the solid wood, a silhouette in the night. "Where's what?"

"The kitten stuck in the tree."

"There is no kitten." Her voice was a mixture of laughter and seduction. Sunlight and heat.

Steve grinned even as blood pooled in his groin. "So why are we outside, hidden behind a tree, searching for a nonexistent cat?"

"Come here," she said, "and I'll show you." Her voice dropped several notches, and his body reacted instinctively,

155

stirring and tightening.

"What are you up to, Penelope?"

Her voice was soft. "Remember the other night when you asked me if I was wearing panties?"

Oh, Jesus. His cock grew a good three centimeters at the question. "Uh huh."

"Ask me again."

Four centimeters. "Are you wearing panties?" Fuck knew she'd better be. They were standing in his parents' backyard.

"Not anymore. I took them off when I came out here the first time." She flicked her arm and something warm landed on his face then slipped to the ground.

He leaned over and picked it up. Though the color was hidden by the dark, he felt the lace, and he saw it was a thong. A wet thong.

Eight centimeters and growing. "Pen...my mother's in the kitchen," he warned.

"I know, and we're in the garden, in the dark, behind the biggest tree in Sydney. Saving cats."

"Without underwear."

"My bra's still on." Her laugh caught him in his balls and tugged. Ten centimeters. He stepped closer to her.

"My parents..."

"If you're worried about your parents, you shouldn't have looked at me with those fuck-me eyes in the kitchen," she said and cupped her hand over his dick. Twelve centimeters.

She'd confused his look of love with lust, but he didn't correct her. How could he when her fingers made short work of the buttons on his fly? Fifteen centimeters by now. At least. No way could he walk back into the house looking like this. "If you think those were fuck-me eyes in the kitchen, you should see what they're saying right now."

"Stop talking, Sommers," she said. "You have a cat to save."

Their mouths met in a heated kiss. Her lips were warm and moist and opened easily to his seeking tongue. She had his dick free from his clothes and pumped it with both hands by the time he slipped his own hand up her skirt and palmed her naked butt.

He groaned into her mouth. "Pen, my parents are inside."

She wriggled her ass and shifted from one leg to the other. Before he knew it, his hand touched the wet heat between her legs. "Then you better be quiet so they don't come out to see what all the fuss is about."

Unable to talk, he let out a strangled groan. A soft one that wouldn't attract attention.

He thrummed her clit, traced his fingers through her slick folds and kissed her again. While a part of him worried his mother might walk out to see about the nonexistent kitten, a bigger part knew there was little chance. Joyce was probably making her way to the dining room at this very moment to tell his father he was proposing to Pen.

Pen gasped as he dipped a finger inside her. She was all feminine fire and soft moans, and his dick felt in serious danger of exploding in her hot little hands. Christ, she was so wet. He gently massaged her with her own cream, running his finger over her clit, through her silken folds and lower, until he touched the crease of her ass.

She trembled. "Fire it up, Sommers. Quickly."

He needed no further invitation. Yanking his wallet from his pocket, he grabbed a condom and sheathed himself with it. And then, right there, against his parents' gum tree, he caught Pen in his arms, positioned her just so and slid inside her.

With one leg wrapped around his hips and the other balancing on the ground, she took him in, her inner walls clenching around his cock. It didn't take either of them long.

Pen rocked against him, encouraging him, urging him on. Faster and harder, until the two of them were lost in a frantic dance older than time.

And right there, against his parents' gum tree, Pen clamped down around him and came hard, the intensity of her orgasm knocking Steve's rhythm out of whack. Right there, against the gum tree, Steve came too, shooting his release into Pen, filling her with the essence and the strength of his love.

When his heartbeat had returned to something resembling normal and he'd released Pen from the death grip he had on her, Pen chortled in his ear. "Better give me back my panties now, or the proof of the nonexistent kitty will be dripping down my thighs for the rest of the evening."

"Shit, Penelope." Steve's cock jumped at the thought. "You are bloody determined to give me a heart attack, aren't you?"

"Not a heart attack. No. Just a good enough orgasm to last us the rest of our lives."

"Marry me, Pen. I'll give you good enough orgasms every night for the rest of our lives."

"I told you, I don't want to discuss marriage again."

Steve shrugged, unrepentant. "I had to ask." he said. "My mother told me to."

"Your mother—" Pen's voice broke off in a laugh that turned to a hiccup.

Ah, jeez, they'd done this before. At the hospital. Steve hauled her against him. "Don't cry, Sunshine. Please, don't cry."'

"I want to marry you, Steve," she gasped. "I want to so much. You have no idea. But I can't. I won't. Even if your mother wants me to." She couldn't talk anymore, and he didn't make her. He simply held her. At least now he was one step closer to his goal. At least now he knew she wanted to marry him. Thanks to his mother.

Pen pushed him away. "I'm a mess," she said as she tried to catch her breath. "My face is hot and I smell of sex."

Steve inhaled. She was right—she did smell of sex. He got semi-hard just breathing in the scent. "You smell incredible," he said and gave her the panties. "Now put these on and we'll go back inside. I'll distract my parents with some nonsense about the cat, and you can head straight to the bathroom and clean up a little." He grinned at her as she hiccupped again. "If my parents find out what we did in their garden, I swear they won't let you leave here without a ring on your finger."

Pen hiccupped. "Trust me, Sommers, by the time I get out of the bathroom, your parents won't suspect a thing."

He slipped off the condom, pulled up his jeans and silently gave thanks for the large garbage bin outside the back door. "They may not suspect a thing, but I will not be able to concentrate worth a damn until I have you home and naked in my bed."

She ran a hand through her hair and then looked at him, her good mood seemingly restored a little. "Play your cards right, and you won't have to wait 'til we get to your bed." She pulled on her panties, straightened her skirt and headed towards the house. "It's a fair distance from your parents' home. Anything could happen in that time."

Anything did happen. With the windows of the car closed and the doors locked, the subtle scent of sex and desire permeated the air, driving Steve nuts. Pen looked at him with a wicked smile and dropped her knickers in his lap. Then she hiked her skirt up over her legs, giving him an enticing view of naked thigh and more. He had a burgeoning erection by the time he pulled up at the first red traffic light.

Without a word, Pen leaned over and nestled her nose in

his groin. Before the light had changed, she had his dick free of his pants once again, and her hot mouth settled around his length.

Her lips and tongue were all over him, wreaking havoc with his concentration. Barely able to breathe, let alone steer a car, Steve turned into a darkened side road and pulled over. She did not lessen her onslaught one bit. In less than two minutes, Steve's balls recoiled, tightened and let rip, spurting come into Pen's mouth. She swallowed every last drop, lifted her head, licked her lips and kissed him soundly on the mouth, giving him a taste of what she'd swallowed.

Then she pulled away. "My turn," she told him, and hoisted her skirt up a little higher, revealing parts that should have been covered by her panties. It was Steve's turn to lick his lips and hers, and he did so in heated anticipation. The taste of her mouth was only the beginning of his late-night feast.

Chapter Thirteen

Tyler was being released from hospital tomorrow. He was going home with Katie. Well on the road to recovery, he'd been transferred out of ICU and into his own private room the day before, and given an almost clean bill of health not five minutes ago. Steve and Katie had walked off with Dr. Lavine, obviously cross-questioning her on every last detail of Tyler's health, which left Pen alone with her brother for a while.

It was good to spend quiet time with Tyler. They'd only had a few hours of privacy over the last few days. Pen cherished them, knowing they would be the last she and Tyler had alone together for a very long time. It was time to leave. Tyler was almost one hundred percent recovered—which meant Pen was on her way back to London. While Dr. Lavine had examined Tyler, she'd slipped outside and phoned QANTAS. Her return flight was confirmed for the next morning.

She shuddered as she accepted what that meant.

There were so many people she'd have to say goodbye to apart from Tyler. Katie for one. Quite unexpectedly, they'd grown extremely close over the last few days. Once Pen was able to let go of her jealousy and resentment, she'd found a lot to talk to Katie about. They'd shared the highs of Tyler's recovery and the tension of the preceding few days. She knew Katie would make both a wonderful wife for her brother and a fantastic sister-in-law for herself—when Tyler finally proposed to her—and Pen did not look forward to their farewells.

Then there were Stan and Joyce. There was no way she could say goodbye to them face to face. She'd fall apart. But she couldn't leave without closing that chapter in her life, either. As impersonal as it might be, a phone call from the airport was Penelope's best option.

And then there was Steve.

God alone knew how she would manage that one. She didn't think she could utter the words and remain sane afterwards. As it was, she was limited in her number of sane days. Saying farewell to Steve might dement her altogether.

Perhaps instead of making tonight about endings, she'd make it about a celebration. A celebration of their love and their time together. The grand finale, so to speak. She had an idea in her head, a way to bring the curtain down. With a gift. A gift she'd never been ready to give him before. But now, well, the time was right. Yes, it might mean relinquishing control for a while. But it was a special night—their last one together—and Steve was worth it.

Her hands trembled fiercely thinking about it. A mixture of lust, apprehension and misery overtook her.

"Pen?" Tyler's voice shook her from her reverie.

"Mm hmm?" She looked up at her brother.

"You thinking about going back to London?"

She narrowed her eyes. "How did you know?"

"Because you've got that look on your face. The same one you have every time you know you have to leave him."

She sighed heavily. "I can't stay, Ty. I'll be hurting him."

"He loves you, kiddo. Your leaving will hurt him more."

"For now, perhaps. But when the symptoms start, you know he'll be relieved he's not a part of all of it."

Tyler frowned. "I don't think so. If anything, he'll feel worse.

That he's so far away and can't do anything to help."

"I don't want him to help," she said vehemently. "When the symptoms start I want him as far away from me as possible. I *never* want him to be in the same position Mom was in with Dad. I never want him to have to shoulder that responsibility. By the time I get sick, I want him happily settled down with at least three kids."

"He wants that too. With you. Even if it means he only has you for a limited time."

Pen drew her shoulders up, feeling somewhat betrayed. "What are you doing? Why are you saying all of this? You...you know how I feel about Steve." She gulped in a mouthful of air. "You know better than anyone that if circumstances had been different, I would never have let him get away. I would have hogtied him to a bed until he agreed to spend the rest of his life with me." Her chest shuddered, making speech difficult. The thought of marriage to Steve, of having a family together... God, Tyler knew how much she craved that. "Cir-circumstances aren't different. Th-they are what they are. And I have to go back."

"To what? Jeremy?"

Pen started. Christ, Jeremy. She'd made a mental note to email him days ago and promptly forgot. She stared at her brother, appalled.

He grinned at her and said with a shake of his head, "Don't tell me. You forgot to let him know you were coming here."

She lowered her gaze guiltily. "I forgot twice. First when I left and then again when I realized I hadn't contacted him. Things were too hectic. Too stressful. I just forgot about him."

"You've been seeing him for almost six months now and you forgot to phone him and say goodbye?"

She glared at her brother. "I thought you were going to die. It's okay to forget."

"You'd never have forgotten Steve, no matter what happened to me."

She pursed her lips together and didn't answer.

"You don't love Jeremy."

"Of course I don't love him." Pen suppressed a snort of derision. "That's the whole point. Not to fall in love again. Jeremy is...company when I'm lonely." And a warm body on especially desolate nights.

"That's what you're going back to? Company when you're lonely?"

"What should I do?" she spat at her brother. "Stay here so Steve can watch me decay? Watch me spiral into madness? No, thank you."

"I think you're making a mistake."

"What?" Her voice was louder than it should be.

"I think you're making a mistake. I think your future—the good part of it—is with Steve. Here in Sydney."

"Oh, and the bad part?" she asked cynically.

Tyler held her gaze without flinching. "I think it's with Steve, here in Sydney."

She sat back in her chair, glowering. "Dr. Lavine was wrong. She said your MRI results were fine, but you obviously injured your brain. You're talking like a blithering idiot."

He smiled gently. "I'm talking like your big brother. I only want what's best for you."

"Really? And since when have you decided that Steve watching me die will be best for me? Weren't you the one who refused to have any contact with Katie whatsoever until the day you discovered you *didn't* inherit the gene?"

Tyler flinched.

Fuck, Pen shouldn't have thrown that in his face. As it was, Tyler felt wretched he'd escaped unscathed while she'd inherited the disease. Rubbing it in was spiteful. But damn it, why had Tyler all of a sudden changed his mind? He knew, he understood, everything she'd gone through—the effort and the strength of will it had taken her to make her decision. He empathized with every bit of her need for pride and dignity. Hell, he'd chosen the same path—until he'd been diagnosed as normal. Now he wanted her to stay with Steve.

Well, fat frigging chance. She was getting out of this place. The sooner the better.

"I want you to be happy. You've been miserable for two and half years. And it's had nothing to do with your test results. You've been hiding behind the likes of Jeremy, pretending to have a social life, pretending to be happy, when all you can think about is Steve."

When she opened her mouth to protest he stopped her. "Don't even try to deny it, Penelope. I was the one who dried your tears every time you cried. I was right there with you every single minute. Don't give me any crap about you being happy without him. You live for him. You always have. Since the first time he came to our house almost twenty years ago you've loved the man." His mouth twisted. "And he loves you."

"Why are you doing this?" Pen asked, shaken. "You know why I'm in London. You know it's because I love him so much that I'm there. I want him to get married. I want him to have children." Her heart burned at the thought. Sweet Lord, Steve would make a wonderful father. A wonderful, kind, generous, loving dad. Unfortunately, he would never be a father to her children. She would never have children. She would never leave them with the legacy she'd inherited. That was another reason why she had to abandon Steve. She would never, never deprive him of that right, of that future. Steve was meant to father children. Sons. Like him.

"Please," she begged her brother, "please don't make me second-guess myself. It's hard enough having to leave," she said on a sob. "Don't make it even worse."

"I'm not trying to make it worse," Tyler said. "I'm trying to make it all better. I'm your big brother, kiddo. It's my job."

Penelope shook her head. "Your job is over. Officially. You've had as bad a last few years as I have. Now you get to live the life you've always wanted. Stop worrying about me. Stop looking after me. Live your life, Ty. Be happy. In fact, be doubly happy. It's on your shoulders to be happy enough for both of us." She looked at her brother, tears straining against the backs of her eyes. "It's enough for me, knowing one of us gets to live our dream. When I thought you might not survive the accident, I was shattered. It was the most unfair thing in the world. But you did survive. Now it's time to forget about me. Live your life and be happy. It'll be enough for me to know one of us survived."

"Forget about you?" Tyler's face turned scarlet. His eyes blazed and his chest lurched, and Pen knew he was about to blast her into the next galaxy.

She held up her hand. "Don't. Don't say one word. I'm going now. Steve and I have dinner arrangements. It's our last night together, and I intend to make it count. I'll be back to say goodbye to you tomorrow before you leave the hospital. You can get as angry as you like, brother dearest, but this is the right choice for me, and we both know it."

"For fuck's sake, Pen—"

She ignored the onset of his tirade, kissed him on the cheek and slipped out of the room. If Tyler felt good enough to lambaste her with such choice words, he was going to be fine. At least she could leave Sydney knowing her brother would have no long-term consequences from his brush with death. A bittersweet smile pulled at her lips as she walked down the hospital corridor. Behind her, nurses ran towards Tyler's room.

Pen was pretty convinced the cacophony of cursing and

irrational threats to ground all outward-bound flights for a year had medical staff racing to find antipsychotic meds and any neurosurgeon, neurologist or psychiatrist on duty. They didn't need them. Tyler was going to be fine.

Chapter Fourteen

Pen had been the perfect date all through dinner. Beautiful, charming and gracious. They'd talked like they used to in the old days. About nothing and about everything. They'd gazed endlessly into each other's eyes like enrapt new lovers. If Steve hadn't already loved her with all of his heart, he would have fallen head over heels while sitting in their old favorite restaurant in Paddington.

He wasn't oblivious to the fact she'd barely touched her food. Neither was he oblivious to the gentle play of her fingers on his thigh or the steamy looks she shot him from beneath her lashes. In fact, when it came to Pen there was nothing he was oblivious to. He couldn't remember what he'd ordered or what the waiter looked like, but if he closed his eyes, he clearly recalled every item of clothing Pen had on. From the low-cut, sleeveless white blouse that showed more braless cleavage than would usually be considered decent, to the slim three-inch heels of her strappy sandals.

He also recalled every single thing she'd said so far and every expression on her face as she'd said it. From the dreamy look of passion in her eyes to the joyful relief when she spoke about Tyler. He'd also noticed the tiny tremors of tension that ran through her shoulders the whole evening.

Regardless of the pleasant décor and romantic surroundings, she'd made no secret of her wish to return to his flat. Her wish to be alone with him. Just the two of them. And when she'd sipped her last drop of wine and smiled at him with a promise of...well, of everything and anything, he'd settled the bill as fast as possible and whisked her out of the restaurant.

They hadn't made love since this morning, since before they'd left for the hospital, and Steve thought he might bust a gut with wanting her. Christ, she need only breathe and desire washed through him, sweet and demanding. He'd been semi-hard the whole night, and the vixen knew it. The gentle play of her hands on his thigh? Every now and again, her fingers had trailed a little higher, grazing over him. Brief enough that no one else would notice, long enough to instill in him a slow burn. Very slow and very hot.

She had him all tied up in knots. He'd firmly intended to tackle her on the question of marriage once again, but she'd effectively sidestepped the issue and kept him in the semi-permanent state of arousal the whole night. He couldn't think straight like this. No way could he logically convince her to marry him. Tomorrow he would use every single power he possessed to persuade her to become his wife. To spend the rest of her life with him. Tomorrow he would convince her that he would cherish her while she was healthy and care for her when she became sick. Tomorrow.

Tonight would be spent showing her how deeply he still loved her.

As much as she had him tied in knots, he wanted to tie her in knots. Or rather, tie knots around her. Christ, he wanted to throw her on his bed, secure her to the damn headboard and keep her there forever.

Contrary to Pen's belief, his fantasy had nothing to do with some unleashed desire to experience bondage. He wasn't interested in binding Pen to his bed so he could have his wicked way with her powerless body.

The real reason he'd always longed to tie her up was much

simpler than that. He did not want her to leave. End of story.

How many times had she slipped in and out of his bed without ever making a commitment? How many times had he searched, unsuccessfully, for a way to keep her with him?

Ropes or scarves were a quick fix to a problem he'd never found a solution to. Now, more than ever, the need to tie her up raged in his stomach. Pen couldn't leave this time. She just couldn't. He had to, *had to*, keep her with him.

It was useless suggesting the scarves again. As arousing and erotic as her behavior had been the whole night, there was still no chance she'd go for the whole bondage theme. In all the years they'd been together, she'd never once given him the go-ahead. There was no reason tonight should be any different.

Tomorrow he'd tie her down. If not with ropes, then with a ring.

When they were finally home and alone in his flat, he caught her in his arms and lowered his mouth to hers. Flames erupted as soon as their lips met, sparks flying all over the place.

"Did I tell you how amazing you look tonight?" Steve asked when they came up for air. The sheer black skirt fluttered around her calves, hinting at the luscious curves of the rest of her legs.

Pen smiled. Her mischievous, sexy smile. "Once or twice. Did I tell you I left my bra off for your sake?"

Steve swallowed. Christ, he'd watched the swell of her breasts spill over her plunging neckline the whole evening. "You mean...?"

Her eyes glittered. "I wanted to get you hot as hell for tonight."

"You did," he growled and kissed her again, skimming his hands over the exposed flesh of her breasts. Fuck, he couldn't get enough of her. If he made love to her for a million years it wouldn't be enough.

She whimpered, and her nipples tightened and poked at his palms. He slipped his hands beneath her shirt and ran his thumbs over the taut beads of her bare breasts, all the while staring deeply into her eyes. Words tumbled out of his mouth. "I love you, Penelope Bonnard. I always have and I always will."

Pain shot through her expression. Grief stripped her face of pleasure. But only for a second before Pen pulled away, took his hand and walked towards his bedroom. She threw her purse on the bed, then she settled on the floor and opened her arms.

Still reeling from the momentary anguish on her face, he sat beside her. "Pen, sweetheart? What is it?"

She pressed her index finger to his lips. "No questions. Not tonight. Tonight is for lovers, for us. No thinking, no talking, just...experiencing." This time she kissed him, cradling his face in her hands with such tenderness he did not doubt her love for him. As she said, tonight was for them. For lovers.

The tenderness did not hide the intention, the thoroughness and the directness with which she kissed him. It did not stop his erection from growing its full length or his heart from pounding. It did not hide her heartbeat either as it raced in time with his.

At length, Pen turned on her knees and reached over onto the bed to where she'd dropped her purse. Her butt poked out prettily and Steve froze, taking in her stance. He grew harder as he sat behind her, watching, wanting.

Then her fingers touched the bag, and he was propelled in to action. Fast, before she sat back down, he settled his hand on her lower back. The contact burned his palm, and he broke out in a sweat. Pen didn't struggle. She turned her head to look at him over her shoulder. Her eyes smoldered and her lips were full and pouty from his kisses.

"Steve—"

"Shhh," he hushed her, and knelt behind her so his erection pressed against the sexy, semi-transparent skirt covering her bottom.

Her arms dropped to the mattress, supporting her upper torso, and she pushed back into him. Christ he loved fucking her from behind, loved to watch her back arch and her ass cheeks tense as he thrust into her.

He traced the outline of her spine beneath the soft silk of her shirt. She shivered under his touch. "I like that you're not wearing a bra," he said as he brought his fingers back up to where her strap should have been. No, he frigging loved it.

"I know." Her voice was wicked.

His dick swelled against her backside. "You're a tease."

"Perhaps," she acknowledged, "but only when I know what I can gain from the teasing."

He dragged his hand under her skirt and up her outer thigh. "And what is it you're hoping to gain from your lack of underwear?"

"That's easy." She grinned. "You."

"You have me, Sunshine. Always." His hand ran over the curve of her satiny hip, and then he swore out loud. "You're not wearing panties either."

"I know," she said again, and he cupped her butt cheek and pinched the firm, rounded flesh.

She moaned. "You can't imagine what a turn-on it is, walking around with nothing but this skirt covering me, knowing you're standing next to me the whole time."

"Lady, if I'd had any idea you weren't wearing knickers, I'd have had you flat on your back hours ago," he rasped.

"You can have me flat on my back now," she said as he kneaded her behind.

"Not a chance. I want you right here, right now, like this."

He slid his finger over the smooth divide between her butt cheeks, dragging it down until he touched hot liquid. He groaned out loud. "You're so wet."

"You have no idea," she said in a hoarse voice. "I've been horny the whole day, wanting you. Wanting this." She jiggled her hips, and his finger slipped between her slick feminine folds.

"Aahh."

Steve wasn't sure who'd moaned. He didn't care. All he cared about was fanning the flames of the woman before him. She was moist and warm, and the slightest movement of his finger had her writhing on his hand. He couldn't wait to slide into her wet heat.

Leaning over her, his finger still firmly lodged between her legs, he used his other hand to caress her breasts, one at a time. Her petite frame allowed him easy access to both sides, and in seconds her nipples were rigid pebbles, prodding his fingertips. He caressed the tight buds as he seduced her with his other hand, dipping first one and then two fingers deep inside her.

Pen moaned incoherently as he added his thumb to the action, sliding it over her clit. Her tremors started deep within her body, and he massaged her a little harder, fucked her a little faster. When he gently twisted a nipple between two fingers her orgasm came in earnest, ripping through her body. Her inner walls clamped down on his fingers.

"That's it, Sunshine. Come for me," he whispered as her body gripped him in passion.

His balls were so tight they hurt, trapped in the confines of his jeans. He wanted nothing more than to rip his pants off and bury himself in her depths. Hell, he wouldn't even have to move. Her inner muscles would milk him so fast and so hard, he'd come before he was fully lodged inside her.

But he repressed his hunger, intent on seeing Pen's pleasure through. Sweet Lord, she was so hot. On fire. And he couldn't even see her. Her skirt hid her sweet ass beneath layers of material.

Several moments later, flushed and panting, Pen crawled onto the bed and collapsed on her stomach. Steve shucked his pants and tore off his shirt in less than three seconds before meticulously removing her clothes. He raised her upper body slightly to draw her shirt over her head then slowly dragged her skirt over her hips and down her shapely thighs.

The sight of her butt, still quivering in the aftermath of her orgasm, nearly stopped his heart. It glinted beneath the soft glow from the bedroom lamp, wet from her passion. His lungs ached with a physical pain. Christ, loving her this much hurt. It filled him so completely there was space for nothing else in his chest, not even air.

"Take a few deep breaths, Sunshine," he said. "Get a little energy back. You're going to need it."

She responded with a soft groan he felt all the way down his shaft.

"Did you like that?" she asked as she looked back at him with a smug, lazy smile. "Making me so hot I climaxed in about ten seconds flat?"

Like, it? "Sweetheart, I fucking loved it!" He clasped her hips, gently pulling her up until she knelt on the bed with her upper body stretched forward. "But I'm going to love it even more watching you come on my dick."

How could she ever possibly consider not marrying him? Consider not spending the rest of her healthy life making love with him, sharing something so special it spanned years and miles and would not quit—despite the ruthless attempts Pen had made to break them up?

How could she continue to keep them apart knowing they

were this good together? Knowing how much he loved her? Tomorrow, he swore, tomorrow he would change her mind. By lunchtime he would have a ring on her finger and a promise of marriage. Tomorrow he would tie her down. Pen was not going back to London. Not for anything more than to pack up her things and hand in notice at her school. From now on, every night would be like this one, a shrine to their love. Every day would be a sweet example of the blissful ordinariness of marriage.

No matter what her future held, their present was wrapped up in each other. They were meant to be together. He was meant to love her and to make love to her, like he did now.

The combined headiness of his resolve and the wild abandon of her inhibitions had his cock loaded like rifle. Large, long and more than ready to fire. Sweat trickled down his back. He was fast losing control. He needed to be inside her.

Pen must have felt the same way. She grabbed handfuls of doona in her fists and shook her hips enticingly. "Fire it up, Steve." She arched her back invitingly.

Steve almost roared as primal male urges rocketed through him. He sheathed himself with a condom, knelt behind her on the bed, pulled her hips close and settled the tip of his aching shaft at her slick entrance. Then he thrust once, lodging himself in her burning heat.

He froze, terrified if he moved he'd lose control right then, before he'd even started. He gritted his teeth and fought the impulse to come.

Pen didn't help. She pushed back, taking him deeper. He grunted out loud from the exertion he used to reel himself in.

"Oh God," Pen gasped. "That's good." She moved her upper torso sensually against the bed covers. "Feels so hot. Like fire." Her back arched again, pushing her hips higher in the air, squeezing his cock.

●

Steve wasn't sure how he did it, with Pen a wild vixen of desire, but he scrunched his jaws together, tensed his entire torso and somehow managed to rein in his lust as her inner muscles clenched around him in a loving, sensual vise. When, at last he was sure he could move without ending all their pleasure prematurely, he began to plunge into her, slowly at first and then a little faster, loving the sensation of her hot, wet core wrapped around his hard, needy dick. Loving the sight of her butt pushing back to meet his thrusts.

"Steve. God, you're going to make me come again." Pen trembled. The tiny quivers vibrated through her inner walls, tormenting his sensitized flesh.

Perspiration beaded on his shoulders and ran down his spine. So much for reining in his lust. He gave himself a minute, tops, before his aching balls erupted.

Pen shook in earnest, sending sweet waves of heaven careening through him. Steve grabbed her buttocks and pulled them apart, determined to watch every last spasm wracking her body. Fuck, she was sexy. If he were physically able, he'd lean down now and lick her. Taste her luscious lips at the exact point where they swallowed his cock.

"I love fucking you, Pen," he growled. He did. More than anything in the world. "I love the way you feel wrapped around my cock. How warm and wet you are. How sexy and sensual." Her ass tensed as her inner walls clenched around him while he spoke, and he had to bite back a tortured whimper. "I love how responsive you are. How you come when I touch you and how you come again when I do. I love you, Sunshine."

He thrust into her grasping depths. Fast and rhythmically. Over and over.

"Steven!" Her voice was strangled. Her breath came in shorter, sharper puffs, and her moans filled the air.

He bit down hard on his cheek, searching for any form of

pain to dampen his excitement a little. He couldn't find it. Especially not when Pen let out a long, steady groan and convulsed around him.

God, he wanted to keep his eyes open, wanted to watch as her orgasm ripped through her body, but the need was too extreme. The pain too agonizing. Pen had teased him the whole evening, and he couldn't hold it any longer, couldn't stop his release. Wrenched from his balls, it tore out of him. His eyes closed of their own accord as streams of come pumped through his dick. He couldn't see her climax, but he could feel it, and the combined effect of their mutual orgasms was perhaps the most intense pleasure Steve had ever experienced.

Several moments passed before Steve could muster up the energy to move. He withdrew from her—slowly because he was still ridiculously sensitive—and went to the bathroom to dispose of the condom. When he returned, he had a warm, wet washcloth which he used to lovingly wipe Pen clean.

"Steve?" she murmured.

"Hmm?" His vocal cords weren't quite ready to kick into full force.

"I have something for you." Her voice was throaty and soft.

"Oh?" It was hard to concentrate when he washed her so intimately.

She shuddered as he moved the cloth away and rolled a finger over her clit. "Mmm. Nice." She sighed. "I tried to reach it earlier, but you... Aaah, very nice," she muttered on a sharp intake of breath. "You kinda distracted me."

"Sorry, love. Won't do that again," he lied and swept the same finger over her swollen lips.

"Tease." She gave a hoarse laugh. "I bought it especially for you. You'll like it."

He gazed at her ass and traced the cleft up to her spine and then back down again. "What is it?" He only half concentrated

177

on the conversation. The rest of his attention was diverted to the exposed lower part of her glorious body.

"It's this," she said and reached for her bag.

Steve took advantage of the slight change in her position to dip his finger between her lips, into her slippery channel and then out again. Several times. So intent was he on his task that it took a while before his mind registered the flowing streams of color spilling from Pen's hand.

His breath stuck in his throat. "Pen," he rasped unevenly.

"Told you you'd like it," she whispered.

"Oh, fuck, Pen." Words failed him. What could he say? The wispy strips of silk stole his vocabulary.

She'd brought him scarves. Two of them. Bright slashes of reds and blues that contrasted sharply with his khaki doona cover.

He swallowed convulsively. *Scarves.*

No, they were more than scarves. So much more. They were Pen's blessing to him to secure her to his bed and keep her there. Forever?

"Are you sure, Sunshine?" Not forever, no. He and Pen did not have that much time. But perhaps for as long as the disease allowed?

"I'm sure." To prove her point, she rolled onto her back and handed him the scarves. "Tonight I give you control."

Spellbound, he accepted both the scarves and the control.

She stretched her arms above her head and reached for the headboard.

The symbolism of her offer almost brought him to his knees. Steve wasn't just going to bind Pen to the bed, he was going to bind her to himself. Permanently.

"I love you, Sunshine."

"I love you too." She wriggled her hands. "Now do it."

Before she had a chance to change her mind, Steve swept into action. First he secured a scarf to the headboard, and then he wrapped the other end gently around her wrist. He tied two knots, tight enough so they would hold and loose enough that he could pull them free at any time.

He took a minute to admire her half-restrained form before circling the bed and securing her other arm in the same fashion.

Pen didn't pull on the scarves or test the strength of the knots. She simply watched his movements with big, trusting eyes.

Steve went to stand at the foot of the bed, motionless. She was a vision. An exquisite vision he couldn't get enough of. With her arms stretched behind her, her breasts were pulled upwards, and her nipples—her lush, rosy red nipples—pointed at the ceiling. Her waist tapered below her ribs, accentuating the gentle curve of her belly. Rounded hips led to long, toned legs. One knee was bent, the other lay flat on the bed.

"Spread your legs for me, Pen."

He didn't need to ask twice.

A muscle twitched in his throat. "Now bend your other knee."

Pen lifted her left leg as per his request.

He could see, but not enough. "Wider."

She drew her thighs further apart.

His mouth went dry. God, she was beautiful. Every last inch of her. From her slender throat right down to the tips of her toes. But it was the half-shadowed spot between her legs that captivated him the most. Her inner folds were puffy and pink. Puffy from his ministrations. Pink from her natural color. He couldn't draw his gaze away.

Pen gave a soft groan and shifted on the bed.

A low-grade ache started in his lower abdomen, growing sharper with each passing second. His cock, already half erect, grew to full size.

She thrashed her legs. "Fire it up, Steve."

He almost smiled. If she thought he was going to fuck her and free her just like that, she was sadly mistaken. While Pen was bound to the bed he was determined to make every second count.

"Soon, sweetheart," he promised and went to kneel between her legs. "First I need to adore you."

And adore her he did. Starting at her neck and making his way down, he kissed and adored every inch of her body. Using his lips, his teeth, his tongue and his hands, he covered her with tender kisses and gentle nips, passionate strokes and warm licks. When his mouth swept over her nipples for the first time, she pulled against her restraints.

"Damn it, Steve," she growled. "I need to touch you."

"No," he disagreed between licks. "You need to be touched."

When he pressed his lips against hers and drew her tongue into his mouth, she moaned out loud and yanked at the scarves.

"Please let me hold you," she begged when the kiss ended.

"You will, Sunshine. Later." He kissed her again and again, until she stopped tugging at the scarves and simply lay quivering beneath him.

As much as he yearned to drop his head between her legs, he held off. Instead he focused acute attention on the sensitive skin of her inner thighs and the soft, ticklish bits behind her knees. He massaged her calves and ran his hands over her legs until he'd memorized by touch every square inch of her flesh.

Then, and only then, did he allow himself the gratification of tasting her. Just the lightest lick to tempt them both. Pen cried out as his tongue swept over her and was gone. Steve lay motionless with his eyes closed and breathed in the scent of the woman he loved. The same woman who, after years and years of refusal, had capitulated and granted him his wish.

He was completely happy. In a way he'd never been before. Pen was his.

With his eyes still closed, he nuzzled her slick folds, touching and teasing without actually giving. It took seconds and Pen writhed against his lips, pleading for more.

Steve could withhold no longer. He opened his mouth to her and loved her. He loved her with painless nips and long, wet licks. He loved her with chaste pecks and hungry kisses. He loved her until she exploded around his tongue and sobbed on her release.

And then he loved her some more. Even before she'd ridden through the waves of her orgasm, he placed his hands beneath her butt and lifted her higher. Closer. He laved her from her clit over her slit and down until his tongue touched the sensitive ring of muscle between her buttocks.

Pen bucked wildly, the tremors in her body increasing substantially. Whether it was a second orgasm or a reinforcement of the first, Steve was unsure. He didn't care. All he wanted was for Pen to experience the same intense joy and pleasure she had given him when she'd handed him the scarves.

Over and over he licked, from her clit to her ass and back again, reveling in her high-pitched moans and ongoing release. It was several moments later when he finally pulled away. When the manic undulation of her hips settled to a calm quiver.

Even then he could not resist the temptation of one last orgasm. Pausing only to breathe, he buried his face once more between her legs and loved her until, screaming, she came in his mouth.

His previous orgasm had been a godsend. If he hadn't already come once tonight, there was no way he could have done what he just did without losing control. As it was his balls were full to bursting. His painfully erect cock hurt each time he moved. Christ, he needed to find a haven. Needed to drive into Pen and release every iota of pent-up frustration, lust and adoration. He needed to come again, and he needed to come inside Pen.

"I have to be inside you, Sunshine."

"I have to have you there, Steve."

He sat up when he heard a catch in her voice. She wore a stunned expression of rapture, but Steve was shocked by the tears that stained her cheeks. He immediately wiped the moisture with his thumb.

"Pen?"

"Fire it up, Steve," she said in a shaky voice.

"You're crying."

She closed her eyes and shook her head. "With pleasure. Now, please. Please, please, please, just fuck me. I need you inside me. *Now.*"

He needed no further invitation. Stopping only to roll a condom over his shaft, he once again knelt between her legs. Then he leaned forward to kiss away the tracks of her tears.

She moaned and drew her thighs apart as the head of his dick touched her lower lips.

"Not too...fast," she whispered. "Too...sensitive."

It almost killed him, but he went slow, pushing into her gradually. Residual contractions from her orgasms rippled through her inner muscles, making the fit more snug than usual.

Oh, Christ, she was so tight, so hot. Slowly, slowly, inch by tormenting inch, he slid inside her. The effort nearly killed him, but he gave her ample time to shift and take the full width of his girth as he buried himself completely in her depths.

She wrapped her legs around his waist.

From this angle, his balls nestled against her ass—the same ass he'd just licked—and he felt unbelievable. Unfuckingbelievable!

Pen's thighs trembled, sending tiny vibrations racing down his cock.

"You okay, sweetheart?"

"Mmmmm," was her only response.

He had to move, had to fuck her. He pulled out slowly then inched back into her. He did it again and again and again, using unhurried and gentle strokes. She moaned, encouraging him. Together they built a good, steady rhythm. With each thrust she relaxed further, urging him to move a little faster. With each rotation of her hips he fell a little more hopelessly in love with her.

She let out a muffled groan and lifted her pelvis. "Harder," she demanded, and he complied instantly, thrilled by her response. His shaft felt heavy and hot, and the friction against it did his head in.

Not quite willing to withdraw all the way, he pulled out far as he could go and plunged back into her. She let out a throaty cry which was quickly followed by his.

It was too much. The pressure built. Unbearable tension tore through his dick and his balls. He couldn't contain it much longer. She was too hot. Too fucking sexy.

He hastened the pace. "I'm close, Pen," he warned. "Real...real close."

She whimpered, driving him fucking nuts.

"I want you with me, Pen," he urged. "Come with me." Jesus, he wanted her to explode. Wanted to feel those tremors shake her as she convulsed around him. He moved faster, harder, and she took everything he gave and pushed back for more.

He had five, maybe ten seconds and that was it. Damn, he was so in love with this woman. "Penelope," he ground out as she rose to meet him, once, twice, a million times. His balls pulled tight against the base of his dick. "Goddamn, Pen, I can't...stop it."

"Don't!" she screamed.

He didn't. At the exact moment the tension erupted and his balls exploded, Pen let loose her own orgasm. The walls of her vagina clamped down around him, tighter than anything he'd felt before. They squeezed him, milked him for everything he had. Steve came, shooting into her depths, over and over again, riding them both through an earth-shattering climax.

Even after the ecstasy began to subside and the white lights stopped flashing behind his eyes, Steve remained wedged where he was, inside Pen, tortured by the last few climactic shivers wracking her body. It was only when her trembling legs dropped from his waist that he slipped out of her. His heart still slammed against his ribs.

This time when he returned from the bathroom after disposing of the condom, Pen was sound asleep.

Gently, so as not to wake her, he unfastened the knots around her wrists, freeing her from the restraints. He experienced no reluctance at her liberation. Pen had finally tied herself to him.

Sated and shattered from the physical and emotional intensity of the experience they'd just shared, Steve climbed onto the bed beside her and fitted his body against hers. "Tomorrow you will be mine completely," he whispered, before he too fell into an exhausted and contented sleep.

Chapter Fifteen

Steve woke up cold the next morning. The icy chill on his flesh had nothing to do with the rain slanting against the window or the wind howling outside and everything to do with the empty space beside him on the bed.

Penelope was gone.

He didn't need to look to know her bags, which he'd helped her pack and move to his place two days earlier, would not be there. Pen had taken whatever she'd brought with her and left. Hours after she'd allowed herself to be tied up, she'd run away—again. She'd chosen the day he'd selected to finally win her over to leave.

Steve rolled over on his side, wrapped a scarf around his hand and stared sightlessly ahead. Pain washed through him. Christ, pain would be a blessing. The agony of her departure tore at his chest, cracked open his ribs and slashed his heart.

He could go after her. He could speed through the streets of Sydney, search the hospital, stop her at the airport. He could call out the National Guard and insist a state of emergency be declared.

He didn't. He lay where he was, crushed.

✧

It was a couple minutes after six in the morning when Pen walked into Ty's hospital room for the last time. Katie was curled in a ball in an armchair beside the bed, asleep. Tyler was staring at a muted TV.

He watched in silence as she set her suitcases on the floor.

"You're going," he said, his voice whisper-soft.

She nodded. "I have to. It's time."

"You know I would never usually second-guess you, kiddo, but you're making a mistake."

"Maybe," Pen acceded, "but it's my mistake and my choice, and I have to make it."

Katie stirred and opened her eyes. She yawned and stretched and smiled at Tyler. Less than a second later, her smile vanished and she swung around and looked at Pen. Horror drew her mouth into a twisted knot.

"Morning, Katie. I'm sorry I woke you." That's it, Penelope, she told herself, stay calm and sedate and you'll be fine.

Katie checked her watch, rubbed her eyes and looked at Pen's bags, aghast. "What's going on?"

"I came to say goodbye. My flight leaves in three hours and I wanted to see Tyler and you before I go." Good. Her tone was even. That didn't mean her heart wasn't rupturing beneath her breast.

"Your flight?" Katie asked tentatively.

Tyler glared at her from the bed, an angry frown telling her more than words ever could.

"To London. It's time to go. Tyler's going to be fine and I have to get back to work. There's no need to stay any longer."

"Yes, there bloody well is." Katie lurched to her feet. "There's one incredibly good reason to stay."

Pen shook her head, tranquil, knowing if she so much as uttered a syllable the tears would start.

"There's Steve," Katie shot at her. "There's a man who loves you beyond reason." Her voice rose, and her cheeks turned dark red. "I know how much he loves you. I know what you mean to him, damn it. I was engaged to him and he never once, not ever, looked at me the way he looks at you. You cannot go now. You *cannot* leave him again."

Katie's loss of temper couldn't shake Pen. No amount of anger, blame or finger-pointing could make Pen feel worse than she already did. It was official. She had reached the lowest point in her life. True, things would degenerate further once the symptoms began, but to date, this was the absolute worst she had ever, ever felt. If Katie attacked her with a mallet, she couldn't inflict more pain than Pen had inflicted on herself.

She gave her brother's lover a benign smile. "I don't have a choice, Katie. I'm too proud. When I start developing symptoms, I don't want Steve around. I want him as far away from me as he can get, so I don't have to face the humiliation of him watching me deteriorate."

The color drained from Katie's face. She opened her mouth, but nothing came out.

"Yes." Pen nodded. "I inherited the gene. I am going to develop Huntington's Disease." She wasn't telling her to justify her reason for leaving Steve. She was telling her so Tyler would no longer need to keep secrets from the woman she knew would become his wife.

Katie staggered, sat back in her seat with a thump and gaped at Penelope.

"In a messed-up kind of a way, I was relieved when I heard you and Steve were getting married," Pen offered. "There was comfort in the thought he'd found someone else." There was also comfort in staring at a knife, knowing she had the option of digging it into her own heart—but Katie didn't need that much information.

"He never wanted me." Katie's voice was gruff. "Even at our most secure times, he only wanted you. He still does, Pen."

"That's what he says," she agreed and marveled at the serenity in her voice. How she maintained her composure when all she wanted to do was fall apart was a mystery. "Give him time. Let the reality of the news settle in. Let him come to terms with my future. I think we'll all agree soon that my leaving here is the only possible option." The calm was a farce. Every muscle in her body ached with the effort she made to sustain her charade.

"You're wrong," Katie argued fervently. "You are Steve's reality. Without you he only half exists."

The words struck like a slap across the face. Without Steve, she'd only ever felt half alive. "I'd rather he be a little miserable for a while than lumped with a woman who has no life. No future worth living."

"Steve would disagree." Katie worried her lip with her teeth. "Does he know about the Huntington's yet?"

"I told him a few nights ago."

Katie's eyes closed but not quickly enough to cover the grief and the sympathy she tried to hide. "Does he know you're leaving?"

A wave of nausea washed over Pen, so potent it made her head spin and her stomach reel. Once more she'd snuck out on the man she loved. She'd left like the coward she was, too scared to say goodbye. At least she'd given him something of herself before she'd left, something intensely personal, something he knew she'd never give to anyone else. At least she'd given him that.

Her gaze flicked to her wrist, checking her watch. "By now he does," she said hazily, her mind in Steve's bedroom, wondering at his reaction to her disappearance. But she didn't ponder it too long. Didn't give herself the time. If she thought too long about the effect this would have on him, her resolve might crumble.

Maybe he'd gone surfing, even in the horrendous weather. It would be a very Steve thing to do. Hit the waves and work through his frustration on his board.

Katie stared at her for a moment before she stood again. This time she did not try to hide her anguish. "I'm going to leave you and Tyler to say goodbye now. I think you need the privacy." She looked at Tyler. "Steve needs me. I'll be back in a couple of hours to take you home."

Her brother nodded. "Go to him, my sweet."

Katie walked up to Penelope. "I think you're making a mistake, Pen," she said, her voice soft. "I speak from my personal experience. If Tyler had inherited the gene, I would have stuck with him, just like Steve would stick with you—if you let him. But it's not my place to judge or criticize you— especially under your circumstances. No matter what you decide to do, or where you do it, you have my support. If you need me, ever, for anything, I will be right here with your brother. A phone call away. Even if you're in London, you're not alone."

Then she hugged Pen tight and Pen hugged her back, profoundly grateful for the understanding and support she'd offered. A lump wedged in her throat, making speech impossible, so she hugged Katie tighter and nodded.

When Katie pulled away, a single tear trickled from her eye. "See ya," she said and walked out of the room, leaving Pen thankful she hadn't made some inane comment like "Godspeed" or "I'm sorry" or "May the force be with you".

"Thank you," Tyler said when the echo of Katie's footsteps had receded. "For telling her. I know it was difficult for you."

"She needed to know."

"He won't let it go," Tyler warned, getting straight back to his objections to her departure. "He's going to come after you."

A slice of her broken heart caught on a rib and Pen almost shrieked in pain. With Katie gone and only Tyler around, her composure slipped. "Not this time." She shook her head. Small tremors started in her belly and rippled outward. "This time he'll know it's over. He's not coming after me. Steve and Pen are truly finished, once and for all." Her hands began to shake in earnest so she shoved them in the back pockets of her jeans.

"You don't have to do this alone," Tyler told her. "You don't have to be a martyr."

A cold sweat broke out behind her neck and on her forehead. "I won't be alone. I know you'll be there when I need you, but that's not going to be for a while yet. In the meantime, let's live the lives we planned before you left London. Enjoy Katie, Ty. Be happy. You're lucky to have her."

"You could be happy too, you know. With Steve."

"No." She shook her head. "I couldn't be happy knowing I was bringing his future down along with mine." Prickles of anxiety ran along her spine. She'd done the right thing, but her future loomed before her, dark and uninviting, and as much as she knew she had to step back into it, she did not want to go. "This is the best decision for both of us. The only choice."

Exhaustion crept up on her, making her suddenly too weary to argue or explain anymore. She didn't want to do this. She wanted to say goodbye and leave. As Tyler began to speak, she held up her hand, stopping him. "No more, big brother. I don't want to hear it. I'm about to say goodbye and tell you I think you and Katie are going to be very, very good together. Enjoy her, Ty. Enjoy your life double as much as anyone else, so I can live vicariously through you. That and only that will give me any measure of satisfaction and contentment."

"Pen—"

"Not one more word." Fortunately Tyler wasn't one hundred

190

percent yet, or she'd never have been able to cut him off—two days in a row. She had to go. Had to get out of the room. Ty was the only person who'd seen her break down before. The only person who understood why she reacted the way she did. He was the only person—other than Steve—she'd ever felt comfortable enough with to let go, and she was seconds away from losing it again. "If I fall apart now, I will never, ever be able to pick up the pieces. I will not be able to drag myself to the airport and board the plane. Above everything else, that is the one thing I have to do. I have to go. For Steve's sake."

Tyler must have sensed she was hanging on by a very, very fragile thread. He didn't push her. Instead he opened his arms, as far as he could get them in their bandaged state, and Pen stepped into them. When she embraced her brother, her body moved into full-blown Steve withdrawal. She shook violently and pain burned through the muscles in her arms and legs. She needed a fix, needed Steve. He was the only one who could take the longing and the craving away. He was the only drug who could treat her in any way. The problem was he could never cure her. He could only ever offer her a temporary solution to her ailment.

"This isn't over. Not by a long shot," Tyler warned. "Steve is going to come after you, and I am going to encourage him." He pressed his cheek to his sister's. "Don't get too settled in London. You're not going to be there long."

Pen shuddered. "That's where you're wrong. Last night I made good and sure Steve would know it was over once and for all. Look after him, please. Make sure he's happy and finds a nice woman to marry." She hesitated, then grinned crazily at her brother, hysteria less than a heartbeat away. "And don't fuck it up for him this time. Make sure he goes through with it."

Tyler's eyes glittered. "Bet on it, kiddo."

His response didn't reassure her. "Someone other than me, I mean."

Tyler made no response other than to raise an eyebrow.

Pen sighed. There was no use arguing with him now. Neither Bonnard was likely to give in. Instead, she kissed her brother's cheek and walked to her suitcases. "I'll phone you when I get in," she promised. "Remember, Ty. Be happy enough for both of us." Then she slipped out of the room and hightailed it to the public bathrooms, where she retched violently over a toilet bowl.

Cold turkey had begun in earnest, and she doubted she'd get through it anytime soon.

"Open the door, Steve! I know you're in there."

Crap. Maybe the pounding was real and not an incessant beating against his skull. Steve dragged himself out of bed and groped around for his jeans.

"I have a key, and I'm not afraid to use it."

Muffled though it was, the voice was unmistakably Kate's.

"Damn it, Steve." More pounding on the door. "Open up."

Steve looked around the room, noticed the tangled covers, the messy pile of clothes on the floor, the scarves still tied to the headboard. He swore and pulled the door closed behind him. No point letting Kate see the telltale signs of Pen's last night with him.

"Okay, Sommers, I'm coming in."

Pen's last night with him.

"I'm putting the key in the lock."

Steve grimaced. *Their last night together.*

"I'm turning the key now."

With a shake of his head, he walked to the front door and

opened it. "You don't have a key anymore, Kate. You gave it back to me the night we broke up."

She grinned sheepishly. "I know, but I figured if you felt threatened enough you'd haul your ass out of bed and put on some clothes in case."

"And then once I was up, I'd open the door anyway?"

She shrugged. "See? It worked."

"Come in." He moved aside and she walked inside.

"I bought coffee and croissants." She held out a cardboard container with two takeout cups and dropped a bag on the table.

His stomach rolled at the thought of food, but Steve accepted the coffee gratefully and collapsed on his couch. "You're here early." A glance at the clock told him it wasn't yet seven-thirty.

Kate shook her hair, spraying tiny droplets of water around. Outside, rain still pelted the window, but the sound was drowned out by the howling of the wind. "Pen was at the hospital even earlier." She took a seat on the other couch, her expression careful as she appraised him. "She came to say goodbye."

Steve gave a derisive snort. "Well, then you're one up on me."

"She left without telling you?" Kate's smile was sad. "Sounds like Pen's slipping back into her regular pattern of behavior."

"Not really," he conceded. "She warned me all along she was leaving. I refused to believe her." More than that, he'd believed she'd changed her mind and decided to marry him. He'd believed she could finally see the potential in their future together—no matter how limited it might be. When she'd given him the scarves he'd assumed they were finally on the same wavelength.

Wrong!

"With all her heart she thinks she's doing the best thing she can for you, Steve. She's safeguarding your interests by leaving."

Steve looked at her sharply. Did she know the full truth? "And you agree with her?"

"It's irrelevant what I think, but I understand why she chose this path. She doesn't want you exposed to her imminent deterioration."

"She told you about the Huntington's." That was huge. For someone who'd kept a secret almost her whole life, it was a big step to share her results with Kate.

Kate grimaced. "This morning. To explain why she'd left you."

"She's going to get sick." He spoke the words out loud, but in truth he was reinforcing the reality for himself more than for Kate.

She nodded.

"Pen's going to get very, very sick. For a very long time. And then she's going to die."

Kate nodded again. "She is, Steve, and there will be nothing you can do to stop it."

"I can make it better. I can help her deal with it every step of the way."

"Oh, honey. I know you want to help her. I know you want to make it better, but you're not God. There are things that are out of your control, things you cannot change, no matter how much you might want to."

Steve's smile was cynical. Fuck knew he wasn't God. If he was, Pen would never have been damned with the disease in the first place. "I love her. Doesn't that count for anything? Surely being there to support her counts for something?"

"Of course it does. It counts for a lot. But the question you need to ask yourself is, in the bigger picture can it count enough?"

Steve took a large hit of caffeine. The pungent bitterness of the scalding coffee didn't improve matters at all. The unbearable, ongoing ache in his chest could never be eased by a hot drink. He held the cup up to Katie. "You couldn't find anything stronger?"

"I got you a double. I didn't think your stomach could handle more so early."

Steve eyed the liquor cabinet. It wasn't his stomach that had trouble handling the bitterness. He curled his upper lip, took another mouthful and gave up trying to pretend he didn't need something harder. "Fuck it," he muttered as he hauled his ass off the couch, opened a new bottle of scotch and added a liberal serving to his coffee.

This time when the liquid hit his stomach the burn did not come from the boiling drink.

"Alcohol won't take away the pain," Kate warned. "It'll only mask it temporarily."

"Temporary is good," Steve answered and took another sip. "Anything that masks the fucking pain is good." He finished the coffee, slammed the cup on the bar and poured himself another scotch. Straight. And he made damn sure to fill the cup. "You ever been smashed before eight in the morning?" he asked over his shoulder.

She shook her head. "No, and I don't suggest you try it either. Scotch will leave you with a bitch of a headache."

Steve drained the cup, set it down on the bar and returned to the couch. He took the Black Label with him. "Already got a headache, babe. The scotch ain't gonna make a damn difference." He tossed the lid over the couch and idly wondered how long it'd take him to do in the bottle. Five, maybe ten minutes tops. He tilted his head, brought the bottle to his lips and poured the liquid down his throat. Not more than five. More like two or three—taking swallowing into account.

The drink burned a path down his throat and settled with a fiery warmth in his stomach.

Damn, where were his manners? He lowered the bottle, took a deep breath and slanted the scotch in Kate's direction. "Want some?" he offered gallantly.

Kate shook her head. "Uh, not for me, thanks."

"Okay, but don't say I didn't offer when there's no more left," he warned her.

Kate raised an eyebrow.

"Cheers," he said before tipping the scotch back into his mouth and glugging it down.

Firm hands jerked the bottle away from him. "I need you sober by lunch, Sommers. Tyler comes home today, and I can't get him out of my car and into the house without your help."

Steve swallowed what was left in his mouth. "Right. Today's discharge day." His head seemed to fill with fuzz. "The big guy gets out of hospital. Sure I'll help you. Tell me what time to be at the hospital, and I'm there."

Wait! Tyler was well enough to go home. *Fuck it.* He hadn't put two and two together. If Tyler was about to be discharged, Pen had no further reason to remain here. Hadn't she told him all along she'd only stay until Tyler was healthy? She'd pinpointed the day of her departure for him, but he hadn't listened.

Kate lifted the almost-empty bottle and stared at it with a frown. To his credit, he thought with pride, he hadn't drunk the whole thing.

"Not before noon," Kate assured him. "Probably closer to one or two p.m. That ought to give you time to sleep off some of the drink."

Steve leaned back in the couch as the scotch pooled in his stomach and flowed sweetly through his veins. Yep, it may not mask the pain forever, but temporary would do. He felt better already. "I'll be there at one."

She nodded and disappeared behind the back of his couch. He'd have twisted around to see where she went, but the effort didn't seem worth it.

"Know what, babe?" he asked instead.

"No. What?" She crossed the room screwing the lid back on the Black Label.

"I think Pen's right."

Kate replaced the bottle on its shelf and turned to him. "How so?"

"I don't need the stress in my life. I don't need the crap that comes with her. Hell, I'm young. I have my whole life ahead of me. I'm gonna find me a healthy woman and settle down."

Kate raised an eyebrow. "You are?"

"Sure. And you know what else? I'm gonna have a good time finding her." He grinned at his ex-fiancée. Suddenly the idea seemed brilliant. Nobel Prize brilliant. If Pen didn't want him that was okay. "There are plenty more fish in the sea," he told her. "Mephatorically speaking." Nope, hang on, that didn't sound right. "I mean metarophically speaking."

"Metaphorically speaking?" Katie asked.

"Yeah. That's it. See? You understand what I'm saying. Metaphorically speaking." He'd never noticed before how much space his tongue took up in his mouth.

"You mean you're going to sleep with anything in a skirt?" Kate clarified.

He grinned again. "Pretty much." Chances were high he wouldn't have as many good orgasms as he'd had with Pen, but hell, it didn't matter. Long as he had a lot of them, that was what counted.

"Like you did last time Penelope left."

He nodded like a fool. "Pretty much." Okay, and he'd never explore bondage again because, really, what was the point? Tying someone up didn't mean you were tying her down as well, so why bother? "Only this time, the healthy one I find is not going to leave me for her ex-boyfriend."

Kate eyed him pityingly. "She's not going to hang around while you brood over your ex-girlfriend either."

"Who's going to brood? I'm going to celebrate. I'm a free man. It's not up to me to worry about Pen getting sick. I have no cares and no repons...respos..." *Shee-it.* That was one tricky word.

"No responsibility?" Kate prompted.

"'S'right. No responsibility. And you know what else? I don't have to worry about my kids getting Hut...getting Hung...getting that crappy disease. I can have healthy children and a healthy wife. See?" he finished victoriously. "It's win-win situation."

"Yep. I can see how you all come out winners in this."

"She did me a favor, you know? Going back to London. Love's overrated, anyway. Who needs it?"

His lids were heavy, and he yawned suddenly.

"Feeling sleepy, Steve?" Kate asked. Her voice seemed to come from far away.

"A little," he muttered and sank further back into the couch. "Not sure why, though. I got a great night's sleep after Pen and I—"

"That's enough," Kate cut him off. "No need to finish your sentence."

"After Pen and I had the best sex of my life," he finished anyway. Damn, it had been fucking incredible. He'd tied her up.

Finally. Although her reasons for letting him do it baffled him now.

"Okay, that's more information than I needed," Kate said.

"We did things—"

"Steve!" Kate's voice was louder this time.

He grinned at her. "We did some good things." Nope, they'd done some fucking unbelievable things. To what purpose, he had no idea. But they'd been fucking unbelievable nevertheless.

"I'm sure you did." She disappeared again and came back a couple minutes later with a large glass which she placed on the table in front of him.

"Whassat?" he asked hopefully and yawned again. "Vodka?"

"Water. And Panadol. You're going to need them when you wake up."

He registered mild surprised. "Am I going to sleep?"

"Yes, Steve. You are. You make a lousy drunk. Now close your eyes, put your head back and get some rest."

"'Kay."

"I'll see you at the hospital at one p.m."

"Kate?" he said, seconds before she let herself out his flat.

"Yeah, Steve?"

"I'm sorry you can't be one of the healthy ones I sleep with this time, but Tyler promised he'd hunt me down and kill me if I ever laid a hand on you again."

Chapter Sixteen

Steve smiled and waved at the bearded, blond-haired man walking towards him. Granted, it was a strained smile and the first one he'd worn in a while, but it was a smile nevertheless. The answering grin on his brother's lips faded the closer he got to Steve.

By the time Sam drew up in front of him and dropped his backpack on the ground, his eyes had filled with concern and sympathy.

Sam folded his brother into his arms. "Jesus," he said in a tortured voice. "Ty didn't make it, did he?"

"What?" Steve spluttered over Sam's shoulder.

Sam let go of him and raked his eyes over Steve's face. "I'm sorry, bro. He was your best friend."

"What the fuck? What are you talking about?" Steve eyed his brother right back. He was hairier than usual. Probably hadn't shaved the entire time he'd been in Africa.

"It couldn't have been easy for you." Sam swallowed and smoothed down the bush that was his beard. "When did it happen?"

"Sam, nothing happened. Tyler's fine. He pulled through with no complications."

Sam's shoulders sagged in visible relief. "He did?"

"He did. He's at Kate's house right now." Probably still

eating. He hadn't stopped since they'd lifted his dietary restrictions.

"Jesus. Thank God." Sam leaned over, put his hands on his knees and took a couple of deep breaths. When he seemed a bit more controlled, he pinned his brother with an insightful stare. "I took one look at you and assumed the worst. You look like shit."

Steve laughed out loud. Another first in a while. "*I* look like shit? Have you seen yourself in the mirror lately?"

Sam smoothed down his beard again. "A bit much?"

Steve nodded. "Mom's gonna have a fit when she sees you."

His brother grinned. "I grew it for her 'specially."

Steve grinned back. "Shit, Sam. It's because of you she still treats us like kids. She threatened me with a belt last week."

Sam's eyes danced with amusement. "What did you? Refuse to eat all your peas?"

Steve stooped down and picked up the backpack. He busied himself putting the bag on his shoulders, avoiding eye contact. "Something like that. Come on. She's waiting at your place with enough food to feed an army." He led the way through the airport to the car park.

"An army? Bugger, I'm just one person." His girlfriend, whom he lived with, hadn't returned home with him. She'd gone on to South Africa to visit family.

"Yeah, but you're one person who's been in Africa for a month, and you know Mom. She's convinced you haven't eaten since you left Sydney."

Sam chuckled like a kid. "Wait 'til I tell her they served us goat on our first night."

Steve laughed right along with him. "As long as they gave you dessert afterwards, she'll be happy."

Steve dumped Sam's gear in the boot, and the two brothers

climbed into the car.

"You still haven't told me why you look like shit," Sam said as he did up his seatbelt.

Steve sighed. "Pen came home to see Ty."

"Oh," was Sam's reply. "Fuck."

As warned, Joyce met them in Sam's apartment with a mountain of food. After kissing and hugging her son like he'd been away for five years, she sent him to shower.

"And not one morsel of food to eat until you get rid of that monstrosity on your face," she yelled at his retreating back.

"I left my razor at home, Ma," Sam yelled back at her. "It was an honest mistake."

"For someone who runs a multimillion-dollar company, you'd think he'd remember to take a few simple toiletries on holiday with him," Joyce griped at Steve.

Steve smirked and waited for the tirade that was sure to follow.

Only it didn't come. Instead his mother busied herself with laying out glasses and drinks. The sound of the shower running echoed through from Sam's bedroom as she put the kettle on to boil and turned on Sam's espresso machine.

Steve frowned. Something was up. His mother was never this silent. Ever.

On cue, Joyce turned to him, folded her arms across her chest and studied his face, her manner unnervingly similar to Sam's. "Okay, I've kept quiet about this long enough. But I'm your mother and I love you, and I will not hold my tongue any longer. Steven, you look like crap," she said at length.

Steve shuddered. "Mom, please. Language." Joyce and *crap* did not blend well together in conversation. But then neither did Joyce and *I will not hold my tongue any longer.*

"You have since Penelope left."

Steve sliced himself a piece of carrot cake. Anything to shift the focus.

"So?" his mother prompted.

"So, you've outdone yourself with the spread, Mom. Everything looks delish. Especially this cake. Bet Sam's looking forward to some home cooking." He had to give the old diversionary tactic his best go.

It failed dismally.

"Of course Sam's looking forward to my cooking. Don't change the subject. We were talking about you."

"We were?" God, no. Please. Anything but him.

"We were." Joyce nodded and picked up where she'd left off. "So?"

Steve suppressed a shudder. "What?"

"Why didn't you ask her to marry you?"

Trapped.

Steve shook his head in defeat. Damn, he should have made good on his threat to Kate and gone out and found himself another woman or four. As abhorrent as the idea seemed now he was sober, it was a tad more appealing than discussing Pen's rejection with his mother.

Reluctant to answer, he methodically made his way through half the slice of carrot cake.

"Steve?"

He sighed to himself. Even if he left now, he wouldn't escape her questions. She'd phone him a million times on his mobile and then drop by his place every day for a week. Or worse, she'd drop by the medical rooms and make a general nuisance of herself until Tina, their receptionist, hustled her into his office.

It was hardly the easy way out, but he opted for the truth. "I did ask her, Mom. She said no."

She accepted his answer with unexpected calm. "I see."

"Good." *Now drop it. Please.*

"She inherited the gene, didn't she?"

Steve's plate tilted in his hands, spilling the remaining cake on the floor. "What did you say?"

"I asked if she inherited the gene."

"Mom..." *Jesus.* "I..." He shook his head, floundering. "How do you know about the gene?"

His mother's expression was gentle. "You and Tyler spent a lot of time together as kids. Dorothy Bonnard and I became friends in our right."

Steve nodded, thunderstruck. It had never occurred to him Pen and Tyler's mother might have confided in Joyce, but it made perfect sense. The two women had shared many coffees while their sons hung out together. He was pretty damn sure they'd discussed wedding venues for him and Pen too, but he didn't dare ask—he did not want to know.

"Dorothy told me all about the disease. The symptoms, the genetics, everything. She also told me when her children were old enough to understand the pattern of inheritance, they'd both vowed not to undergo any predictive testing."

Steve sighed and put the plate on the counter. "They changed their minds." He crouched down on the floor to clean up cake crumbs and gather his thoughts. Tyler had filled in a few missing details for him, and when he stood again, he relayed them to his mother. "Pen took the test a couple of months after Dorothy died. Both Tyler and Pen reckoned their mother had suffered enough with her husband. They didn't want her to know if either or both of her children had landed the same fate as him. They made a conscious decision to wait until she was gone before they did anything."

His gut clenched. He'd held Pen after Dorothy died, comforted her, dried her tears day after day after day. What he hadn't realized was the tears were not only caused by grief for her mother. They were also tears of fear. She'd blended her anxiety about the testing in with her mourning. She had a valid reason for being so depressed, a reason Steve would never have questioned.

"Dorothy was a strong woman," Joyce said with a gleam of admiration in her eye. "She might not have liked the result, but she would have coped with it. Like she coped with her husband's slow demise." She nodded thoughtfully. "Tyler must have taken the test too."

"He did. After Kate and I got engaged. When he found out he was home free he came back to fight for her."

The flat filled with silence. Even the running water had ceased.

"That's what I thought. I worked out then Pen must have discovered she had the gene."

Bless his mother. He felt a rising tide of affection for her and almost laughed out loud at the different ways their minds worked. While Joyce had come to the conclusion Pen hadn't returned to Steve because she had the gene, he'd concluded she hadn't loved him enough to take the test. He'd refused to acknowledge the possibility Pen might actually carry the gene. His mother refused to acknowledge the possibility Pen might not be in love with her son. Far as Joyce was concerned it was an utterly ridiculous notion. Of course Pen loved her son.

Fuck. He wished he'd been right and not his mother.

"So you proposed knowing she would develop Huntington's?" Joyce asked.

"And she turned me down cold."

Behind her, Sam, clean-shaven and wearing only a pair of shorts, slumped onto a kitchen stool. "What the hell is

Huntington's?" he asked.

Reluctantly, Steve told him and watched as his brother's expression turned from curious concern to utter devastation.

Joyce *tsked*. "That girl is too stubborn for her own good. If I'd known she'd said no to you, I would have tanned her hide, never mind yours."

Steve and Sam exchanged a silent *yeah-yeah* look. For all her threats, their mother had never raised a hand to either of them as kids. And that was no mean feat considering the shit he and Sam had gotten up to.

"You still think I should marry Pen, Mom?" Steve asked, amazed. "Even knowing how sick she's going to become?"

His mother shot him the have-you-grown-another-head look of disbelief. "Of course I think you should marry her. I've always thought you should marry her. We all have. Including Dorothy."

Shee-it. He was right. The mothers *had* discussed wedding venues. Steve glanced at his brother, looking for moral support, but Sam only added his two cents' worth by nodding in agreement.

Steve had to set them straight, introduce them to reality, Pen's reality. "She's going to lose her mind. The disease is going to nullify her capacity to have even the simplest of conversations or make the most basic of movements."

Joyce's eyes filled with tears. "I know, dear."

"She has a one in two chance of passing the disease on to any child she has."

She nodded sadly. "I know, dear."

"She wants to be left alone so she can retain what little pride and dignity she still has. She doesn't want me to watch her being stripped of it."

"I understand that too, dear, but pride and dignity will not keep her safe from herself. Nor will they bring her any measure of comfort or love. You, on the other hand, will."

He gnawed on his lower lip. "Knowing all of this, knowing what will become of her, in about ten or so years, you'd still want her as a daughter-in-law?"

Joyce looked at him askance. "Of course we would. What kind of a question is that?"

Again Sam nodded in agreement, the look on his face a dead ringer for their mother's.

"Haven't we always told you?" his mother said. "Family stick together, no matter what."

"She'll become a burden. Not only to me, but to all of us. Like her father was a burden to her mother." He used the arguments Pen used on him, but who was he trying to convince? Himself, or his mother and brother?

Joyce frowned. "That's what Pen and Tyler told you? That Dorothy saw their father as a burden?"

Steve nodded. "They never wanted Kate or me to go through what their mother went through."

"If Dorothy was alive today, she would challenge every word. She loved her husband. Until he took his last breath she loved him. Sure she was angry about the injustice of it all and crushed by the progression of the disease. And yes, she went through all sorts of hell trying to take care of him alone, but she never saw him as a burden. She admitted his death was a blessing, but she cried when she spoke about it. Years later she still missed him. For everything she had to go through, she would not have traded places with anyone else. Not for a minute. Henry Bonnard was her life, both in health and in illness. Although she hated the disease and what it did to her family, she never regretted being with him."

Joyce took a deep breath. "She once told me if she was given the choice to do it all again, knowing from the beginning what she only learned in the end, she wouldn't have changed a thing. For her the good was worth the bad. Period."

Steve gawked at his mother, at a loss. There was another side to the story. A side Tyler and Pen hadn't taken into consideration. In their haste to protect him and Kate, they'd neglected to look at the positive side of their parents' marriage. They'd only seen the bad. The disease.

Pen had done her best to convince Steve there would only be the bad. She absolutely refused to see what could be the good parts of their future together.

Joyce broke through his musings. "If Dorothy and Henry hadn't married, Tyler and Penelope would not have been born. That in itself was enough for Dorothy. Henry gave her two children." His mother looked pointedly at him. "Your best friend and the woman you love. Imagine if they had never been born. Imagine if Henry had never married because he wanted to retain his pride and dignity."

A world without Pen and Tyler. Steve couldn't imagine it. Even for the two years they'd both been in London, they'd impacted his life every single day.

"You and Penelope would make beautiful children, Steven. Beautiful grandchildren for me."

Pain almost had him gasping. Jesus, he wanted to have children with Pen. He wanted to start a family with her, but he wasn't the one standing in the way of his dreams.

"I asked her to marry me, Mom. She said no. What more can I do?"

"Ask her again," Sam suggested helpfully.

"Exactly," Joyce agreed. "Only this time, try to be a little more persuasive."

"More persuasive? The woman is in London. The only way I could be more persuasive is to get on a plane, fly over there, tie her up and drag her home."

"What are you waiting for?" Joyce looked at him expectantly.

"International customs doesn't take too kindly to kidnapping."

"I'll bail you out," Sam offered generously.

"Gee, thanks," Steve shot at his brother.

"Penelope belongs in Sydney. With us," Joyce said.

"Mom," Steve answered in exasperation. "It's not that simple."

"Yes," Sam argued. "It is."

Steve stood in the kitchen, floundering.

"Go and book your air ticket, Steven," Joyce told him in her I'm-your-mother-and-I-won't-accept-nonsense-from-you tone of voice. "It's time to bring Penelope home."

Chapter Seventeen

Pen shut the door behind her and slumped back against it with a sigh. She closed her eyes and wished with all her might it was Steve who'd seen her home and not Jeremy.

No. She did not. It was a blessing Jeremy was the one she'd spent the evening with. Steve was safely ensconced in Sydney, moving on with his life.

It wasn't important that since returning to London over two weeks ago, Pen had been miserable. Utterly, totally and completely miserable. It wasn't important that the satisfactory life she'd made for herself here had lost every ounce of its appeal. That the icy wind which usually invigorated her now made her cold. That the steady downpour of rain she'd always viewed as a symbol of life and rebirth now made her wet.

What was important was that she'd spared Steve from her destiny.

At night she fell into bed exhausted, praying for the oblivion of sleep, but her dreams haunted her. More often than not she woke up in a cold sweat, her arms open, reaching for a man who was not there. Who could never be there.

At least at night there were short snatches of time, snatches of restless sleep, when she could hide from her thoughts. Daytime offered no relief. With the rising sun came the rising awareness she was alone again. She would never be with Steve.

What little joy she'd been able to create for herself here in England had been lost in the devastating aftermath of leaving him again. Emptiness had taken residence in her belly, a hollow nothingness she couldn't fill. The ache for Steve echoed in its endless depth.

Without him, she'd only ever felt half alive. Now she went through the motions of living. The world happened around her. Inside she slowly died.

A desperate sob escaped her throat as once more the pain of loss enveloped her. She'd known it would be this bad. The last time she'd left Steve the wound had never healed. Now she'd reopened it she doubted it would ever close. She'd ripped a band-aid off a bone-deep cut. What little protection she'd given the lesion in the first place had been permanently removed. There was no way to cover it up again.

Her injuries lay raw and exposed, festering in a life she did not want to live.

For the first time she looked forward to the oblivion Huntington's would eventually bring. At least then the hurt wouldn't be so bad.

Her one consolation in this godforsaken life she'd been handed was that she had done the right thing. She'd given Steve his full and happy future. He might be hurting now. He might not yet understand her motivations and her reasoning, but when he did, he would thank her, and then he'd move on. He'd already proven to her he was able. His engagement to Katie had not been a mistake—even if his choice in fiancée had been. He'd wanted marriage and children and the white picket fence, and he'd gone after it. He would again.

The tears started in earnest, pouring down her cheeks as sobs wracked her body. She didn't question them, didn't panic from fear they might be an early symptom of the disease. She accepted them for what they were: an outlet for her insufferable grief. A grief that would preoccupy her for a very, very long time.

The voice that murmured in her ear almost stopped her heart.

"Aw, Pen, sweetheart, please don't cry."

Her breath caught on a sob as blood drained from her upper body. Shock set in, paralyzing her.

Strong hands pulled her against a hard, male chest. Arms wrapped around her, holding and supporting her. "Nothing can be that bad, can it?" he asked.

Pen repressed a hysterical moan. An unsteady shaking in her stomach grew and expanded until shivers overtook her. She couldn't move, but she couldn't stop shaking either.

Oh... God. He was here. In her flat.

"It's okay, Sunshine," he whispered as he ran his hand through her hair. "It's okay. It's all going to work out."

He'd come after her. He hadn't listened to a word she'd said.

Her knees faltered, and her legs gave in. Before she fell, Steve tightened his hold on her, keeping her upright.

It was another dream. It had to be. Steve wasn't in her flat. He couldn't be. It went against everything she'd worked so hard to achieve. She shook her head, tried in desperation to clear it, to drag herself to full consciousness. The difference was, in her dreams she couldn't touch him. Couldn't feel him. Now she couldn't not. Pressed against the solid length of his body, with his warmth surrounding her and holding her up, every breath she took filled her lungs with his scent, his essence.

Oh, sweet Lord, he was here.

For the briefest minute she allowed herself to remain in his arms, to draw from the strength he offered and to relish the contact between them. But only for the briefest minute, and then she stepped back.

It took several seconds before her breathing evened out and

she could calm her pounding heart long enough to speak. Then she made the mistake of looking at him, and whatever oxygen she'd stored in her lungs evaporated.

Oh, his face. How she loved it. Cherished it. She had its image stored in her heart and her head, and she'd taken it out to look at so many times she'd thought she'd memorized every line and angle. She hadn't. She'd forgotten how she got lost in his blue eyes. How the rest of world faded around him and he was the only thing she focused on. How she couldn't tear her gaze from him. She'd forgotten how he took her breath away.

"Wh-what are you doing here?" she managed to stammer.

"I've come to take you home, Pen." As much as she couldn't tear her gaze from him, so it seemed he couldn't stop looking at her.

He stepped towards her, his intentions clear, but her sense of self-preservation took over and she stepped back. Uh uh. No touching. If he touched her again, she'd be done for.

"I am home," she said in a shaky voice.

"You're in a flat in London, with a few of your possessions. I'm taking you back to your family, to the place where your heart is and where people love you."

Too shaken by his response to muster up a real answer, she asked stupidly, "You are?"

Steve nodded. "I am."

Slowly, slowly, the shock began to recede. Anger inched into its place. She'd almost killed herself getting out of his life, coming back to London and freeing him from her future, and now he had the audacity to follow her. No way. It was not going to happen. She'd worked too hard, come too far to let him ruin her plans. How dare he? How dare he walk into her flat without her permission and announce he was here to take her home?

She narrowed her eyes. "Really? You and what army?"

"No army, Pen. Just me."

"Well, I'll tell you what. Why don't you take you and get out of my flat?" He couldn't be here. *Could not.* Already her resolve weakened and the pull to step back into his arms was close to irresistible. Her body responded to his proximity. Her breasts heaved and her nipples felt tight and needy.

"I will," Steve nodded affably. "As soon as your bags are packed and you're ready to leave with me."

"Sure." Pen gave him a sweet smile. "That'll be in about...oh..." She looked at her watch. "Never."

Steve grinned at her. "Aha. You are in there. I thought I'd lost you to all those tears."

She opened her mouth to blast him and hiccupped. "I'd like you to leave," she said instead, with as much dignity as she could muster.

"I'd like you to marry me," he countered.

At which point she lost her temper altogether. "Get out, Steven. You are not welcome in my home. You do not belong and I don't want you here."

Steve nodded. "I'll go, if that's what you want. But I'll only come straight back in as soon as you close the door behind me, so it would be rather pointless."

She glared at him. If she didn't smack the smug look off his face, she was going to jump him. It was a close call either way, since being in the same room as him had her as hot and horny as it always did, yet it also had her cold with fury and ready to lash out. "You're not going to leave, are you?" she asked with disdain.

"Not unless you come with me."

Smack him, definitely. She curled her fingers into a fist. "How did you get in here in the first place?"

"Tyler."

"Tyler?" she spluttered. "My brother?"

"Yep. He figured you wouldn't let me in if I knocked, so he gave me his key."

She wasn't going to smack Steve, she was going to deck her brother. Hell, she'd punch his lights out. In a flash of sudden insight, she understood why Steve had hit him. Infuriating pig.

"Don't blame him." Steve's voice was soft. "He only wants what's best for you." His gaze raked over her. "We both do."

"Let's see. You and my boorish brother sat down, had a chat and decided what? You're best for me?"

He shook his head. "Not just Tyler and I. My mother, father, Sam and Kate agreed as well."

Her eyes widened in disbelief. "You had a conference? All of you together? About me?"

"No. Not all together. First my mother lambasted me about letting you go. Then Sam suggested I kidnap you. Later on, Tyler shat on me for not being man enough to hold onto you, and my father, in his usual tactful way, phoned to ask if you and I were engaged yet. Kate said if I wanted you I should come after you—for both of our sakes."

Damn it. Damn it, damn it. He'd brought family into it. Played his trump card. He knew how much she adored everyone he'd mentioned, how much she'd love to be a part of the Sommers clan, and he'd worked the issue. Damn him. "Your family wouldn't be so keen to have me back in Sydney if they knew the truth."

Steve's face grew somber. He walked through to her lounge and sat on a couch. "There's something you should know, Sunshine, and you might want to sit while I tell you."

So much for getting him out of her home. Steve was not leaving. Okay, fine. She'd hear him out and once he'd finished saying whatever it was he'd come to say, once he'd done as much convincing as possible, then she'd kick him out.

Permanently, this time—right after she'd taken Tyler's key from him. She walked with reluctance to her lounge and perched on the couch opposite him. "Right, Sommers. What do I need to know that I don't know already?"

His face was filled with such tenderness, a rush of love welled in her chest. She couldn't force it down, couldn't fight it, so she left it there, sitting right where her heart was, refusing to be ignored.

"My parents know the truth, Pen. They've known all along."

His words left her reeling. "Impossible," she denied. "How could they?"

"Your mother told them."

She knew her mouth hung open, but she couldn't seem to close it.

"Our mothers became friends when we were kids. They spoke about a lot of things. Within the first year of Ty and me knowing each other, they had discussed Huntington's in great detail. Every aspect of it, including your father's illness and death."

He fell silent then, and she took the time to digest his words. It took a while. They didn't make sense at first. For so long she and Tyler had hidden their secret and now she discovered Stan and Joyce knew all along? How could it be? "My...my mother told her? Everything?"

"Everything, Pen. She obviously couldn't have told her about your undergoing the testing, but my mother figured it out. She assumed, when you didn't come home with Tyler, that you'd done the test and found out the result."

She'd never considered it for a minute—her mother had spoken about the Huntington's. Well, why not? It might have been something she and Tyler had stuffed into their cupboard, but their mother never had. Of course she'd have needed to speak to someone about it. Wanted to speak to someone—and who better than a warm, understanding, loving couple like Stan and Joyce. "Your parents know I...have the...gene. They...know."

No, please. Not them. She didn't want the Sommers to know what was to become of her.

Steve nodded.

"And Sam?" she asked with dread.

"He was there when my mother brought up the subject."

"Oh God." She dropped her head in her hands. She could almost feel their pity radiating through Steve. "I didn't want them to know. I didn't want them to feel sorry for me."

Steve was by her side before her head touched her hands. He put his arm around her shoulder. "Aw, Sunshine. They don't feel sorry for you. They feel sorry for me."

She lifted her head and stared at him. "You?" Then she nodded. "Ah, for being stupid enough to fall for someone with such a dismal future." Christ, that hurt almost as much as knowing his family pitied her.

"No." Steve slumped back against the couch. His arm remained around her shoulders, his hand tangled in her hair. "They feel sorry for me because you dumped me. Again."

She should push his arm off, should pull her head away, but she didn't have the strength. It felt so good there, raking through her hair, feathering over her scalp.

"Don't misunderstand me. My mother may not feel sorry for you, but she is upset. She's also terrified of the idea you'd consider battling this disease alone. She wants you to come home, Pen. She wants you to officially become the daughter, or daughter-in-law, she never had. Both my parents do." He hesitated, and when he spoke again, she heard a smile in his voice. "They want to be grandparents."

His words sliced through her, making her tear away from

his touch and spring to her feet. Okay, so he'd nearly had her. He'd nearly seduced her into thinking perhaps she could go home with him, but his last sentence had annihilated any hope that might have begun to blossom.

"Fuck you, Steven," she spat at him. "Fuck you for coming here and for disrespecting every single one of my wishes. All I asked was that you leave me alone to accept my future with a little pride and a little dignity, and you couldn't do it. I never, for one second, gave you reason to believe I would marry you or stay in Australia. I never led you on or promised things I could not deliver. I gave you...everything..."

She stumbled over her words as she thought about their last night together—the intense, profoundly personal and deeply intimate night they'd spent. She'd let him tie her up and in doing so had relinquished her control. It had not been easy. Not one bit. In a few years' time she'd have no choice but to forego what little control she had left. Giving it away had been a task tougher than she'd ever imagined. But she'd done it. For Steve. And the pleasure and the intimacy had been worth it.

Her breath came in short, sharp bursts. "I gave you everything. I could not have given you more." She was angry and cut to the bone by his last remark, and she couldn't handle the extent of her own emotions.

She'd been so sure she'd wrapped it all up when she'd left Sydney. She'd said her goodbyes and closed that chapter in her life once and for all, and now Steve was here, reopening it, forcing her to once again finish something she should never have restarted.

"How...how...?" She floundered. "How dare you come here and throw your parents and your brother in my face. You know how much I love them, how much I long to be a part of your family." Her voice caught. "For you to bring them into my apartment and then talk about grandchildren—" She couldn't complete her sentence. Couldn't articulate the hurt he'd inflicted.

Grandchildren. Steve's parents wanted to be the grandparents of her children. It was too cruel to contemplate. Too incredibly painful. If there was anything in life she wanted, it was that. That and everything having their grandchildren entailed.

Bile rose in her throat, choking her with its bitterness. "How could you?"

"How could I what? Bring up my family? Or bring up the family I want to have with you?"

She couldn't turn around. Couldn't look at him. "Both," she croaked, for her voice would not work properly anymore.

"My mother made an interesting point," Steve said. "She asked what the world would have been like if, like you, your father had decided not to have children. You know what, Pen?" Steve asked roughly. "I couldn't even think about the answer. The thought of neither you nor Ty ever being born... Christ, it's inconceivable." He took a deep breath then added, "Your mother thought so too."

Her hands trembled as she put them over her mouth to stop the gasp of pain. This wasn't fair. Steve was not playing fair. He knew, *knew* she was not prepared to bring a child into the world with the same risks she faced.

"I wouldn't have had a best friend," Steve said softly, his voice uneven. "I wouldn't have had you. It's...unthinkable."

She shook her head. "Go away. I don't want to hear any more."

"Know what PGD is?" Steve asked as if she hadn't even spoken.

"Go back to Australia." She would never, ever have expected Steve to behave this cruelly towards her. Ever.

"Preimplantation genetic diagnosis," Steve told her.

She refused to listen any longer. "I don't want to talk about marriage and futures and grandparents. Leave. Now."

"It's used after in vitro fertilization to isolate embryos which have inherited abnormal genes. Only the embryos which are not affected are implanted in the uterus."

She shook her head. It was gibberish. All of it. She didn't understand a word he'd said.

"It means you can have a baby free of this genetic disease, Pen. There are tests available that can be carried out before you even fall pregnant."

Slowly she turned to look at him. When she'd had her test done, the genetic counselor had spoken about it. But Pen had already firmly decided that she would never have children. She never wanted her children to watch her demise the way she had watched her father's.

Steve continued speaking. "Several eggs are fertilized through IVF, but only the embryos free from Huntington's are used." His gaze held hers. "Parents with genetic disease can give birth to normal children. You can have a baby, Pen, without worrying that he or she will inherit the gene."

For the second time that evening her legs gave. With no one there to support her, Pen collapsed on the floor. Steve was beside her in seconds.

"You can have my baby, Pen. We can be parents without worrying about passing on errant genes."

Her body was boneless, her arms flopped uselessly at her sides while her stomach rolled beneath her ribs. Steve pulled her onto his lap and cradled her, supported her. "Be my wife, Pen. Have children with me." His hand was in her hair, his lips on her forehead. "Come home and complete my family. Please."

Her resolve steadily weakened. He'd combated every argument, provided solutions for all her concerns. All except one. The big one. The one that he could never resolve: her inescapable fate.

She allowed herself the luxury of remaining in his arms. Leaned into him, absorbed his body heat. She pressed her breasts against his chest and remembered again the sweet deliciousness of making love with him, the gut-wrenching, heart-aching beauty of being filled by him. For the briefest fraction of time, she allowed herself to imagine the joyful bliss of being married, of having his child, raising his child.

And that's when reality cut in. As he sighed into her hair and his body shifted beneath her butt, his attraction still as potent as hers, she pushed him away for the last time. Her body screamed its frustration, crying out for Steve's touch, but she ruthlessly repressed her desire. It didn't matter that she could have normal children. It didn't matter if his whole family wanted her to come home to them. It didn't matter Steve wanted her to be his wife.

It only mattered that she couldn't because she didn't have a future.

She crawled from his lap, put a few good meters of space between them and cleared her throat. "I'll say it for the last time, Steven. Go home. Leave me in peace to live and die with dignity. I will not bring children into this world and let them watch their mother slowly lose her mind. I will not bring them into the world and then deprive them of a parent. I will not marry a man when I cannot offer him everything, and I will not become part of a family only to have them watch helplessly while I rot away."

"I love you, Penelope. We all do. We refuse to leave you alone. You have several good years ahead of you. Several years that should be lived to their fullest and not seen as preparation for the bad to come. Hell, you could be hit by a car tomorrow. Tyler was. There's no guarantee it won't be you next. I could be run over by a bus. It doesn't mean I'm going to live every minute preparing for my ultimate end. No, I'm going to enjoy my life from now on, and I want you to enjoy it with. I want us to live together and celebrate the time we have left."

He raked his hand through his hair, trapped her with his gaze and would not let her turn away. "I know I have to lose you sometime, Pen. I've come to terms with that. But I refuse to let you go until there is no choice in the matter. When the disease finally takes you to a place I cannot reach, that's when I'll say goodbye. Until then, I am not going anywhere. We have time now. Stop wasting it. When you're gone, I'll mourn you, but I refuse to grieve for you while you are still healthy and vibrant and alive and so beautiful it hurts to look at you." He took a deep, harrowing breath. "I don't want to say goodbye until I have to, Sunshine."

Oh, dear Lord. He almost made her believe in happy endings. Already the sunset wedding on the beach was weaving its way through her head, lulling her into thinking it was possible.

Pen steeled her resolve. It wasn't possible. Not if she wanted to preserve her pride and her dignity. She had to get him out of her apartment, now, before she did something stupid, like agree to marry him.

Pen stood, slowly, although the effort close to killed her. "The door is this way, Steve. I'll show you out."

Chapter Eighteen

Goddamned stubborn fool. She refused to listen. Didn't matter how many times he said it, she would not hear his words. He wasn't going anywhere, at least not until he'd played his last card.

The door was behind his back. The only way for her to access it was by walking past him. He waited until she'd almost cleared his legs before he strategically stuck out his foot and tripped her. Thrown off balance, she fell heavily, but he was one step ahead of her. Arms outstretched, he caught her before she hit the ground. Then, using a neat little maneuver which impressed even him, he flipped her over on her back and covered her with his body.

Got her.

Stunned eyes looked up at his.

"You don't listen, Pen. I'm not leaving you now."

"Steve, get off—"

He didn't give her a chance to finish. Taking full advantage of her open mouth, he swooped in and kissed her. There was only one language he and Pen communicated effectively in, and he'd talk it now. Without giving her a chance to object, his lips took full possession of hers. His tongue swept over hers, brushing away anything she might have said.

His body took less than a second to bounce back to life.

Minutes ago, when he'd held her on his lap, he'd responded to her closeness. Now his erection, already primed by the sweet rise of her butt against his groin, grew to full strength. Pen might be stoic enough to refuse him clothed, but he'd put money on it that once he had her naked there would be very little she'd say no to. Including him. Including their future.

Pen might have refused his offers of love and marriage, she might have refused his promises of happiness, but she couldn't refuse his body. She'd never been able to. That was why, no matter how many times she'd left him, she'd always come back for more.

It had taken a long time for Steve to understand why she rejected him on every emotional level possible yet accepted his physical advances. It was the only way she could cope with the intensity of her feelings. The only way she knew to show the extent of her love for him.

She'd always held herself back, never fully committed, even when they were together for extended periods of time. The one place she'd let herself be with him one hundred percent was in the bedroom. There she let go and gave him everything she had.

She'd allowed him to tie her up. In her eyes it was the ultimate gift she could give him, the ultimate expression of her love for him. Physically, she had surrendered to him. The problem was, she'd held back emotionally. And that was the side of her Steve needed the most.

He might have heeded her protests, might have taken notice of the way her hands beat against his arms, demanding he release her, if she hadn't fully responded to his kiss. Even as she banged her fists on his sides, her mouth consumed his. As he hungrily rediscovered the hot, wet promise of her kiss, her lips fused with his. Her tongue was everywhere, tangling with his, following it into his mouth, teasing it back out again.

No matter what her fists said, her mouth told him she wanted him there.

Steve kissed her for an eternity. He kissed her until her hands ceased their struggle. He kissed her until she lost the stiff edge to her posture and her body became soft and pliant beneath his. He kissed her until she moaned into his mouth, wrapped her arms around his neck and held him as though she would never let go. And then he kissed her some more.

It didn't matter where they were, in London or in Sydney. Heck, they could be in the South Pole for all he cared. Right here, in Pen's arms, he was home. He was where he belonged. Even though he'd intended to break through her objections to their marriage, it was he who was making breakthroughs. He who was realizing the only place he could ever be content was in Pen's arms.

Pen finally broke contact, but only for a minute and only long enough to pull off his shirt, and then her mouth was on his again and she was kissing him and murmuring against his lips. He couldn't understand her words, didn't try. He just kissed her and held her and gloried in her touch as her hands ran over his back and her palms burned through his flesh.

He hadn't lied. He couldn't deal with goodbye before there was no longer a choice. Only when the disease took her to a place nobody could access would he feel halfway prepared to let her go. Until that time, he wanted to stay right where he was, right where he'd always wanted to be. Home with Penelope.

He broke the kiss this time, but only for the minute it took to make short work of her shirt and bra. He cursed her jumper, which proved to be trickier to remove than he'd counted on, but at last it was gone. Her shirt lay torn beneath her and her bra was somewhere on the other side of the lounge. Then he kissed her again and they both groaned as her breasts were crushed against his chest, as the sensation of skin against skin tilted their universe several degrees off center.

Christ, he couldn't think straight in this position. He couldn't think at all. He knew he should be trying to convince

Pen to marry him, but all he could do was feel, and all he could feel was Pen, and she felt so damn good. It wouldn't stop him, though. He'd passed up the last opportunity. He wouldn't be fool enough to pass up this one as well.

Outside, night and rainclouds blackened the sky. Inside, his own little ray of sunshine burned strong and alive, and he groaned as her hand skimmed over his thigh and moved higher, seeking his erection. She could have it. For now. She could have anything of his, provided she took it on the grounds on which he offered it: forever.

He shifted, letting her hand find him, cover him, and he groaned again.

Once more, Pen muttered against his lips, but he swallowed her words as he took her mouth with his. No talking. No speech. This was about convincing Pen in the only way he knew how.

Refusing to part with her lips, he was forced to remove her jeans while he kissed her. It was a bit of a struggle, but he persevered, freeing first her button and then her zip, and shoving the black denim over her hips and helping her kick them off. He didn't take as much care with her thong. He held the dainty material between his thumbs and forefingers and ripped. An instant later, Pen was bare beneath him.

Steve wondered if he'd ever wanted her this much. His body was on fire. Was it possible to want someone more every time they made love? Was it possible that instead of satisfying the lust and the need and the desire, it fanned the flames? Because every time with Pen was like the first, a raging need that increased in intensity with each passing minute. He could not get enough. The more he touched, the more he wanted to touch.

She shimmied beneath him, rubbing herself tantalizingly against his groin, and he very nearly came right then. Willpower alone prevented him from doing so. He would not take this any further until Pen was with him. On every count.

"Damn it, Steve," she moaned as she shimmied again. "Take off your pants."

He clenched his jaw and fought against the pleasure of her movements. Her hands tugged at the waist of his cargos with little effect, so he tipped his weight to the side, giving her access to his belt. In seconds his pants were undone, and he kicked them off, along with his boxers.

And then there was nothing between them. It was just them. No barriers, no covers. Only the two of them. Surely, in this state, she could no longer deny him? Surely, with nothing but their naked bodies, their needs and their desires had become one?

Side by side they lay. While Pen closed her eyes and sought his mouth with hers, her palms closed around him in a gentle squeeze. She held him in her hot hands and pumped, slowly, rhythmically. His resistance slowly crumbled. A groan rose in his throat. He ran his fingers down her thigh, found her knee and hooked his hand under it, bending her leg, exposing her inner treasures.

Christ, she was so wet. Her folds were slick and slippery, and his fingers glided over them, evoking muffled sounds of bliss from her lips. When he pressed lightly against her clit, she tore her mouth from his.

He nearly busted a gut with longing. Surely she had to see that being together for whatever time they had left was the only viable option? The only choice they had?

She quivered, and he drew wet circles around her slit. When he dipped his finger inside her, she cried out.

"Fire it up, Steve. Now." Her body had erupted into full-blown tremors. She shook and shivered beside him, and whatever blood he'd had in his veins emptied into his dick. He was like Pavlov's dog, responding to a direct stimulus. Pen moaned their catch phrase and he reacted.

Only this time he didn't.

This time, though it nearly killed him, he rolled onto his back, away from Pen, and shook his head. "No." He retracted his hand too, leaving her with nothing.

"Steve..." Pen groaned, and he turned and watched her arch her back and reach for him. She was too entrenched in their lovemaking to comprehend his actions.

He forced himself to sit up and move a few more inches away. His dick screamed its protest, punishing him as his balls jerked in pain.

Pen opened her eyes, searching for him. Her face was glazed in confusion.

He knew his actions were extreme, but Pen had left him with no alternative. He'd never refused her before. Would she respond in the way he desired if he refused her now?

He palmed his shaft. "This what you want, Penelope?" Jesus, he was stiff as a fucking lamppost.

She wet her lips with her tongue. "You know it is."

He shook his head. "You can't have it. Not anymore." Again, his balls tightened, and he pumped harder—partly to relieve the pain and partly to taunt Pen.

Her breasts heaved as she dragged in a deep breath. "Steve," she begged, "please..."

He had her exactly where he wanted her: as desperate for him as he was for her. Now all he need do was persuade her to marry him. He could not, would not put it off any longer. Though, God knew, if he took too long convincing her, he might never be able to father her children.

"I told you once before, Pen. I'm not a giant dick. I'm not here to bring you off when you're feeling horny. I may have been that to you before, but no more."

Her eyes widened, her pupils began to constrict, and

suddenly her gaze was focused again. "Bastard," she uttered quietly.

"Perhaps. But I won't be your little joystick anymore." He pointed his dick in her direction. "You want this, then you take everything that comes with it. Me, marriage, kids, the works."

Her gaze locked on his hand and his lap. "You did this on purpose." Her voice was wispy, her mouth swollen from his kisses. "Got me all worked up because you know I can't refuse you."

"Wrong, Pen. You have refused me every day for years now. You've turned your back on me more times then I can count because of some misplaced sense of pride. I won't stand for it anymore. From this point on I come as a package deal."

Pen was silent for a long, long time. Then she closed her eyes and turned her head away.

His heart lurched. Fuck, he wasn't reaching her. Maybe he'd taken too forceful an approach, but what else could he do? How else could he convince her? He'd come too far to give up now. "You thinking about it, Pen? Or are you trying to work out how you can get me to fuck you with no commitment? You still want me. I can see that clearly. Your arms are still trembling at your sides, and your nipples are still stiff little beads." For a second, he had to close his eyes as they rolled back in his head: a reaction to the further hardening of her nipples. When he looked at her again, it took every ounce of restraint to hold back and not launch himself at her.

"I bet you wish I was touching your breasts right now. Kissing, them, nibbling them, sucking on your nipples." His voice broke then because she lifted her hands and covered her breasts, stroking them like he wanted to. Her hips twisted, drawing his attention downwards.

"Christ, Sunshine, look at you." The words were torn from his mouth. "You can barely keep still you want this so much."

He was going to have a stroke. Without a doubt. "You're wet, as though you can't stop your body from reacting to my words." He stopped then. Drew in a few deep breaths.

"I'm yours, all yours. You can have me, Pen, as long as you take all of me."

She whipped her head from side to side, tormented. Fuck, he didn't know who this was harder on: Pen or himself.

"I can ease the hurt, sweetheart. I can make it all better. Say you'll marry me, and I'll satisfy every ounce of lust in your body."

Pen groaned and shook, but her fucking pride held her silent.

"Say the word, Pen. I'll slide inside you and make the frustration go away."

She squeezed her eyes shut, and a single tear slid down her cheek. Time stood still. The world stopped spinning. Steve held his breath. It was here. Pen's moment of reckoning. Would she accept him, all of him and everything he had to offer, or would she say no? Again?

Without looking at him, she shook her head.

And with that rejection Steve's hopes died.

His body went limp. The fight drained from him. Whatever energy he'd used to seduce her fizzled away. The challenge was over, and he'd lost. He couldn't breathe—there was no air. His chest burned from lack of oxygen.

There was nothing more he could do to convince her.

He'd tried. He'd used every weapon, every piece of arsenal he possessed. He'd crossed oceans to be with her. He'd tried love, and he'd tried family. He'd tried her brother and his parents. He'd used his brother and her mother. It hadn't helped. He'd proposed and he'd promised. He'd given himself physically, and he'd denied her completely. Pen would not give a fucking inch.

He gave up trying. He had nothing left to fight with. Pen might love him, but that was as far as she was willing to take it. She'd placed her pride and her dignity before him, and nothing he said or did had made her change her mind. She would not accept him in her life any longer.

For several minutes he sat where he was, bewildered. He searched his reserves for a means to accept her rejection but found nothing. His strength was all used up.

Though his body still pounded with caged desire, he barely noticed. Compared to the horrifying reality of his situation it was insignificant. Pen would not marry him. Not now, not ever. He might not be prepared to say goodbye yet, but she was. She just had.

He'd been a fool to hope. An idiot to dream. His family and hers had encouraged him to come after her, encouraged him to take a chance. Well, he had. He'd taken a calculated risk, and it backfired.

He closed his eyes and let the pain wash through him. In a minute he'd drag himself off her floor and dress. In a minute he'd walk out of her flat and out of her life and leave her forever, like she wanted. For now he was incapable of movement. The pain had crippled him.

He should have listened to her. He hadn't.

He would not make that mistake again.

His chest burned so bad it brought tears to his eyes, but he gritted his teeth and bore it. He'd get through this. He'd have to. Pen had refused him, and there was nothing, *nothing* more he could do to change her mind.

"You're wrong, you know?"

Her voice came from so far away it was difficult to comprehend her words. But he got the general gist. He should never have made the trip to London.

Pen needn't have said anything. She'd already made it abundantly clear his decision was a mistake. Steve sat with his eyelids drawn shut and his jaw clenched and allowed the humiliation and the devastation of her continued rejection to hit home.

Something touched his knee.

"It...it's not just about sex with you," she said shakily.

His senses went on instant alert.

"It never was. The rea—" Her voice broke. "The reason I keep coming back to you is because you represent—no, you *are*—everything I have ever wanted. You...you're love. And family. You're l-life, Steve."

Just not *her* life, apparently. He raised his head slowly to look at her, though the effort was harder than he could ever have imagined. He didn't want to stare into her eyes while she turned him away yet again.

Her hair was mussed and her skin flushed. Tears streaked down her cheeks.

Pen took an uneven breath. "M-making love with you is my way of living a bit of that life. Of tasting what I can't have. I come back over and over because no matter how much I know I have to give you up, I can't quite convince myself to do it once and for all." She squeezed her eyes shut. "I can't give up on the dream of having a family. Of raising children. I h-have to, but I can't." She swiped at her cheeks and looked into his eyes again. Hers shimmered with tears. "The first time I met you I saw the future I'd always coveted. I saw marriage and children and happiness. Even as a child I understood what you represented in my life."

Her hand, which had been lying on his knee, now gripped his thigh.

"I don't want to say no anymore. I'm sick of putting my pride before your love. I always believed my dignity was so important, but compared to you it means nothing. What's the point of having my pride if it doesn't give me any joy?"

Her lips quivered and her body shook. "The truth is you make me happy. Happier than maintaining my pride and dignity ever could. I'm tired of being depressed all the time. I wa...I want...to marry you. More than I want to take my next breath. I always have. I c-can't fight it any longer. I'm just not that strong."

His heart ceased beating. His lungs stopped functioning. He heard her words but dared not believe them.

"I want you, Steve. I want all of you. Every last bit of you. Whatever you're offering, I'm accepting."

A spark of hope flared in his heart. Still, he had to make sure. "You're accepting my proposal?" The question seared his throat, leaving it raw.

"If you'll have me. If...if you honestly believe you cannot be happy without me. If you can look into your heart and know regardless of my future you want to be with me, I can't say no." Her voice caught. "I never wanted to. Ever. All I have ever wanted was to be with you. Since I was twelve. Since the first day Tyler brought you home, I've dreamed of being with you." She gulped air loudly before continuing. "I love you. I fall asleep at night thinking of you and I wake up in the morning longing for you. Without you I feel like I'm half a person, like I'm not actually living."

She couldn't go on. Great big sobs stopped her words.

Steve's heart beat in a rough, uneven rhythm. His arms felt heavy as lead and he couldn't lift them. His ears had *not* deceived him.

"I...I still think it's a mistake," she rasped. "You...you'd be giving up your life for mine."

Words escaped him, so he shook his head, negating her comment.

"If you stay with me you won't get a happily ever after. My life doesn't come with that kind of guarantee. I don't have a future, Steve. You do. Don't waste it on me."

Fuck, she was accepting his proposal and pushing him away at the same time. Could she still not see that she *was* his future? "My life is wasted without you, Pen. Since the day you knocked on my door and proved to me you weren't just Tyler's kid sister, you've been the only woman I've ever wanted. I don't care what your distant future will bring. I care what our present can give us. And with you and me together, our present can give us everything. Enough to make up for what's to come. Share it with me. Share my life. I'll make you happier than you ever believed possible."

It was her turn to answer without words. With tears still streaming down her face, she nodded. Just nodded.

"Yes?" Steve could hardly ask out loud. Hope had returned. It lodged in his heart and beat against the walls of his chest.

"Yes," Pen nodded.

"You'll marry me?"

"If you'll have me."

"You'll come home to Sydney?"

"I...I would love to come home to Sydney."

"Children?"

She hesitated. Fear ran through her eyes.

"Children?" Steve said again. He couldn't imagine a world without Pen and Tyler. He refused to imagine one without Pen's children.

Her face paled.

"Your children and mine, Pen. Our children."

"I..." Her gaze darted behind him, unseeing.

"Girls with faces of angels and boys with mischief in their chocolate brown eyes."

"Steve—"

"If your father had chosen your route I'd never have met you. Christ, I'd never have known you. Never have loved you." *Inconceivable.* "Don't deprive the world of the chance to meet your children."

"I..." She shook her head. "I can't have babies and then abandon them before they're grown."

"You won't abandon them, Sunshine. You'll love them while you can and...and when you can't...you'll leave them with me." Ribbons of pain wrapped themselves around his neck, strangling him. She wouldn't be there to raise their children to adulthood. She might not even see them enter their teens. "I'll take care of them. I...I'll love them. Always. Enough for both of us. I'll bring them up to be the kind of people you would be so proud of. " His voice was hoarse. "I swear it. When you can't be there for them anymore, I will be. I'll be there for them always."

More than that, he'd make sure they remembered their mother as the person she was now and not the victim she would become.

"I want children, Steve." Pen sobbed. "Little blond-haired boys who love surfing."

His stomach lurched at the image. "We can have them, Sunshine. Just say yes."

Tears streamed down her cheeks. An indeterminate length of time passed. "Yes."

"Yes?"

"Yes."

Steve almost wept as her answer swirled around in his head. "You're really going to marry me?" he asked, desperately needing the confirmation.

"I really am."

"You won't run out on me in the dead of night?"

"Only if you decide you don't want me."

"Never."

She took an unsteady breath. "Then I promise I won't leave you again. Not until the disease takes me away."

"Even then, I'll be with you. I'll help you through the hard times. I swear you won't have to be alone again. Ever. I'll be with you un-until—" His voice broke. "Until the...end."

"And I..." Like him, she struggled to talk. "I will be so grateful to have you there."

Suddenly the reality of her acceptance hit him. Suddenly, the fight was over. He'd battled her for so long it took a full minute to come to terms with the fact there was no further opposition.

Pen was his.

At last.

"Sunshine..." Suddenly the tears were not Pen's. They were his. "Sunshine..." He shook his head. It was real. She was his.

And then Pen was in his arms and he was kissing her. And kissing her and kissing her and kissing her.

She was his. For as long as the disease would allow, she was his. He laughed and he cried and he kissed her and he held her, and this time, when Pen uttered those words, when she told him to fire it up, he did not pull away. Not when he knew she was asking him for his love.

He gave it to her. All of it.

His little ray of sunshine might one day burn out, but for now she glowed bright enough to sustain him through their future. Pen was his. Finally. And he intended to make every day count.

About the Author

To learn more about Jess Dee, please visit her website at www.jessdee.com or her blog at http://jessdee.wordpress.com. Or you can contact her via email at jess@jessdee.com

Love…or friendship? Does she really have to choose?

Only Tyler
© 2009 Jess Dee
Circle of Friends, Book 1.

Katelyn Rosewood is facing a moral dilemma, one that's six-foot-two, sexy as sin—and her fiancé's best friend. Katie spent a lot of time getting over Tyler Bonnard, but now that he's back in Sydney, he's turning her carefully reconstructed world upside down.

Her relationship with Steve Sommers may be short on heat and desire, but after Tyler left her two years before, she'll take security and solid friendship over wild passion any day. Except Tyler seems to have a good—if outrageous—explanation for why he's returned.

After a tragic family secret tore him out of Katie's life, Tyler is glad to be back with his two best friends. But one thing is out of place: Katie's in the wrong man's arms. And if her reaction to his return is any indication, she's not quite over him. Which could mean hope for Tyler, heartbreak for Steve…

And another devastating loss for Katie, who must choose between the man to whom she's committed her future, and the man who still holds her heart.

Warning: Keep a tissue or two handy while reading this book. While it does contain a few steamy love scenes, the rest of the story might just make you cry.

Available now in ebook and print from Samhain Publishing.

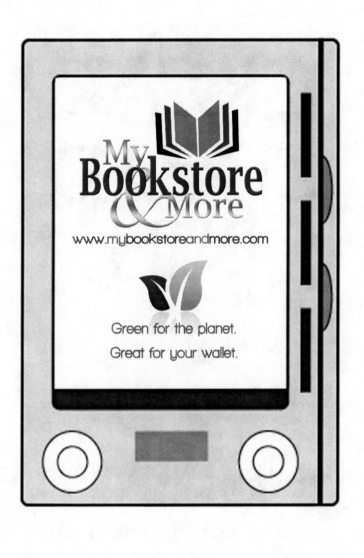

LaVergne, TN USA
05 December 2010
207476LV00001B/111/P